By ROSE MASTERS

Spades

Published by DREAMSPINNER PRESS
www.dreamspinnerpress.com

SPADES

ROSE MASTERS

Published by
DREAMSPINNER PRESS

8219 Woodville Hwy #1245
Woodville, FL 32362 USA
www.dreamspinnerpress.com

Spades
© 2024 Rose Masters

Cover Art
© 2024 L.C. Chase
http://www.lcchase.com
Cover content is for illustrative purposes only and any person depicted on the cover is a model.

Trade Paperback ISBN: 978-1-64405-665-3
Digital ISBN: 978-1-64405-643-1
Trade Paperback published April 2024
v. 1.0

For my mom, who has always supported me in everything I do.

CHAPTER 1

"CALL." OWEN'S heart leaped, but he maintained his poker face.

"Straight," an older gentleman said, sounding satisfied.

This time Owen did smile. "Full house," he said, feeling satisfied himself. He jumped slightly at the sound of muffled clapping. He knew the game was fierce but hadn't noticed the crowd building around them.

He quickly collected his winnings and went to cash out but paused for a moment as the woman at the register reached out to hand him his money. A strange malice emanated from her. He carefully peeled off the leather glove on his right hand, trying to make it appear natural. Then he purposefully brushed his bare skin against her fingers as he took the money. *Warning, cheater, punish.* He jerked involuntarily but hid it with a cough.

The woman glanced briefly to her right. Owen walked away to the left as fast as he could without raising suspicion. He made it to a nearby bathroom and locked the door behind himself. All the urinals and stalls were empty; he was alone. He overturned a garbage can and propped it under a set of high-up windows, but as he'd suspected, he couldn't fit through.

Owen hopped back down and moved the can to block the door. He brushed the hair out of his face. This was bad. He had been far too careless this time. Although he hadn't played too many games, every game he played, he won. Big. He'd thought no one would pick up on it. Apparently he was wrong.

Someone banged on the door. No one yelled. They wouldn't want to disturb the guests. Owen heard the chime of a key being worked into the lock. Crap. This was it. He glanced briefly into the mirror, then froze. His eyes. His left eye remained a plain, undistinguished brown. His right eye, though, reflected a bright violet iris. Fuck, he'd lost a contact. Thank God he had at least four spares on him at all times.

Owen fumbled with the opening of his leather satchel. Behind him, he heard a click, and the door pushed against the garbage can. It held shut. For now. Owen fumbled with a brown contact lens, popping

it in as the can crashed to the floor and the door flew open. Four men—
wow, were they big—quietly entered the bathroom. Owen immediately
masked his fear. He knew better than to say anything. The only move he
made was to slowly pull off his left glove as well.

"Sir, can you please come with us?"

With a small nod, Owen walked toward what he was sure was not
going to be a fun time. The man who spoke, a tall and surprisingly thin
man with blond ringlets cascading around his face, lightly pressed a hand
to the back of Owen's shoulder as if to guide him; there was a little too
much pressure for that to be the case. Owen said nothing and watched
everything.

He walked a quick six yards to a hallway behind a private door,
followed by a left, a right, then stairs. They walked about four flights
down. Each landing brought more and more dread to Owen as he realized
they were heading to a basement. Crap. Usually when he was made, they
started with an office visit. Then it was some light conversation peppered
with threats. Basements, though, they were different. The conversation
was usually much less… light. They must have been tipped off about
him. Owen ground his teeth together.

It wasn't even as if he were cheating! Owen could sense what he
liked to call "truth." When he was around people, he could read feelings
and the echoes of what people kept hidden behind a smiling face. He
found that people proved to be deceptive more often than one would
think. It was why he came to be a (not-really) professional gambler.

Well, no, the "why" was actually because he was a dirt-poor hermit
who was too overwhelmed by being among so many people talking and
thinking all the time to maintain a regular job.

"You may have a seat." Owen heard the blond man say before that
firm grip pushed him into a plain folding chair facing a desk.

Owen's hopes lifted. Maybe this was a really shitty office? The
stone-cold detachment Owen felt pushing against him crushed his hope.
A tingle started at the back of his neck. One of the four guards, a rather
large man with shorn brown hair, was actually putting out a vibe of
sadism. Aw shit.

Despite it all, Owen maintained his calm demeaner. He looked
around lazily, aiming to appear uninterested but in reality scanning for
any way out. None of the men said anything. None of them made eye

contact. Except for one. He looked straight at Owen. His smile appeared pleasant, but Owen could see the slight curve in the very edge of his lips.

Owen heard a swish and turned around to see the door opening. His lips went slack, but only for a second before he reined himself in. Walking casually into the room was the single hottest man Owen had ever seen. He had bright blond hair, draped down his back in a loose ponytail. He wore… was that Michael Kors? Damn.

The man walked past Owen to the desk, sat down, and simply beamed. Owen's heart skipped a beat, but he was careful not to show it. Why was he crushing on this guy; he was about to be fucking killed.

The man pulled a pack of cigarettes from his coat pocket and offered one to Owen. He shook his head, and the man shrugged and lit one himself. He took a long drag before speaking.

"So how have you enjoyed my casino, Jack Smith?"

Yeah, Owen had a few aliases. He had Jack, Jake, Jimmy, John (okay, well, he was drunk when he was coming up with them, and he got into a pattern). He had IDs for each. Considering he spent most of his time holed up in hotels and cheap rentals, he really did cover his tracks well. So what slipped today? Yes, he was gambling big, but he hadn't really let himself stand out.

It had to have been a tip-off.

Owen smiled with all of his teeth. "I have been having a wonderful time. Your casino is really awesome!"

He tried to sound drunk. Maybe that would throw them off. Owen tried to read the man to see if he was buying it. Poker face. Damn, he was good. He had a soft friendly smile that did not change when Owen spoke. He wondered what the guy was thinking….

Wait. Nothing. Owen tried to pull the truth from the man and felt… nothing.

His own poker face fell away, and his eyes opened wide in shock. His mouth fell open. The owner—he had to be the owner, right?—frowned for a moment. Probably because Owen was gaping like a fish. He shut his eyes and relaxed his face.

"Do you know why you are here, Mr. Smith?"

"I have no idea." Owen tried to sound innocent, letting his eyes go wide deliberately this time.

The man laughed in disbelief.

"I am the owner of Spades, Leo Ellis." He dipped his head slightly with a smirk, cigarette between his fingers. "I have to admit... Mr. Smith"—his tone clearly expressed his disbelief in the alias—"I already know your reputation. I have been warned. Sure, I don't mind you gambling here. But this is five big wins in a row at my table, and we don't want our other patrons to get ripped off."

A chill went up Owen's spine. He honestly wasn't sure whether it was fear or arousal. He found himself getting caught up in the owner's bright green eyes. Even actively trying to reach out, he could read no truth from the man. For the first time since he could remember, he didn't know what someone was thinking. It was terrifying, but also kind of exciting.

Leo looked above Owen's head and nodded. Owen squeaked as strong hands hauled him up from his seat and pushed him onto the stone floor.

Ugh, fighting time. Owen hated beatings.

He popped up as one of the guards went to kick him. He dove to the side, sliding his fingers against the man's ankles under his suit. *Give me a weakness*, Owen willed. In that short contact, Owen received his answer. He jumped up and pulled the man's left arm straight against his body. The guard frowned in confusion until Owen pushed his elbow as hard as he could. The man didn't just go down. He *shrieked* and collapsed into a pile. Tendon operation.

Owen's gaze crossed Leo's, and he paused. Leo looked... curious?

Owen gasped as his attention was drawn back to himself. Two arms laced themselves around Owen's own, pinning them behind his back. He had no skin contact. He awkwardly drew his face up and brushed his forehead against the man's chin. *Give me a weakness.* Ah.

Owen dropped his entire body weight, then twisted. The man went flying. Bad balance.

Owen shook himself off, then felt a strong blast of fury. If the feeling itself didn't throw Owen off balance, then the backhand slap across his face sure did.

"Wait," Ellis said calmly.

Owen sat up, dazed, looking up at the guard towering over him. He touched the corner of his lip and saw blood. His head hurt. That was one hell of a blow. He started when he felt a hand on his shoulder. He looked up, right into Leo's green eyes.

"What were you doing?" Leo said in a genuinely interested tone.

Owen was lost. "What are you talking about?"

Leo lowered his lashes. He didn't seem to be in the mood for games.

"That look you got when you fought my men. Strange, distant, and then they were down."

"Um, I don't think...." Owen started, confused. What was he supposed to say to that? Why did this guy even notice? "Um...."

He was interrupted by warm, long fingers steadying his chin.

"What's wrong with your eye?"

Owen blinked. "What?"

"Why is your eye a different color now?"

Owen lost all control of his face. He eyes widened while his chin, still gripped by Leo Ellis, went slack. His contact!

Leo gazed into Owen's eyes thoughtfully for what Owen felt was almost a century but was probably only a few seconds.

A cryptic smile broke across Leo's face. He squeezed Owen's chin gently and pushed him onto his back before standing up and walking over to his desk.

Owen rolled over and sat up, but one look at the glares from the guards and he remained seated. He watched Leo bring a glass and some scotch out of the desk drawer. He calmly poured a drink, then reached into another drawer and pulled out a small glass vial with white powder in it. He quickly dumped this into the drink and walked back to Owen.

"Drink this," he said calmly, smiling slightly.

Owen's mouth dropped open. Every mask and guard he put up flew right out the window. *Who the fuck does this guy think he is?*

"Are you fucking kidding me? I'm not going to drink that!"

Rather than getting mad, Leo's previously cross features lightened up. Owen could feel a swell of disdain and anger coming from behind him, but he couldn't look away from Leo's laughing eyes.

Then he paused. He noticed that even at this range, he couldn't read the enigmatic owner of the casino. He cautiously brushed his fingers against Ellis's, feigning taking the drink, and nothing. What? That had never happened before. He was almost intrigued.

Although—Owen looked at the tumbler that now sat in his hands—*not an ideal introduction.*

Owen thought about throwing the drink away. But even if he couldn't read Leo's thoughts, he could pretty clearly sense the truth in the others. Either he ended up with possibly poisoned whisky in his stomach or he got a severe beating. The drink was the better option. Besides, if this Leo guy was going to kill him, there were quicker, easier ways.

Leo wrapped his hand around Owen's and slowly pushed the glass to Owen's lips, grinning cryptically. Owen stared directly into his eyes as he emptied the glass, coughing as it was pulled away from his hand.

Owen wanted to blame the liquor for the burning in his cheeks as he looked into Leo's eyes. Leo was still smiling. Owen's lips twitched involuntarily, and he bit his tongue to arrest his own small smile. He didn't have any more time to think about it as he slowly lost consciousness. The last thing he felt was a hand catching his head as he fell.

CHAPTER 2

OWEN WAS sitting in a café that he frequented, meeting a young girl he had picked up from his community college psych class. His head was spinning, and he took a shaky sip of coffee, trying to block out all the pressure of a café full of people blasting out their innermost feelings at him. God, he hated being in public. He tolerated it for school and sometimes, like now, for dating, but it didn't make the headache any better.

"Owen!" a petite redhead plopped down on the chair opposite him. "I hope I didn't make you wait. I took the bus, and we hit construction."

Owen flashed her a genuine smile. "It's fine, I've got my coffee fix." He gestured to the caramel latte in his hand.

Then the rest became blurry. Owen remembered really liking her, going out, seeing movies, sleeping with her, distancing himself like he always did, and getting dumped. What a shame.

Consciousness slowly began to come back. Owen opened his eyes halfway and marveled at the burgundy canopy above him. *Huh*, he thought. *Hotel accommodations are getting better.* He turned on his side, feeling silky-soft sheets against his skin.

The sheets too? Wow, I don't remember....

Then it came back to him. The casino, the confrontation, the drink, and bam, now he was....

Where was he? He assessed the room. It looked like one of those high-end hotel suites.

"What the fuck?"

He covered his mouth. That was way louder than he'd intended.

No one else was in the room, and no one came in at Owen's exclamation, so it was time to investigate. The room itself must have been about 300 square feet. It was a palace compared to what Owen was accustomed to. He walked to the huge window and gently pulled aside the heavy drapes, exposing a balcony and a beautiful view of the city. He looked down to the pavement far below and decided that wasn't a way out.

He then evaluated the other exits. There was a closet not too far from the window, and one more door on the opposite side of the room. Must be the way out. Owen stepped as quietly as he could toward the door. The floor was carpeted, so he didn't need to worry too much about being heard.

Owen gripped the door and slowly turned the knob without making a sound. He pushed it open enough so he could peek out. Seeing no one, Owen opened the door fully, revealing a spacious open-concept living room/kitchen. This room alone was probably twice the size of the last apartment he'd rented.

Owen passed the living area and spied the kitchen. He fancied himself a rather good cook. And anyone who knew him knew he was a stress baker. Although he denied it, he knew it was true. The pristine stove, two ovens, and hanging high-quality pans filled Owen with a strong desire to bake his feelings away.

Shaking his head to clear that train of thought, Owen began to examine the room with a clearer mind. The first thing he noticed in the living room was a couch. He pushed his hand on the cushion. Oh God, was it soft. Across from the couch was the biggest TV Owen had ever seen in a person's house. And right in front of the screen on the TV stand sat the Xbox that had just come out a month ago.

Owen gaped at it. His Xbox was at least a decade old. He never had the money to buy a new one, and since it still worked (sort of, it was a bit glitchy), he had never bought a new one. He went to investigate and cursed when his knee collided with the wooden coffee table between the couch and the television.

Owen sucked in air until the pain faded to a bearable degree. He glared at the offending furniture and saw a note on official-looking monogramed paper.

> *Owen Hart,*
> *Welcome to my home. Unfortunately, I have some business to attend to, so you are on your own for a while. I have left you classic video games and a slew of romantic comedies. Should you need anything, simply knock on the door and ask.*
> *Yours Truly,*
> *Leo Ellis.*

Owen was stunned. Those were literally his favorite things. Video games he had always liked. He often invited friends (one or two at a time only) to his apartment to play those stupid arcade-style games.

Wondering if they had Ms. Pacman, he fumbled with the TV remote and the game system. The selection screen came up, and yes, they did. Next he looked over at the selection of DVDs that were laid out on a shelf under the TV.

Rom-coms were the kind of thing that he had made fun of without really knowing what they were. Then one girlfriend had dragged him to see *27 Dresses*, and he was hooked. Of course, one particularly passionate boyfriend had insisted he see *The Time Traveler's Wife*. He had never cried so hard in his life, and he loved every second of it. Turned out he liked romance movies in general.

But how the hell could Leo Ellis know these things?

Owen stiffened. Wait, how did Ellis even know his name? He searched his brain to figure out what information he could have given any of the hotel staff that would tip them off to his real identity.

Owen was a very private person. He was social, but he was careful. He only had a few real friends, and his acquaintances knew nothing about him. The girls and boys he dated came in and out of his life. He was often pegged as loving, generous, and an open book, but all the information he shared with people (other than his closest friends) was calculated and usually only partly true.

Stories about his childhood were always entirely fabricated, even *with* his friends.

Owen looked up and started. He caught a glimpse of himself in the large mirror decorating the wall next to him and had thought it was someone else.

He studied himself carefully, putting his face right up to his reflection. His eye almost glowed violet. He winced. A quick look around confirmed that his satchel (and thus his contacts), was nowhere to be found.

"Hmm." Owen wondered if he should take the other contact out?

But no. Perhaps it would be easier to pass off the unusual color as a birth defect if he left the one brown lens in?

Looking around once more, Owen saw a door partly open to a bathroom and one other closed door in the large room. The latter had to be the exit. Repeating the routine of inching the door open slightly, Owen peeked outside, then froze when two truths curled around in his head. The first was lazy and pleasant, but the other was aggressive, with an underlying anger.

So there were guards. Not that he expected any less. He had begun to slowly close the door when a hand grabbed the side of the door and pulled it open farther. The face of the guard with curly blond hair appeared in the opening.

"Can we get you anything?" he asked with a small smile.

His energy was soothing. He didn't seem to hold any malice toward Owen.

Although an honest aura could always snap into something ugly. Playing it safe, Owen smiled and offered a quick "No thank you!" before pulling the door shut again, trying not to appear as worried about this situation as he was.

Owen's head spun. He could still sense their truths through the door, and it wasn't a nice feeling swirling around his head. He retreated to the kitchen because it was the farthest from the door he could get. His grumbling stomach brought him back into the present.

For a moment he wondered if the food here was poisoned like that drink, then quickly shook the idea off. If they wanted to kill him, it would have happened already. He hoped so at least. Opening the door revealed the best stocked fridge that Owen had ever seen. He closed it, then pulled open cabinets. They had everything.

In a cabinet full of snacks, Owen found a protein bar. Too uneasy to really eat, he had that instead of cooking.

He munched quietly on the bar while lazily opening cabinets, then froze. They had... flour, sugar, spices, even cupcake liners. Owen ingested the rest of the protein bar, practically swallowing it like a snake.

Well, if no one was around to tell him what was going on, he might as well stay busy. Owen collected all of his ingredients and started baking.

OWEN WASN'T sure how much time had passed. He had already made at least fifty cupcakes and was working on another batch. Owen had no control over himself when it came to baking. His friends loved it because they had a constant supply of sweets, and he loved the calm that came over him when he baked. He was violently whipping the batter (there was a stand mixer, but Owen was of a firm mind that mixing that way was cheating) when he heard a *snick*.

He almost dropped the bowl, but hastily placed it onto the countertop. He summoned up his best poker face but couldn't hold it as he grew fearful. Even getting his ass handed to him at crappy casinos couldn't break that façade. But pain was straightforward and predictable. This was neither of those things.

The door opened, and in walked none other than Mr. Casino Owner, Leo Ellis. Owen sucked in air as he took in the man's golden blond hair, his loose ponytail draped over his shoulder this time. He wore a plain black suit. *Gucci?* Owen wondered. Though he could never afford it himself, Owen had an eye for designers.

Leo walked into the room and closed the door behind him. He had a light smile on his face that turned to a slight frown when he looked up.

Owen's heart skipped a beat, meeting the man's beautiful green eyes with what he *hoped* was a cool and indifferent demeaner in his body language.

"Mr. Ellis," Owen started, not really sure what he was going to say.

"Leo," the man said, looking critically at him. "What happened to you?" he asked, his smile growing.

Owen frowned, caught off guard. "Wha...," he started to say as Leo gestured at his own chest.

He looked down and froze. His shirt was *covered* in flour. *Oh wow, nice job Owen. Way to play it cool!*

The look on his face must have been very revealing because Leo started to laugh. Owen giggled for one moment, then shut it down. Maybe it was because he was baking, or maybe it was because he was delirious from the stress of the situation. More likely, although Owen did not want to admit it to himself, Leo's laughter was simply infectious.

Leo's laugh sounded genuine and harmless. Owen had heard many a laugh where there was malice or some other unpleasant emotion behind it. He hated feeling the disconnect between what he heard and what was truly there. Owen focused his energy again, and nope. Didn't get a thing. Leo's laughter, though, had sounded so beautiful and untainted to him. Though he could never be sure.

The block in place between him and Leo's thoughts and intentions wasn't good. He needed to be ahead of the game on this. And yet at the same time, it was kind of refreshing. Leo's voice snapped Owen back to reality.

"How is the suite? Beats a shitty motel, right?" His smile never wavered.

How does he know where I'm living? Strangely, Owen was more annoyed at the breach of privacy than he was worried about what must be a high-level member of some sleezy syndicate knowing where he lived.

"Why am I here?" Owen didn't feel like playing games.

Leo nodded, as if he totally understood where Owen was coming from.

"I'll get right to the point, then," he said in a serious tone. Leo held up one finger, then walked toward Owen. Feeling panicked, Owen stepped back as discreetly as he could until his back collided with the long kitchen island (currently filled with cupcakes).

Owen's whole body tensed as Leo drew closer, and it remained that way until he was passed by. Instead, Leo entered the kitchen and sat on one of the stools at the island. He looked mildly amused as he picked up one cupcake, turning his hand to observe it. He frowned slightly.

"We don't have frosting, though," he said in a serious tone, noting the icing piled onto the cupcake.

Again, Owen felt laughter build up before he shoved it down. Leo sounded like a child.

"I made it from scratch," Owen said, aware of the amusement in his own voice.

Leo must have heard it too because his smile returned. He resumed inspecting the cupcake. He even brought it up to his face to smell it. Owen snickered at this before he could catch it. Leo didn't react, so Owen hoped he hadn't heard.

With one more look and a quick frown, Leo took a bite of the cupcake. Owen was amazed that Leo could somehow devour a cupcake so quickly without getting any of that huge pile of frosting on his face.

"These are very good, Owen," Leo said after finishing off his cupcake. "Are you going to eat all of these by yourself? I can't imagine why you made so many." Leo smirked.

Owen could think of nothing to say… wait, no!

"Please stop fooling around. I want to know what is going on. Why am I here?!"

Leo brushed his ponytail behind his back. If Owen hadn't known any better, he would have thought the man looked a little disappointed.

Owen was off his game. This was the first time he ever had to actively read someone's emotions from the outside. This was new territory.

"I marked you at the casino because I needed to look into you. Rather than throwing you into a holding area, I've brought you home and set you up right here in this suite." He gestured around the room.

"Okay, but why did you need to do any of that? You could have had me beaten, then banned. That seems a lot simpler."

"Ah yes, simple." Leo smirked. "The short answer here is that you are interesting. You did something back there, I don't know what, but I *do* know that you are going to tell me. Eventually. Say what you will of my business practices, I avoid torture where it is not necessary."

He leaned over the counter, grabbed the collar of Owen's shirt, and pulled him over the island, making direct eye contact. Owen braced his hands on the island, feeling vulnerable. He observed Leo's eyes shifting back and forth.

"Which one is the contact?" Leo asked curiously.

Owen instinctively closed his eyes, then forced himself to look back at those eyes, now boring holes into him. If looks could kill….

"Well, I've always been a fan of colored contacts. This purple one was on sale, and I felt like standing out," Owen rationalized. Leo didn't react at all to his statement. With his free hand, Leo stretched his fingers to Owen's eye. Owen quickly shut his eyes, not wanting to share that aspect of himself.

"Open," he said.

Owen took a deep breath, then opened his eyes.

Leo looked very serious, reflecting more the man Owen had met the night before. He again reached for Owen's eyes, and Owen didn't even blink. First, Leo lightly felt for a contact on his naturally violet iris. He did the same with the other, exposing the contact hugging the eye.

"I thought so," Leo said in a calm, yet happy, way. "Why do you wear contacts?" Leo asked.

Owen eyed him in disbelief.

"I try not to draw attention to myself in general. Can you imagine how many looks I got before I discovered colored contacts? And I'm telling you, not all of them were nice. I hated wearing sunglasses all the time!"

Leo let go of Owen's shirt, throwing Owen off balance as he had been pulling against the hand holding him. He looked down at his suit jacket and frowned, trying to brush off the flour that had somehow migrated from Owen to him.

"Okay, okay." Owen was fairly sure at this point he was not in immediate danger. "So what happens now?"

Leo glanced up with a slight pout on his lips. Owen guessed he appreciated his wardrobe.

"Well, I have a proposition for you." A friendly smile reappeared.

When he didn't immediately continue, Owen responded.

"Okay, what is it?"

"I will give you two options. In the first option, I would like to hire you as an escort."

Again, he paused.

"Um, what does that mean?" Owen asked, nervous.

"You would join me at fundraisers, parties, events, certain meetings, etc. And of course, you will live here free of charge should you so choose."

Blood pooled in Owen's cheeks.

"Would we have to…?" Owen was too embarrassed to even say it aloud.

Leo looked confused for a moment before understanding washed over his face.

"The answer to that question is no." His look turned sly. "Unless, of course, you want to."

Owen shook his head so hard he felt pain in his neck. His chest relaxed. But a part of him was disappointed. *It's totally Stockholm syndrome*, he rationalized. Although he hadn't been there more than a few hours.

"Suit yourself," Leo said, shrugging his shoulders. "Of course you can always change your mind," he said with a wink.

"Is that it?" Owen asked.

"Ah, no. I don't think it would do anyone any good for you to do nothing all day. On your days off, I will hire you to wait on the casino patrons at Spades. For all of this, you will be paid five thousand dollars a month."

Owen's brain froze. He had *never* even come close to making that much money. He could imagine the apartment that he would be able to afford, the foods he could buy, the kitchen he could have!

He worried for a moment about how riddled with emotions casinos were. It would be hard blocking enough of it to walk away without the world's worst headache. But for that kind of money....

"So, what is the second option?" Owen asked after a long pause.

He must have pretty clearly expressed his emotions in his body language because Leo was looking very satisfied with himself.

"The second option is quite simple. You can go home."

Owen waited for him to continue, but Leo said nothing more.

"Is that all?"

"Well, yes. But you will be blacklisted by every contact I have, and believe me I have a lot of contacts."

"Ah." Owen didn't suspect Leo knew how big a deal that was for him. Gambling was the easiest way for him to make money.

Poker became much easier to win when one knew the emotions and reactions of everyone at the table. He did work regular jobs, but they were hard to hold because he couldn't concentrate on his work. He usually stuck to seasonal work. And he definitely needed more of an income than that. The poker games could supplement his miniscule income.

Five thousand dollars, though.

"Can I think about it?"

Leo beamed. "Take as long as you want. Feel free to go wherever you would like. There are other private bedrooms, some offices, and some... utility closets that you cannot enter. Otherwise come and go as you please. My guards will remain with you until you become accustomed to the building. If you leave and don't come back, then I will assume that you have chosen the second option. Oh, and I think that it would be nice of you to share those cupcakes with my employees. They're really very good."

With a quick wink, Leo left his stool and walked to the door. Owen suddenly had a thought.

"Mr. Ellis, wait!"

Leo turned his head, a small frown on his lips. "Leo," he said firmly.

"Ah, okay. Leo." Owen stumbled over the name a little. "Did anyone find a pair of leather gloves at the casino by any chance?"

Leo looked curious again. "No, why?"

"They were a gift, and I always wear them. If you find them, can you please return them to me?"

Leo maintained eye contact for a few seconds before continuing to the door. As he stepped out, he waved a hand without looking back.

CHAPTER 3

OWEN WAS stuck. There were so many things going through his head. Escort? Wasn't that only something that happened in movies? And why would a man like Leo want *him*, of all people, going around with him. Surely there were more attractive, better-mannered men than him?

And wow, living in a place like this? Owen had never even *been* in a place this nice, let alone lived in it. Plus the money! No matter how bad the emotional intrusion of working so closely with people would be, that was a lot of money to Owen.

Owen looked next to him at the dozens of cupcakes neatly lined up. *Well, there is always decorating....* Owen snapped himself out of his attempted escape from reality. He needed to think about this.

Owen took a seat, trying to go over his options. He sighed after a few minutes, knowing that there was no way that he could absorb everything right now. So what should he do? He glanced at the door that Leo had exited. Owen revisited the image of that slender frame walking away. He sighed.

Owen stood up, deciding to brave the unknown. He was halfway to the door before he paused, turning around to look at his cupcakes.

OWEN CRACKED the door open, balancing two cupcakes in one hand as he did so. He paused to get a better grip of the cupcakes, and once again, the blond guard opened the door with a neutral smile.

"Can I get you anything?" he asked quietly.

Owen held his hand up.

"I have cupcakes."

The man looked calmly back at him, still smiling mildly. Owen sensed a rush of surprise and confusion.

From beyond the man at the door, Owen was almost pummeled by a wave of irritation and annoyance. He glanced discreetly at the guard to his right. His hair was shaven to stubble. He was big. Both tall and bulky. Mr. Sadist. Owen didn't like that person.

"Why thank you, Mr. Hart," the blond man said, completely in tune with his truth.

"Thanks," the other man said neutrally, his truth anything but.

"Owen," he said quickly, turning to the blond. "So, um, you are...."

Something changed in the man's eyes as his energy swirled pleasantly around Owen. He was happy about something. Was it something Owen had said?

"My name is Jacob. My friend over here"—he gestured at the other guard—"is Seth."

Seth's smile appeared positively villainous. Well, more likely that miasma of anger was distorting how Owen saw Seth.

"Can I, uh, walk around?" Owen asked.

"We'll escort you as you don't know the layout of the building," Jacob responded. "Although you may want to change your clothing," he added with a smile.

Owen looked down at himself again. How did he manage to get... was that sugar? He touched his dusty pants and licked his finger. Yes, it was sugar.

"I don't have any clothes," he said, a little disappointed.

"There is clothing in the closet. If they don't fit you, then tell me your size and I'll arrange to have some things sent up for you," Jacob said.

Before Owen could respond, Jacob once again shut the door. Owen wasn't liking this pattern of doors being closed in his face.

He went toward the bedroom. When he opened the closet earlier, he'd noticed clothing but hadn't guessed it would be for him. Although with everything happening the way it was, he shouldn't have been surprised.

He pushed shirts aside, seeing what was there. Owen made two observations. The first was these were not his clothes. The second, they were such expensive articles, he feared even wearing them. They were all his size. How had they had time to even buy this stuff? Unless they had a lot of clothing lying around for guests. Unlikely.

What time was it? He looked at the sunny afternoon view outside the window. What *day* was it?

Owen changed into a purple T-shirt and black faux-leather pants (at least he hoped they were faux) and then headed back to the door.

He opened the door, stepped outside, and noticed that both cupcakes were gone. He reached his feelers out and concluded that the guards had eaten them. He glanced at Seth and observed the cupcake had done nothing to change his mood.

"Can you show me around?" Owen asked Jacob directly. He wasn't going to talk to someone who would rather be pissy than civil. On the inside at least.

"Sure," Jacob responded.

Jacob reached into his pocket, and for one moment, Owen thought he was going to pull out a gun. He quickly realized how pointless that would be. Instead, Jacob retrieved a phone and handed it to Owen.

His phone!

Owen quickly unlocked it and looked at the date and time. It was 3:00 p.m. on Saturday. That meant he must have been out for most of the day.

"You wanted to look around?" Seth asked coolly.

Owen winced. The persistent negative energy was giving him a headache.

"Come," Jacob said, gesturing down the hallway.

As they walked toward the elevator, Jacob described the layout of the building. "This building is five floors. Above us is the penthouse. That is where Mr. Ellis lives. This floor is comprised only of suites for guests. The floor below has rooms for select staff. Level two is for offices and storage."

Owen frowned at this.

"Um," he interrupted, gently touching the top of the man's hand. *What is in there? Interrogation.* Owen wasn't really surprised. *Drugs?* he quickly asked mentally before the touch became unnatural. *No.* He withdrew his hand and sighed in relief. His mother was a drug addict. Not that having interrogation rooms was much better, but, well, it kind of was to him.

"Oh, sorry, continue. I had a thought but lost it," Owen said quickly.

Jacob didn't react to the interruption.

"On the first floor there's a lobby, a gym, a pool, and a media room. All of these areas are completely open to you. We only ask that you don't spend time on the other levels. You'll have a key to your room. Your room will be cleaned during the day while you are out."

Jacob said all this matter-of-factly.

Owen couldn't help but feel uncomfortable with the idea of living in a place like this without paying. People were going to clean up after him? He almost felt like he would have to keep the room even cleaner than he usually did. He didn't want to be pegged as a slob.

Owen desperately wanted to see the pool. His friends had often referred to him as a fish out of water. In the hot summer months, he would often go to his friend Sal's modest home to sit in a small kiddie pool that Sal bought as a joke when Owen bemoaned the fact that pool memberships were so expensive. Owen didn't take it as a joke, but rather as an invitation to sit and splash in his friend's backyard.

But first....

"Can I leave?" Owen asked. He could hear doubt in his voice.

Jacob's smile reached his eyes. Owen could bathe in the humor that swirled in his mind. He completely ignored the competing negativity.

"We can call you a car to go anywhere you want to go," Jacob responded. "We only ask that you use these services, rather than public transportation. I'll give you the number to the car so that you may return. Feel free to meet any person that you want, so long as this person isn't in conflict with this business. And you are not to speak of anything you see or hear while you stay in the building. In all other aspects, feel free to go or do whatever you want to so long as you inform us of where you will be or if you won't be coming back."

"Oh, okay," Owen responded. This was a good deal. He hated public transport anyway. "Can you call me a car?" Owen asked. Jacob pulled out his phone.

CHAPTER 4

"OWEN, WHY don't you move in with Sheryl and me? We have a spare bedroom, and we won't charge you half as much as you are paying in those shitholes you find to live in," Owen's old friend Aiden said, taking a small sip of his Heineken. Owen sat on an Adirondack chair across from him on the back porch. He was nursing a beer as well, although he dared not have more than one and lose his faculties.

Owen adjusted the dark sunglasses covering his eyes. Aiden always had a spare pair for him. He hated it, but it was a necessary evil. Aiden knew about his unique eye color, but also respected Owen's distaste for it.

"Nah, I like being able to pick up and leave. And anyway, I think I found a really nice apartment for now."

"Oh, what apartment?" Aiden asked, resting his head on his hands dramatically.

Owen laughed lightly. "It's not a for sure. Don't worry about it."

Aiden shrugged and sipped his beer. He was no dope. He knew that if he pushed Owen for more information than he wanted to give, he would just be getting lies.

They sat for a few hours, chatting and enjoying the fresh air. When the sky began to dim, Owen figured it was time to go back. He wasn't ready to turn down Leo's offer yet.

When Jacob had called the car from the building for him, Owen was shocked. The car that came was sleek and black, with tinted windows. He would have been happy with an Uber. He had instructed the driver to drop him off a few blocks from Aiden's home, and he gave the same instructions for picking him up.

When Owen reached the revolving doors to the lobby of Leo's building, he spotted Jacob standing there, waiting for him.

"Did you have a good day?" he asked, sounding surprisingly genuine. Owen was starting to like him.

"It was okay," Owen replied.

"Come, I've been asked to bring you straight to your room when you arrived."

"By whom?" Owen asked nervously. He wasn't sure whether he had seen the whole cast in this crazy play he found himself in.

Jacob didn't respond except to gesture Owen to the elevator. Owen sighed. This would all be much better if he actually believed that he was safe.

WHEN OWEN reached his suite, he was surprised to see another guard at the door. He wasn't familiar to Owen. For all he looked like he was going to die of boredom, Owen sensed a sharp alertness and assessment. Interesting.

The man, who had already seen him from the corner of his eye, turned to Owen with a neutral expression.

"Mr. Ellis is waiting for you inside."

Owen felt a rush of surprise. What on God's green earth would that man be doing in *his* suite at this time? A few ideas popped into his mind before he could shut them down and avoid the blush that he could already feel blooming on his cheeks.

He took a deep breath, and before he changed his mind and ran, he opened the door and walked into the suite. Only to find... videogames? Huh.

Leo sat on the couch playing Galaga on the Xbox. He paused his game, looked back at Owen, and smiled.

"Come," he said cheerfully. "Grab the Wii so I can beat you at Mario Kart."

OWEN TRIED. He tried so hard to even come close to surpassing Leo at the video game. He was almost embarrassed by how low his score was in comparison. True, he wasn't super into Mario Kart, but he still considered himself a decent player. Until now.

"Damn, you're good. Where do you get the time to play while running a business like yours?"

Owen didn't want to let on that he really did know what kind of business Leo was running. Or was he even running it? Yes, he owned Spades, but there might be a few leaders further up the food chain as far as he knew.

"I'm naturally talented at many things."

Leo leaned over, crowding Owen against the armrest. Owen found himself in a position that scared him. He didn't know if he wanted Leo to back off or move closer.

Suddenly, Owen had an idea.

"Your hands look so soft. What do you do to get that skin?" Owen gripped Leo's hand. First, a gentle caress. Nope, nothing. He then held Leo's hand between his own and focused. No, not this way either. Owen recalled one of the lessons he had learned from his guardian. He looked up and caught a bemused look on Leo's face.

Taking a breath and preparing himself for embarrassment, Owen leaned in and kissed Leo. No, even with the closest contact he could achieve, he couldn't read Leo.

Even without the ability to read him, he knew that Leo was shocked. Owen began to feel embarrassed and started to pull away.

Before he could get far, he felt a sharp pain in the back of his head. "Leo! Stop pulling on my—"

Owen was silenced when Leo dragged him onto his lips so hard that Owen felt flesh scrape against teeth. As if to make up for the powerful connection, Leo's tongue gently caressed his lips, pausing to lick up the little bit of blood Owen had from the small cut left behind.

Leo's tongue grazed across Owen's lips, pushing against his teeth, seeking entrance Owen happily provided. Owen explored Leo's mouth. He sucked on Leo's tongue, which caused a feeling that shot right down to his groin. Using his last few remaining brain cells, Owen noticed that Leo's mouth tasted like mint. It took Owen a moment to realize that Leo had sat back. He blinked back to reality and, seeing Leo's hungry look, blushed right down to his neck.

"Uhm." He couldn't even fathom what to say in this moment. Leo simply winked and reached behind the other end of the couch. He pulled out a familiar satchel, and Owen's heart leaped. His contacts! Leo handed the bag to a very grateful Owen.

"Oh, and my people found these," Leo said, pulling Owen's gloves from the satchel. Owen probably should have played it cool, but he was so damn glad to have something to block out what skin contact he could.

"I have business to attend to," Leo said. "Tomorrow is your first day at work. Be ready by four."

With that, Leo left the room. After a deep, ragged sigh, Owen decided that it was time to take a shower.

LEO NODDED at the men guarding Owen's room. He hadn't been surprised to hear that Owen had left the apartment. He did send one of his men to follow him and take note of where he was going. Part of him wanted to order them to drag him back if they had to.

The other part figured if Owen had decided to leave, he wasn't going to stop him. Well, maybe he would play sweet and seduce him into staying. Leo dealt in money, not in human trafficking. Of course he would have been very disappointed to lose Owen before he had figured him out.

What did he know about Owen Hart? First, he had the most beautiful eyes Leo had ever seen. Why he covered them with contacts and sunglasses was beyond him. Second, he seemed to know things. While Owen was fighting off his men, Leo had sensed something. Leo had noticed that each of Owen's defenses began with skin-on-skin contact. He might not have noticed with the first guard, but the face-to-face contact with the second had driven the point home.

He also remembered Owen's face when he'd turned his attention to Leo. Owen had brushed his fingers gently across his own. His expression, though.... Shock showed on his face, followed by confusion. The same thing had happened again with his kiss. Leo wouldn't be surprised if Owen initiated it for whatever reason he touched others.

Not that he was complaining. That wavy black hair that rested on slim shoulders, constantly getting in his eyes. The smooth, pale skin and those kissable pink lips. Yeah, Leo knew this would be interesting.

"Sir."

Leo turned his attention to the petite man who had come up behind him. It was very disconcerting how he could sneak up so soundlessly when he wasn't even trying. He may be small, but Leo had seen him take out opponents nearly twice his size.

"Yes, Alex?" Leo responded, letting his mind focus back to the present.

"Your dinner appointment has arrived," Alex said, his voice almost melodic.

"Good," Leo said, turning to follow Alex. "Why did they send you?"

Leo thought he caught a glimpse of a blush, but Alex turned back around too quickly to verify.

"Well, Jacob is on guard duty, and I figured I would come up to, uh, cover for him."

Leo couldn't hide his smile. Thank goodness Alex was facing away. Cover for him, huh? Everyone knew that Alex was smitten with Jacob. He always found a reason to be nearby. Leo had actually separated them on guard duty because he knew it would be a distraction.

Leo had always wondered if Jacob felt the same way. That man didn't wear his heart on his sleeve. If he had feelings for Alex, he hid them very well. They would make for an interesting pair, though. Aside from their height difference, their energy levels varied greatly. While Jacob was what Leo would call "an old soul," Alex was like the energizer bunny.

Leo sensed energy in Owen also. His reaction to all of this was fun to watch. He seemed to believe he was hiding himself very well, but he had a lot of tells when it came to his true thoughts and emotions. Finding out what Owen was up to was twice as fun now that Leo enjoyed his personality. He wondered how Owen would do working at the casino.

Leo intended to send Jacob to discreetly babysit him.

CHAPTER 5

"OWEN! GET these drinks over to blackjack table two."

"On it," Owen said. He picked up the tray and carried it carefully to the people at the table. He had experience in waiting tables, so walking with the trays was easy for him. He had started his first day at around 5:00 p.m. It had been very slow until about seven, when he started having more orders. Owen minded the crowd but did not mind the tips. On one hand, his head was pounding with the juxtaposition of excitement and anxiety mixed with anger coming from the gamblers. He tried to focus on the former and push the latter out of his mind (literally).

"How is it going, Owen? Good first day so far?"

Owen turned his attention to an Asian woman with long black hair broken up by dark blue highlights. She had been the first to introduce herself, as Yuri. She had worked there for five years, had two dogs and an adopted child, and was happily married to her life partner, Rebecca. She had thrown this information at Owen like a bucket of water in his face, but she had such a good aura and a genuine nature that Owen didn't mind.

"It's going well, Yuri. Is there an alternative dress code? This shirt is making me hot as hell!"

Owen wore a white long-sleeved shirt, covered by a maroon vest, and with a maroon jacket like the cherry on top. Yuri laughed.

"Usually we take the jackets off later in the night when people care less about how we're dressed. We're not supposed to, but Mr. Ellis usually turns a blind eye."

That reminded him. "Yuri, what do you know about Le... Mr. Ellis?"

She looked at him curiously. Owen wondered if his question sounded as nervous as he felt.

"He is a truly kind man. He keeps his word and is very generous with his staff. Not just with things like bonuses and gifts. He is the kind of man who will work with you when you need anything like days off for sickness and family. He actually paid for childcare for Lou, mine and

Rebecca's son, when neither of us could afford it or watch him ourselves. That went on for about a month. When we finally got back on our feet, we tried to pay him back, but he refused to take the money."

Owen didn't know what to say. He stayed for a moment, enjoying the true fondness emanating from Yuri's truth.

She gave him another look before shrugging and taking her orders to the bar.

"You seem like a nice kid. And with your looks, I suspect you'll be getting good tips." She laughed at her own joke. "Now go. Shoo. Do your job!"

Owen smiled and walked his drinks out to the patrons.

YURI HADN'T been kidding. By the time his shift was over, Owen had made almost two hundred dollars in tips alone! That was certainly worth the pain pounding behind his eyes.

Not even a minute after Owen finished his shift, he felt a familiar aura behind him. He turned around quickly enough to see Jacob standing with his hand up as if to tap Owen on the shoulder. He froze for a moment in surprise before lowering his hand and smiling right to his eyes.

"How was your first day?" he asked quietly, gesturing to the exit when Owen didn't immediately follow him.

Owen was still unsure of his standing here, and he felt that it would be smart to keep what he could to himself. But Jacob was so nice! And the eddy of positive emotion coming from him was easing his headache.

"It was fun, actually. I met some new people. Plus I stayed busy, which distracted me from my headache."

"Headache?"

"Oh yeah, I get migraines a lot," Owen said quickly.

"Would you like me to send for something for that?"

"Yes, that would be good," Owen said, knowing from experience that there was no medication that could stop the headaches he had. He always had to wait it out.

They said little else as Owen followed Jacob out of the casino, into the shiny black car, and back to the apartment building. It was almost one in the morning when Owen walked into his own apartment. He shut the door and locked it behind him.

"How did it go?"

Owen yelped and spun around. Leo was sitting at the kitchen island with a laptop in front of him, wearing a pair of glasses that made his eyes pop. Owen was defiantly not used to being surprised by the presence of other people. He would have to adjust that with Leo. Be more mindful.

"Is this, like, a thing? Are you going to be in here every time I come back?" Owen was only half joking.

Leo laughed lightly, gesturing for Owen to join him. "You didn't answer my question," he said with a smile.

"Nor you mine." Owen couldn't stop the contagious smile as he walked over and occupied the stool next to Leo.

"I was sick of being stuck in my office, and I knew you wouldn't be back for a few hours, so I took over your rooms. Apologies for that. I had also wanted to catch you before you went to sleep to find out… how did it go?"

"I would say surprisingly good. Everyone was so nice when I thought I would be surrounded by gangsters."

"Oh, but don't forget that gangsters can still be charming."

"Believe me, I…." Owen's face heated.

"Oh, do finish that thought, Owen."

Owen felt his flush get darker. Something about hearing his own name on Leo's lips sounded so sensual. Fingers lifted his chin until he was looking into Leo's eyes.

"I do wish you would leave the contacts off," Leo said, pouting like a child.

Nervous laughter bubbled up inside Owen but was quickly silenced when Leo lifted Owen's face farther and pressed his lips gently onto Owen's. Leo cupped Owen's cheek, and Owen held on to Leo's wrists as he lazily licked and nipped at Owen's lower lip. Owen opened his mouth to suck up air, and Leo quickly took advantage with his tongue. Hyperawareness suffused Owen's body with each caress of Leo's tongue. Leo's hands burned on his face before one hand dropped to slowly glide down Owen's neck to his chest, then farther, working its way down his body.

Owen felt like something wasn't right, but for the life of him couldn't think of what.

Leo cupped the bulge in Owen's pants, and he moaned into the mouth still covering his.

Had any of the blood that went to his member stayed in his head, he would have appreciated the dexterity with which Leo opened his pants using only one hand. Part of Owen wondered if this was the right thing to do. The other, much larger, part wondered why the hell not.

"Wait, wait, wait!" Owen shouted against Leo's lips, pushing off of his chair and nearly falling to the floor. A look of childlike disappointment crossed Leo's face, but he didn't try to stop Owen's retreat.

"Umm...." Owen tried to catch his breath.

Leo smiled and waved a hand. "It's okay, Owen. Not everyone can handle a catch like me." Leo's laugh was light and genuine. Owen marveled at how unaffected he looked while Owen scrambled to make his brain reboot.

"Umm...," Owen started, then stopped again, totally unable to get more than that out right then. Leo must have realized this, as he smiled knowingly.

"Oh, and this isn't the only reason I'm here. In about a week and a half, there will be a fundraiser at the mansion of one of my business associates. You will be joining me."

Owen couldn't help snorting at the wording. His brain finally unfogged enough for some anxiety to kick in.

"So, what exactly am I supposed to do there?" he asked.

"Well, you are expected to make light conversation. The fundraiser is for some kind of endangered animal organization." He idly flipped his hair behind his back. "Don't ask me for details. I never know. No one tries to talk to me about such things anyway."

Leo smiled widely at Owen, actually going so far as to boop him on the nose with his pointer finger. Owen unconsciously brought his hand up to his nose, feeling the ghost of a touch there.

"You, on the other hand, have to learn enough about this stuff to bullshit your way through. I have a folder with just such information here. There is also a touch of information about the guests," he said, handing over a small file, which Owen noticed was titled Owen Thing.

"Oorrrr," Leo drew out the word, "you can get a sense of—" Leo paused and frowned as if trying to work an idea out in his head. "—something like that," he finished, watching for Owen's reaction.

Inside, Owen's stomach flipped until he thought he might throw up. Why was Leo fishing? He was uncomfortably close to the truth. Owen kept his expression carefully flat and unaffected. Leo searched Owen's face for a moment, then shrugged.

"I'll be busy tomorrow for most of the day. All amenities here are open to you. If you don't leave, you may come with me to lunch at Lola's."

Owen perked up. The deceptively small café had amazing soups, salads, sandwiches, and the best selection of sweet and fancy coffees in town. His thoughts must have shown on his face, because Leo took on a look of pride.

"I funded the whole thing. They paid me back but still find a place to seat me whenever I wish to eat there. They even named a sandwich after me: the Lion."

Owen let out a short laugh. That sandwich had the entire kitchen sink in it. It was chaotic, untraditional, and delicious. Even though it was a pain in the ass to eat. Yes, that seemed like a suitable name for Leo's sandwich.

CHAPTER 6

THE NIGHT before the fundraiser, Owen could barely sleep. He tossed and turned all night, staring at the clock and trying to will himself to sleep. Much too soon the sun came up, and Owen hopped out of his bed with a sigh and a heavy body. No matter how hard he had tried to stave off the thought of being at some party with a bunch of rich people, especially the ones whose work was not very clean, anxiety still took over.

What was he going to say? How was he going to handle shaking hands? He knew he couldn't wear his gloves at a fancy event. And how tight were the quarters? How many people would there be? Would he be able to focus with everyone's thoughts and feelings competing for his attention?

What was he going to *wear*? On one hand, he didn't want to draw any undue attention to himself. But on the other hand, there were so many stylish suits hung up in his closet (he had scoped out his new wardrobe to make sure it was up to par) that Owen would way rather wear than—*so help him God*—a plain black suit.

Owen put on a bathing suit. Every day after he swam, Owen would hang his suit in the shower to dry. For some reason housekeeping, or whoever they were, kept giving him new ones when the wet one was perfectly fine.

He threw on a T-shirt (which had mysteriously appeared when he mentioned to Jacob that he didn't have anything to wear downstairs to the pool) and grabbed a few cupcakes.

Owen stepped outside, and Jacob immediately reached out for a cupcake, which Owen happily handed over. It would seem that Jacob had a sweet tooth.

"Pool?" he asked, clearly already knowing the answer.

"Yup."

When they got down to the first floor, Owen began to hand out his precariously balanced cupcakes to the staff members he passed. This earned a "Thank you" and a bright smile from most of the men and women. Some people declined, but Owen could sense their appreciation for the gesture.

And as of today, he was officially out of cupcakes. He thought about all the smiling faces his cakes left in their wake. He would have to make something else to feed the masses. Not that he was complaining. In fact, his soul felt on fire with the idea that he finally had an excuse to bake an insane number of pastries on a regular basis.

With that comforting thought, Owen went for a swim to clear his head and hopefully lessen that intense feeling of dread growing in his stomach.

OWEN DIDN'T go to work that day, so he was alone with his own thoughts and fears. He played video games and watched movies for most of the day. He couldn't for the life of him understand why he still needed a babysitter. Granted, he no longer needed to tolerate that asshole Seth, and Jacob was great company when he came in for food whenever Owen cooked (that fridge was never empty) or to play a few rounds of cards.

So he didn't truly mind it, but it did make him feel untrustworthy.

Leo's folder had indicated that there would be no sit-down dinner tonight, so he whipped up some chicken parmesan for Jacob and himself.

"Are you nervous?" For all that Jacob was initially intimidating to Owen, he now found his taciturn nature very genuine and kind.

"Well, yes. I've never done anything like this before."

Jacob took a bite of his chicken, appearing lost in thought.

"Honestly, Owen, you'll be fine. Mr. Ellis sees something in you that would make you an appropriate guest. He very seldom makes a wrong decision when it comes to trusting his people. Let's make a deal. I won't be at the fundraiser tonight myself, but I have a coworker, Alex, who is very sweet and has a keen eye. I'll ask him to look out for you, and if you seem to need rescue, he'll come get you as if on some business or other."

"Thank you," Owen said, actually a bit relieved. He encountered very few people who offered this level of kindness and truly meant it. He looked down at his plate as a distraction from how deeply that sentiment had touched him.

"I should have made spaghetti," he said, frowning slightly at the oversight.

Jacob burst out laughing, and Owen couldn't avoid the tickle in the air and joined in.

OWEN NEEDN'T have worried about his outfit. A woman had come to his room bearing a fresh tailor-made suit. Thank God it wasn't black. Instead, it was a sleek, slim-fit slate suit over a dark plum-colored shirt. A gray tie was draped along the hanger. After quickly getting him dressed, the woman checked the fit and look before smiling, patting him on the head, and leaving.

Owen was confused by how fast it had happened.

"Thank you?" he tried to say loud enough for her quickly retreating figure to hear.

Jacob popped his head in before the door closed.

"That suits you," he said, "and be ready in an hour. The car will be waiting."

Owen nodded before he realized that Jacob had already closed the door.

"What the hell am I supposed to do for an hour?" Owen whispered to himself. He really didn't want to be reminded of how close he was to this event. An hour was not enough time to really mentally prepare, and it was too much time to wallow in his anxiety. Owen glanced at the kitchen wistfully.

Nope. Not enough time to bake. And besides, he wasn't about to ruin this suit. He couldn't even imagine how much it cost. Owen sighed, sitting on the couch carefully so as not to wrinkle the suit before he even left his room.

OWEN WAS startled out of his game of Ms. Pacman by a knock at the door.

"Yes?" he called out.

Jacob opened the door slightly at first and then fully when he saw that he had Owen's attention.

"Owen, remember my friend Alex? Well, he's here to take you to the car."

A short man, maybe five feet seven to Owen's six, popped up from behind the door. Tall next to Owen, Jacob's height dwarfed Alex physically, but Owen could already sense the excess swirling energy bouncing around Alex. It made his presence almost larger than life.

"Mr. Hart! I heard so much about you. I hear tell that you make cupcakes?"

Owen thought that Alex was going to come and offer a handshake, but he stayed back.

"Owen is fine. I ran out, but I love baking, so there will be more pastries coming soon."

A look of excitement crossed Jacob's face, then disappeared so quickly Owen wasn't even sure he had seen it. He would have to ask about his favorite sweets—if Jacob would admit how much he liked them.

A short, aborted laugh drew Owen back to Alex, quickly enough to realize that his entire focus was on Jacob. He turned back to Owen when he realized he was caught.

"So, are you ready to go downstairs? Jacob told me you're nervous about tonight."

Owen shot Jacob a look, feeling like a small, whiny child.

Alex continued unperturbed. "If you need a rescue, give me a little wave. Tonight I am personally in charge of your welfare, so I'll notice. And don't worry, you'll probably get a lot of attention from the get-go. People are always curious about Mr. Ellis's companions. He picks well. Which means he picked *you* well too." Alex's smile was as big as his confidence.

"And then it'll get much less interesting as people settle down." Alex nodded to himself as if this were fact.

"Are you ready?" Jacob asked calmly.

Owen took a deep breath. "Yes."

OWEN WAS as wonderful as Jacob had told him. Well, of course his words were "He has a good heart," but by those standards, Alex knew that he would really like Owen. He was glad that Jacob "worked with" Owen. They were a good fit. For a split second, jealousy crept down his spine, but he carefully stomped that down.

Alex didn't know anything about Owen besides what he had heard from Jacob, which was honestly a lot. Jacob was a big gossip when it came to Alex. He liked to think it was because Jacob held Alex in high regard. Maybe even… no. Now was not the time to pine like a schoolgirl.

Alex had been drawn to Jacob since the moment they had met. He was so calm and had such kind eyes. Being with him and speaking with him always tamed the chaotic jumble that was Alex's thoughts.

Owen seemed to be that way too. Alex had been surprised when he met him. Alex had sensed that Owen felt overwhelmed when he introduced himself, which was normal. What wasn't normal was the knowing smile he had given him. And did he imagine it, or did Owen look at Jacob then back at him as if he knew his secret?

Owen walked in front of him. His shoulders were back, and he walked with an air of confidence. However, Alex noticed Owen pressing his thumbnails into the palms of his hands. Well, at least he could say Owen bore his anxiety well. Alex watched him, trying to get to know his subtleties. Owen had a calming presence. Almost like Jacob, but of course no one could reach that Zen nature of his.

Finally the elevator rang for the first floor, and they were off to the car.

"Owen," Alex said quietly, "I won't be with you in the car. It will be you, Mr. Ellis, his personal guard, and a driver. I will see you again at the venue."

He leaned in closer and whispered, "You've got this," in a muted yet still very excited tone.

OWEN HAD no idea how a grown man could buzz with as much chaotic energy as Alex. It didn't hurt his head or drown out his surroundings, it just sort of swirled around.

Owen had tried to build himself up for this event as best he could. It wasn't until Alex had come for him that he really felt the panic. And it wasn't only for the event. Leo had cancelled on their lunch date but instead had started eating dinner with Owen. Well, it was food Owen made for himself that Leo sort of stole. After the first two nights with the surprise dinner guest, Owen started cooking for two.

Owen had to laugh at himself. For all that Leo was a confusing source of sexual attraction, not to mention his childlike attitude, Owen was taken by him. It was new and scary because he was going in blind. This must be what "normal" people felt like. He didn't know if he loved it or hated it.

Still, it had been over a week, and Owen was starting to feel more comfortable with Leo. Even liked him for more than the base attraction that he couldn't shake.

Alex opened the door to the street.

"Owen!" came a loud, familiar voice.

"Uhh…," Owen was caught off guard by the sheer energy in that voice. And then by the person that voice was coming from.

Leo was leaning lazily against a sleek black town car. When Owen got closer, he uncrossed his arms and reached out to ruffle Owen's unruly hair. Before he could think of what he was doing, he knocked Leo's hand away, earning a laugh.

"You can't mess up a man's hair," he said indignantly, running his fingers through his hair to try to tame the chaos.

"I'm sure its fine," Leo said, opening the car door and gesturing him in, like, well, an escort.

Leo followed him in, and they sat face-to-face in the very roomy back seat. There was some light in the car and drinks and snacks. Owen was too nervous to touch anything. Leo opened a small fridge under the seat.

"Pick your poison," he said, gesturing to the beer, soda, and then the liquor next to it. Owen shook his head.

"No, thank you. Already I am not confident in my knowledge from that truly crappy file you gave me." Owen was irritated all over again. It seemed that the same level of competence had been used in the information gathering as in the naming of the file: Owen Thing.

Leo laughed.

"I assure you that it was I who named the file but not I who made it. I take only half the blame."

Owen smiled despite himself.

LEO FELT his heart swell at Owen's smile. And at the level of comfort he seemed to be showing. Yes, Leo could see the anxiety present on the fringe, but nothing like it had been before.

Any boredom Leo had experienced before getting in the car was wiped right away by how amazing Owen looked in that suit.

And if nothing else, Leo was known to be a good judge of character. He wasn't trying to string Owen along and show him off as a pretty face.

Leo knew that he was fit for this role he'd put Owen in. If he hadn't been sure, he would never put him through such an ordeal. No, this would work.

Leo had been so excited for this fundraiser. Usually these events bored the living shit out of him, but tonight he had *Owen*. He was so anxious to see how Owen would respond to this situation. He was honestly hoping that Owen would slip up and expose whatever it was he could do. Leo was reasonably sure that it was some kind of knowledge Owen obtained through skin-to-skin contact, but he wasn't sure what that did and did not entail.

Owen had a great personality. He was kind, friendly, stubborn, and apparently trustworthy. And he had an air of decorum that was so appropriate for his job as an escort. Should tonight go as Leo desired, he hoped it would convince Owen to stay on.

Leo took a closer look at Owen.

He gripped Owen's face, a cheek gently placed in each hand.

"Wha…?" Owen said, but Leo shushed him. He squirmed uncomfortably.

"Why are you still wearing those contacts?" Leo asked.

Owen's features deflated as if in relief, then twisted up in annoyance.

"Listen, I respect that this is your thing, and I want to live up to your expectations, but please stop asking me to take them off. I hate standing out because that means more attention, and more attention means bigger headaches, and…." Owen trailed off, murmuring to himself inaudibly.

Leo smiled. That was the most honest thing he had heard from Owen since they met. But he caught something.

"Owen?" he asked.

Owen looked at him, frustration still in his eyes.

"Owen, why would attention give you a headache?"

Leo watched Owen's body tense up. He waited for a moment to see if Owen would say anything useful, but instead he redirected.

"How long does it take to get there?" he asked.

Leo smiled tightly, disappointed but not willing to push it.

"We have about ten minutes," he said.

Owen nodded sharply. And that was enough sour attitude for Leo's taste.

He pinched one of Owen's cheeks, hard.

"Hey!" Owen yelped, but his body language softened.

Leo smiled and gave him a quick wink. The corners of Owen's lips started to turn up despite his obvious effort to fight the feeling. Leo wanted to know what Owen had meant exactly. Did Owen have some sort of empathy? Leo couldn't quite nail it down. However, Owen was going to have enough on his plate tonight without worrying that his precious little secret was out, so Leo let it drop. Speaking of....

"Owen. I'm not going to make you take out those boring contacts tonight. But. Going forward you will not wear them when you're with me. And maybe not at work because you would probably get amazing tips. Okay?"

Owen gave him a look of disbelief. "Can we revisit this when I'm not being faced with so much anxiety already?"

Leo smiled, seeing that the response was irritation but not anger.

"I will happily discuss this another time. Anyway, we are here."

OWEN WAS bamboozled. Leo had at least distracted him enough on the ride over to calm the fear that was now setting in, but he couldn't believe that he had let slip even the slightest detail about his "gift." Leo couldn't possibly guess the specifics, though.

The driver opened the door, and Leo gestured for Owen to step out first. Owen wasn't sure what he was expecting. Maybe a ton of news paparazzi or undercover cops trying to nab a crime ring. In reality, Owen stepped out into the quiet night at the end of a very long driveway leading up to a *very* large white house. Men and women were dressed to the nines. Some people milled about on the grass, getting into conversations before even gaining entry.

Leo stepped out behind him, placed a hand on each of Owen's shoulders, and whispered, "It's going to be fine. You will do wonderfully."

Owen took a deep breath, Leo's warm words comforting him a little bit.

"Ready?" Leo asked quietly.

Owen nodded, and with a gentle pat on the back from Leo and a quick glace behind at Alex (who gave him two thumbs up quickly enough that no one noticed), Owen headed up the driveway to the mansion.

CHAPTER 7

"OH, HELLO, dear. You must be Leo's new companion! My name is Charlene, and you are?"

A middle-aged woman offered her hand, and Owen took it. For the third time so far, he sucked up any important information to generate a brief yet enjoyable conversation for the both of them. He had no idea where Leo was. He had disappeared almost immediately with a mock salute.

"I'm Owen. It's a pleasure to make your acquaintance."

Charlene gripped his hand with both of hers briefly, then let go.

"So what do you think of this noble cause we stand for tonight, Owen?"

Owen could hear in her voice that she expected him to be caught off guard, assuming he was there just for show and wanting to drive that home for him. Passive aggression at its genteel finest. Well, tough shit, lady.

"Oh, you know, saving the wildlife is so important, but I can't help thinking that we are spending more time on animals than we do our own people."

Charlene made a sound of surprise. Excitement filled the air around her.

"Charlene, have you ever heard of the organization called Invisible Children?" Owen continued.

"Oh yes, I have! I've been planning a bit of a fundraiser of my own for that very cause."

"I can barely imagine a world where children must fear for their lives, facing death or enslavement, which is nearly as bad. Yet no one pays them any mind. These children and their parents must live in fear every day that they will be taken."

"Oh, how lovely to hear someone who sees what a truly humanitarian cause this is," Charlene exclaimed.

"I am sure your fundraiser would be wonderfully helpful."

"Believe me, you will be invited, with or without Leo Ellis." She turned around at the sound of her name being called.

"Ah, excuse me, Owen. I must away. It was wonderful to meet you."

Owen waved, resisting the temptation to flip her off on her way. She was the third person (of three) to come talk to him with the distinct objective of making him look stupid. Which would have reflected poorly on him but more importantly on Leo.

For the moment Owen was alone. He took a quick glance around the room and spotted Leo, head down in conversation with two important-looking men in a distant corner of the room. Owen took another brief look around and spotted Alex, eyes sharp and directed at him. Owen took a couple of steps before yet another person walked toward him with ill intent. He discreetly waved his hand at Alex and turned to a man approaching to say he was needed elsewhere.

Without even hearing him come, Owen felt a hand on his shoulder.

"Excuse me. Mr. Hart, you are needed for a moment."

"Thank you, Alex," he said before turning to the gentleman. "Excuse me, sir."

"THANK GOD for you, Alex, Owen said with a weary sigh once they had stepped out to the relative privacy of the patio.

"That was great, Owen! I tell you, not one of Leo's other escorts have ever made him look so good. It's like you always know the exact right thing to say."

Owen blushed at the praise. Still....

"Alex, I feel like I've run two marathons. When do we leave?"

Alex's smile turned gentle. It reminded him of the rare moments when his mother had smiled at him like that.

"Owen, you can leave whenever you want to. Leo wanted you here, but he didn't expect you to stay for the whole party, not your first time. He actually said something to me about you getting overwhelmed easily."

Owen pouted at the comment, then seriously considered it.

"Yes, but do you know how much more of the event is left?"

"I would say maybe two hours."

Owen nodded.

"I'm good. I just need a break." Owen looked around as the people milling outside increased in number. "Do you have another hiding spot?"

Alex smiled. "Of course."

Alex led Owen to a bedroom set far enough away from the party that no one would look for him.

"There are rooms set aside for the guests who may need to spend the night because of business dealings. This one is for Mr. Ellis. Only he or you would enter."

Owen nodded. "Thank you."

"I'll be right outside the door. If you need me, come get me."

Alex gently closed the door, leaving behind a mist of compassion and excitement. Although he always seemed to be excited. Owen laughed to himself.

He sat on the comfy king-size bed, bouncing a few times before lying down. He was about to do some breathing exercises to get back in shape mentally for the party when he was struck by an overpoweringly negative and hateful energy. He shot up in the bed and tried to locate the source. He could feel it coming from the doorway.

Knowing what to expect, Owen jumped off the bed and went flat on the floor. Not under the bed; it would be too hard to escape. He heard the door open, and before he could even think of what to do, he was struck by a thought. Where was Alex?

He reached out his feelers and felt a small energy, probably knocked out? It was tainted with pain, but the residual sensations were still there, so Alex was alive.

Now what? Owen peered around for some kind of weapon. He didn't see anything.

Fuck.

With no other option, Owen rolled under the bed as the intruder moved toward his side. When he looked up, he saw a hunting knife taped to the underside of the bed. Weird, but who cared at that point?

Owen pulled the knife away from its hiding spot, and without hesitating, he slashed it right across the man's Achilles tendon. He heard him shriek and hit the floor.

Owen continued to roll out from under the bed on the other side and ran for the door. He stepped behind it as another man walked in, likely in response to his comrade's screams. His was the only energy remaining besides Alex, who was still down for the count.

The man burst into the room wielding a gun. Owen snuck behind him and stabbed him in the arm holding the gun. He dropped it to the floor, and Owen quickly grabbed it and pointed it at him.

"Who are you, and what are you doing here?"

In his anger, his hands and his voice shook. No one should treat Alex like that. He was too much of a sweetheart.

"We came for Ellis when we heard someone come up here, but what we got instead was his little whore."

Owen thought he was going to lose it. "His *what*? Are you fucking kidding me?"

"Come on, kid, you're not going to shoot me."

Owen couldn't count the times that people thought he was some frail little boy with no experience in the dirty side of life. Well, they were wrong.

"Just give me the—" the man started.

Owen steadied his hand and shot the thug right in the kneecap.

"Fuuuuuuck!"

He hit the ground like a bag of bricks.

Owen glanced back at the other man, whose eyes were focused on his partner in surprise.

"Do you want to lose a kneecap too?" Owen threatened. "Or was the ankle good enough for you?"

The man shook his head quickly, raised one hand in the air, and left one hand on his wound. Owen could only imagine the pain a wound like that would evoke.

As he was heading toward the door, maintaining eye contact with his attackers, he felt a burst of pain and worry.

"Alex, are you okay?" Owen asked before opening the door all the way.

"I'm fine. What happened? Are *you* okay?"

"I'm fine," Owen frowned down at the floor.

I don't see how they are going to get this blood off the carpet, he thought.

Alex's eyes went wide, and Owen realized that he had said that out loud. Before he could give an excuse for the clearly inappropriate remark, Alex burst out laughing, then covered his mouth to stop himself. At least he felt well enough to laugh.

"Are you okay?" Owen repeated. "What happened to you?"

"Oh, fine. I just got a bump on the head." Alex frowned. "Not very good at my job tonight, I guess."

Owen patted him on the back, gun still aimed at the closest goon. "Que será," he said. Then Owen had a thought. "Alex, why was there a hunting knife taped under the bed?"

Alex looked surprised for a moment and glanced at the intruders. When he saw the stab wounds, he smiled.

"This house is a no-gun zone. While this is often respected, Mr. Ellis doesn't want to take any chances, so he leaves the knife there in case of emergency. It seems that his caution has paid off."

Alex considered the man cradling his knee, smearing blood all around himself. He took a step forward and kicked him hard enough in the face that he lost consciousness—and probably a few teeth. The other man was (smartly) staying put.

Alex pulled a cell phone out of his pocket and quick dialed.

"We have a situation in the bedroom. Two unidentified males, incapacitated, needing special attention."

Owen somehow felt that last bit was rather sinister. And it may well have been, what with the anger that was emanating from Alex now that the shock was over.

"Yes, yes. Owe—Mr. Hart is fine. Please have Mr. Ellis wait until we can confirm that the area is clear. What do you mean—" Alex cut off as Leo burst into the room.

"Owen? Are you okay? What happened?" Leo said in a rush for answers. It was only after he had done a quick check on Owen, both looking and feeling for wounds, that he stepped back and took stock of the room. His worry subsided in exchange for cool indifference. Owen was happy that he wasn't the cause of that look. It was terrifying. Nothing like the Leo he had come to know.

Leo assessed the two men on the ground. "Alex, what happened?"

Alex bowed his head slightly but appeared calm and collected. Nevertheless, Owen could feel the anxiety flowing out of him in waves.

"Two hostiles surprised me and knocked me out. You'll have to ask Owen for the details after that, but it appears he found your emergency knife and... took care of the situation."

Owen thought he saw Alex's lip twitch as if he was hiding a smile.

Leo gazed at Owen for a moment, then at the two men, then back at Owen.

"Did you do this?" he asked, surprise clear in his voice.

"Um. Yes?" he responded.

Leo laughed and reached his hand out toward Owen. "You won't need that anymore."

Owen looked at him strangely until he realized that he was still holding the gun. He handed it over.

"Can I assume that this is not your first time firing a weapon?"

Owen shook his head and shrugged. "I learned about guns at a young age."

Leo suddenly looked very interested. "While I have no information on your younger years, I would very much like to hear more about this when this whole"—he waved his hand around the room—"mess has been taken care of. You may go home with Alex."

Owen wasn't surprised that Leo lacked information on his childhood. He was off the grid for most of his younger years. He had lived with the professor, his mentor and surrogate father, since the age of thirteen, and he valued his privacy. The professor was eccentric, but he had been good to Owen, helping him learn about what he could do and how he could control and filter all the swirling emotions that existed within people.

And of course, he had taught Owen how to fight.

"Come, Mr. Hart. The car is here."

Owen nodded as Alex patted his shoulder before leading the way to the exit. As he walked, he noticed that no one even turned in their direction. It seemed no one had heard the gunshots. The room must have been soundproofed.

They made it outside and down the driveway. Alex ushered him into the car and then took a step back to close the door.

"Wait! Alex, um," Owen paused, not sure if asking would make him seem weak.

"Yes, Owen?" Alex smiled as if they shared a secret. His energy was so, well, energetic. With a hint of shame.

"Do you think you could ride with me? In the back?"

Alex looked surprised for a moment, then smiled knowingly. Owen would never have asked such a thing in a situation he didn't totally comprehend, but Alex's aura was comforting.

"Sure thing." He went to the passenger door and said something to the driver before jumping into the seat across from Owen.

"Wow, feels fancy," Alex said, taking stock of his surroundings. "I'm not really used to being on this side of the car." He mused, "So, Owen. Would you be up for this again?" The tone of his voice was light, but Owen could sense that he was also being serious.

Owen shrugged. "Pack me a knife in my suit, and then we'll talk."

Alex laughed again, dissipating the tension. "Unfortunately, I don't think that I will be on 'Owen duty' for quite a while after this." He frowned, "I'll tell you a secret." He leaned in and whispered, "You're the most interesting person in this whole damn organization."

Owen chuckled, feeling the stress from the ordeal melt further away. His headache, though, was there to stay for a while. He closed his eyes against the ache.

"Owen, are you truly okay?" Alex asked quietly.

Without even opening his eyes, he nodded and leaned his head against the seat.

"I have a migraine, that's all," he said.

Alex didn't respond, but Owen could almost sense a nod. He must have fallen asleep, because the next thing he knew, Alex was gently shaking him awake and guiding him to his room. Without even bothering to change, he hit the pillow and drifted off.

CHAPTER 8

LEO STOOD in the cold, unfinished basement of the house. He could feel rage bleeding into his every thought and feeling. He could feel it buzz inside his body. Leo held all of his employees in high standing and would be furious if they were harmed, but Owen? This was different. Owen was *his*. Well, not really. He had only known him two weeks, and even the knowledge he had on his background was (as he'd realized tonight) shaky at best.

But he was so kind. Jacob had kept him abreast of all of Owen's comings and goings and how he seemed to leave many friends in his wake. He was fun and beautiful and….

He was nearly killed.

Leo almost growled. He stopped and took a deep breath. This was not going to work if he didn't keep his head. He turned when he heard grunting as two men were tossed on the floor in front of him. They were bound, but both were conscious and aware, their wounds tended to enough that they wouldn't bleed out.

Leo gestured to one of his guards and was handed a gun.

"Who the hell do you…?" the man with the shot kneecap started to say before Leo blew a hole through his head.

The other man looked shocked.

"I only need one of you. Now, either your fate could be worse than his, or you can tell me who hired you and I will kill you kindly."

LEO FIRED his last shot into the body of the low-level guard on the ground. It was his last bullet as he had felt that the man's death should be a slow one despite his candor. So Maxwell Balor was out to get him now.

Balor had been a thorn in Leo's side for years. He constantly interfered with Leo's business dealings. Specifically, he had an eye out for Leo's casino. It was one of the best money-laundering venues in the state.

The brazenness of the current attempt was even more pronounced because of how poorly his underlings were able to keep his secret in the face of death. Leo surrounded himself with loyal people. He liked to think that most of them would go to the grave before betraying him. He knew in his heart that Alex had nothing to do with this. That was the only reason he had sent him home with Owen.

But things were getting complicated now. This attempt was an audacious one, and it was getting harder to avoid an all-out war with the syndicate.

And they had gone after Owen.

That was another question Leo hadn't thought to ask in his anger. How did they even know that someone had gone to his room? Only he and his men should have known which room was his. Even the house staff wasn't in on assigned rooms.

This whole mess reeked of a message. But who knew? And they'd said they were gunning for Leo, but if they had followed Alex and Owen, they would have immediately known that Leo wasn't there.

Maxwell was becoming a bigger pain in the ass every day.

"Clean this up for me," Leo said, handing over his gun to Seth, who took it and gestured to his other people to take care of the blood and the bodies. It would be rude to leave behind a mess in a host's home.

Too angry to even exchange pleasant goodbyes, besides, of course, with the host, Leo made his way out to the car waiting in the driveway. His people would make their own way home.

He had to go see Owen.

"OWEN." A VERY serious voice pulled Owen abruptly from a deep sleep.

"What? Who?" He shielded his face with his hand and squinted at the figure in the doorway of his bedroom. Leo.

"What time is it?" he asked groggily.

"Owen, are you hurt at all? In any pain?" Leo asked with a seriousness that Owen was not accustomed to hearing from him.

"No, I'm really fine," he replied, growing more alert. He would rather sleep, but Leo seemed to be worried about him. Which was kind of nice.

"Are you okay mentally? Any shock or upset? You could have been killed." The last part held a hint of anger that Owen sensed was not directed at him.

"No, Leo. I'm fine. I hate to break it to you, but that wasn't the first time someone tried to take me out," Owen said, too tired to come up with a lie.

Owen couldn't see the face that Leo made because his back was to the light coming from the other room.

"I'm going to be the nice guy here and let you go back to sleep, with the understanding that you are going to explain that little tidbit of information to me in the morning."

Owen opened his mouth, but Leo interrupted him. He was only going to agree. He felt that this was relevant information for the first time in his life.

"And is there anything you want or need before I let you go back to sleep?"

"No," Owen said, feeling oddly comforted that Leo was so worried about him. He wondered if he was this way with everyone.

Leo looked at Owen for a moment. Owen was wondering what his expression might be when Leo walked over and placed a gentle kiss onto his forehead.

"Good night, Owen," he whispered.

He was up and gone before Owen could respond. The door closed, and Owen flopped back down on the bed. Not awake enough to change but awake enough to realize he was going to ruin this beautiful suit by sleeping in it, Owen peeled off his clothing, dropped it in a controlled pile on the floor, and jumped under the covers.

Owen took a deep breath and felt the pull of deep sleep. Maybe it was the adrenaline that made him feel so glad that Leo hadn't been hurt or attacked too. And maybe that same reason explained how he actually felt kind of... happy to share a piece of himself.

OWEN JERKED awake. He blinked dazedly at the canopy above him. His brain still wasn't working when he heard pounding at the door. So that's what woke him. He pulled himself out of the comfort of his bed, realizing before he got to the door that he was naked.

Well, that would have been embarrassing. He rushed to the bathroom and threw on a robe before opening the door to a bright-eyed Alex.

"Good morning," he said cheerfully.

"Good morning, Alex," Owen said. "So do you know what happened last night? After we left?"

Owen had been too tired both physically and mentally last night to really think about anything like that.

"Ah, well, that's not something that would come from me. You should ask Mr. Ellis. What I am here for is, first of all, to find out if you are all right."

Alex paused, and Owen didn't say anything, taking the moment to read the slice of worry in Alex's truth.

"Well, I know Mr. Ellis has already spoken to you," Alex went on, "but I wanted to know. For myself."

Owen snapped back to the conversation. "Alex, I promise you, I am fine. I slept like a baby last night: no fears, no nightmares."

Alex took a long look at Owen before apparently finding what he was looking for and nodding.

"I'm so glad to hear it."

The usual excited happiness in Alex swirled around Owen. He could never help but smile in its presence. Which reminded him....

"Alex, do you know where Jacob is? He's usually on guard duty during the day."

Alex pouted. "It's not really *guard* duty. It's more like—"

"Babysitting," Owen finished, laughing.

Alex looked for a second like he was going to argue but shrugged.

"Jacob is helping Mr. Ellis with some work. I'm surprised that Mr. Ellis is trusting me with you again after... you know." A look of shame crossed his childlike features.

Owen patted him on the back. "Alex, I could do way worse than you as a babysitter."

Alex laughed, and humor tickled Owen.

"So do we have an agenda today, or can I go to the pool?" Owen asked.

Alex smiled and gestured to the hallway. "Ready when you are!"

LEO WAS *tired*. He had spent all night interviewing both his people and those who were relevant from the fundraiser. Mostly staff. He had his men comb over surveillance video to verify exactly what had happened last night. He'd heard testimony from well over thirty people. The only thing keeping him going was the rage that Owen might have lost his life *directly* because of him.

Owen had nothing to do with his dealings, and even if Leo hadn't liked him or found him interesting, Owen didn't deserve to be brought into Leo's problems like that.

Leo felt a hand on his shoulder and realized that someone had been talking to him.

"Mr. Ellis," Jacob said gently, "I think we can go on from here. You should get some sleep."

Leo looked around. There were only a few people still in the room, and most of them were going over video, accounting for who was where, both at the party and in the building.

"I have to go see Owen. I have some questions," Leo said, getting up.

"No," Jacob said firmly. "Go to sleep. Mr. Hart is at the pool and likely will stay for quite a while." He smiled. "He's like a fish. He would live in the pool if he could."

Leo was torn. On one hand, he was glad Owen was getting along well with everyone. But on the other hand, he was a little jealous they knew things about Owen that he didn't.

With a short sigh, Leo gave in and headed to his penthouse for some sleep.

"Due to these recent events, we are going to bump up security to your apartment. Now both the elevator and door will be guarded by our oldest, most loyal staff. Alex is with Mr. Hart, and I will be here with you, along with Tyler. As I said, for now, go to sleep. Owen will still be here when you wake up."

Would he? Leo wondered if that occupational hazard would chase him away. He was desperate to talk to Owen, see how he was doing. He'd been calm last night, but had that been shock? Or was he putting up a front and planning to leave today?

Leo pressed his fingers against his sinuses; he had a killer headache. Still, he was determined to hear Owen's story. Nothing at all would stop him.

OWEN POPPED out of the pool and sat on the edge with his feet in the water. He splashed around for a minute, then looked over at Alex.

"Are you hungry?" he asked.

Alex shrugged. "Do you want me to order something?" he asked.

Owen rolled his eyes. "You obviously don't know enough about me to babysit. I could whip us up some paninis. They're my specialty!"

Alex smiled. "Whatever you're having, I'll have."

"Good answer," Owen said, pulling his feet out of the pool and walking to the exit. He always wondered why he was the only one in the pool every day. He didn't know if it was a coincidence or if people were kept out while he was there, but he also didn't really care. He loved his alone pool time.

OWEN ATE his sandwich and contemplated what he was going to share with Leo. He wanted to be truthful, but at the same time he wanted to evade some of the details that seemed too personal.

Maybe it was loneliness setting in, but Owen wished there was *someone* in this world who *really* knew him.

He was more nervous than he had been last night. He had been so tired, and the talk had seemed so far away. Now he was anxiously waiting, not knowing how much time he had left.

Feeling well and truly stressed, his thoughts turned to baking.

"Hey, Alex, what kind of sweets does Jacob like?"

Alex snorted. "You could put sugar on a plate and he would eat it." His eyes unfocused for a brief moment, but Owen had caught it. Interesting.

"How about you? What do you want?"

Alex looked a little surprised, then took a moment to think. "I'm one for brownies," he said.

Owen smiled. "Brownies it is."

He thought about starting a batch right then but didn't want to get interrupted. Well, at least he had baking to look forward to. As if on cue, Owen heard a knock on the door. As Alex got up to answer, Owen finished his sandwich in three big bites.

"Hello, Owen. Did I miss paninis?" Jacob asked humorously.

Owen chuckled. "Sorry, today was Alex's turn for lunch."

"Lucky him," Jacob responded. "Mr. Ellis would like to invite you to his rooms. He said that you would know what for."

Owen nodded. He stood up and followed Jacob down the hall. Alex gave a wave and a nod before locking Owen's door and heading down the hall in the opposite direction.

Owen was intrigued. He had never thought about what the penthouse must look like, but now his curiosity was piqued.

OWEN WAITED with bated breath as Leo opened the door to his suite. The first thing he noticed was that Leo looked terrible. He didn't seem to have changed his clothing from the night before, and his suit was a wrinkled mess. He had dark circles under his eyes, and his shoulders were slumped. It was so different from the confidence he normally commanded with his posture.

"Hello, Owen," he said, sounding as tired as he looked.

"Are you feeling okay? I can come back later," Owen said.

Leo shook his head. "Please, come in."

Owen was so concerned with Leo's condition that he hadn't yet taken note of the rooms behind him. If Owen thought his own suite was spacious, it was nothing compared to this. He gazed around. Like his, this room had an open-concept living area/kitchen. From where he was standing, the kitchen appeared even bigger than his. He could bake up a storm in there.

A cough shocked Owen, and he realized he was being rude. When he looked back at Leo, he was smiling.

Jacob was nowhere to be seen; he must have left. Owen wondered if he had gone far. He reached out to the door and picked up a wisp of Jacob's signature pleasant calm. So he must be right outside.

"Owen, have a seat," Leo said, gesturing to the couch. For a second Owen thought Leo would join him on the small couch but was relieved when Leo instead sat on a recliner across from him.

"I was promised a story about someone targeting your life before? And please don't tell me that this has nothing to do with... whatever it is you can do that you are trying to hide. I already *know* something is going on. I'll sit down and write a damn contract with you for nondisclosure if you're so scared of sharing."

Leo sounded so tired that the frustration in his voice was muted.

Owen thought for a moment. He thought. He thought some more. "Okay, we can try this one more time first," he said finally. He closed the space between him and Leo, cupped his cheeks, and leaned in for a kiss. This time Owen was less anxious, and he was able to feel something. It was faint, but he could sense fatigue, frustration, and infatuation. Owen blushed at that last one.

Right before he pulled back, Owen asked, *Can I trust you?* As he leaned away, he got his answer: *To the grave.*

Leo looked confused. His facial expressions were pretty easy to read, probably since he was so tired.

By contrast, Owen was *thrilled* that he had finally gotten something out of Leo. It was faint, but he had felt it. And he trusted it.

"Why don't we settle in, Leo. This is a long story."

CHAPTER 9

IT BEGAN when Owen was ten. Until then he'd had a good childhood. Friends, food, the love and attention of his mother. She was his everything. His father hadn't been around for as long as Owen could remember, but he never missed him. He loved his mother, and she always knew when he had done something wrong.

One day when Owen was eight or nine, he stole a piece of gum from the bodega down the street. He rushed home, heart pounding until he was sure that he wasn't followed. He'd taken two steps into the house when his mom, without even turning to look at him, said, "Why are you feeling so guilty?"

He froze. And then he started to cry. His mother walked over and shushed him.

"What did you do?" she asked gently.

Owen wiped his nose with his sleeve. "I stole a piece of gum. I'm sorry." He sniffed but stopped crying.

"Well, I'm sure it's fine, but don't do it again. Theft is not a harmless crime, you know."

"How did you know?" A question that Owen had asked her every time she seemed to be able to read his mind.

"I can sense your guilt." she would always reply with a laugh.

It wasn't until later that he realized she was being literal.

It was when Owen was ten that something changed. It started with headaches. Owen's head would constantly feel like it was pounding behind his eyes. His only break from the pain was when he was alone in his room. So he stopped going to see friends outside of school. Soon after, something snapped.

The pain, thoughts, and emotions, all jumbled up from people he stood close to. His mind was a chaotic mess, and he took to hiding in secret corners of the house, seeking solitude. At around the same time, his mother started to change.

He confided in her only once about what was happening to him. She had been drunk (as she had been more and more frequently at this time), and she picked up a table lamp, smashed it on the floor, and slurred, "Well, you're fucked. Get used to it."

That sent a chill down his spine, and he never spoke of it again.

Men started coming over. Broken liquor bottles were exchanged for dirty needles scattered on the floor. There was very little food in the house. Owen got used to going hungry.

Owen knew to hide when the men came around. A few had beaten him bloody. Two had attempted sexual assault. In the first incident, he got away and hid. The second happened when he was twelve. He ran right out of the house and never looked back.

OWEN LIVED on the streets after that. He stayed in one of the abandoned industrial buildings on the south side of the city, where he was joined by sex workers, junkies, runaways, thieves, and the generally homeless.

Owen stayed wherever there were fewer people, and he would isolate himself from those who were there. He made the mistake of making friends with a sex worker who must have only been about fifteen. They spoke often when they saw each other. Then one day Owen saw her get into a car and felt an energy so bad it smacked him in the face.

He would have called to her, but she was already gone. He never saw her again.

Owen took to pickpocketing. He learned the trade from a few boys in his building. He had an easy time of it because, as he lived in the chaos, he began to be able to pick out individual streams of energies.

One day—and he didn't know at the time, but this would become his thirteenth birthday—Owen picked the wrong (well, or right) mark. He was a tall broad-shouldered man, with black hair slicked stylishly back. He must have been in his late fifties. He wore a gold chain and rings, and Owen was sure he would walk away with a big score this time.

Before Owen was even a yard away, the man turned around and looked directly at him. Without breaking stride, Owen gazed down at the pavement and made like he was trying to cross the street. Before he could get to the edge of the sidewalk, Owen felt a firm hand on his shoulder.

"I can give you money if that's what you are looking for, but I don't think that's what you truly need."

Owen tensed up. He was *not* a hooker. Well, some of his friends were, but that was beside the point.

The man laughed. "No, nothing like that! Owen, I can feel the discord in your mind. I have some experience in this myself. If you would like help, then come with me."

"How did you know...?"

"Here," the man said, rubbing his finger and touching Owen's bare neck. "You can hear more when you are touching. But I can tell you all of this and more should you join me."

Owen focused *very* hard on the intentions of the man. The sincerity lingered until he was sure that this was no trap set by a depraved stranger.

"Why are you doing this?" Owen couldn't fathom why anyone would go to so much trouble for him.

"I am a rich man, I am a powerful man, but these things also make me a lonely man. I care not for the company of sycophants and leeches. I remember being in your shoes once. I want to help you because I can sense that there is something inside of you worth helping. You may call me Professor. All my favorite people do," he said cheerfully.

"TAKE A DEEP breath in, hold, and exhale all the chaos. Now breathe in again, this time focusing on one single emotional string, then exhale slowly, letting it fall away. For this exercise, I will be moving about the room. Keep your eyes fully shut and try to follow my truth. If you lose it, don't get frustrated. Just reach out again."

Owen followed orders. He had been working with the professor for a few years now. He was sixteen and getting better and better with his quirk. He had learned how to individually identify where the streams of energy were originating from, and he had learned how to mute most energies. He was still completely blown away by strong emotion, but the professor had said that time helped with that.

Though Owen had asked a few times, every question about the explosion of feelings coming from skin-to-skin contact was deflected by the professor.

"Another day," he would say, gifting Owen with leather gloves the first time he was asked about it.

From almost the moment he stepped into the professor's impressively large home, Owen was set up with a tutor. He felt that basically all his time was spent being tutored or learning from the professor. He had no real friends, but he didn't feel deprived. He wondered how his old friends had fared through the test of time.

The professor gave him fighting lessons as well. Over the course of several years, Owen learned basic self-defense, how and when to use a firearm, archery (which was mostly for fun), and how to use someone's emotional waves against them.

"Remember, Owen, there is no such thing as fighting dirty. There is only winning or losing."

All this self-defense was fun for Owen, but he never understood its purpose. Until one night when he was about seventeen and a strange man somehow broke in through the main entrance of the professor's home. Owen hadn't been able to sleep, so he was sitting in the library staring at the shelves and shelves of books, counting them to try to get tired.

He heard the front door click shut. As the professor had taught him, he stretched his senses out to the entrance. He perceived quiet, coolness. A sort of emotionless efficiency. He didn't know what to make of it, but he knew it wasn't good.

The energy came closer, and Owen ducked under the desk. As he hid, he heard—and felt—the intruder grow closer.

It was hard to tell the purpose of this invasion. The man could be here to steal or even to kill. Owen didn't want to take chances. He waited until the man walked over to the desk, soundless except for his truth.

Owen saw the man's legs and pushed the chair in front of him out to knock him over. He fell facedown onto the floor. Owen saw a gun slide a few feet away. The man seemed stunned for a moment, then quickly regrouped and went for the weapon. Owen grabbed his wrist and bit down, *hard*. When he did, he got the impression this person was looking for documents related to property owned by the professor. He had never read anything so specific.

While the man swatted at his head to get him to release the bite, Owen shot up and around him and grabbed the gun.

"Who are you? Why are you here?" Owen asked, breathing heavily both from the reading and from the struggle.

Owen could feel the man smile even though he couldn't see his face.

"You're not going to do anything, kid. You don't have the—"

He tapered off abruptly when Owen fired a round into his shoulder.

"I'm sorry, I don't have the what? The desire to keep people safe? To avoid losing my own life to some low-life criminal? Am I getting close?" Owen grew calmer now that he had control over the intruder.

"Owen, are you okay?" the professor asked, bursting into the library. He saw the man on the ground and Owen standing above him and smiled.

"Wow, you got one! Exactly what I taught you: shoot first, ask questions later." He laughed.

Owen was happy to see the professor but found his reaction a little callous. But then, he was an eccentric man. He had taken Owen in, after all. Owen was sent to bed, and the incident was never spoken of again. Owen could feel that the professor wanted it that way.

This happened once more. That time it was very clear that the person was an assassin. Owen had been hanging out in the kitchen. The professor taught him how to bake, so sometimes when he couldn't sleep, he would whip something up for the morning.

He was making a quiche when he felt a flash of cold ill intent. He put down his bowl and crept toward the hallway, turning off the lights as he went. Luckily, it seemed this person didn't notice, because she continued on her path to the staircase.

After the last kerfuffle he was in, Owen had taken to always carrying a knife on his person. The woman was already at the stairs. She was going slowly because there was barely any light in the house. Owen was used to the layout and could catch up to her quickly and quietly.

He got close enough to see that she had both hands on a gun but that it was dominantly in her right hand. He rushed her and curved his knife so that he slit her right wrist. Not a sound came out of her, likely from experience, but she dropped the gun. Owen dove for it, knocking her legs from under her in the process.

The professor always said the main goal was complete incapacitation. So Owen punched her in the throat with the butt of the gun. This time she did make a sound, a deep croak. The lights came on, and Owen squinted to see the professor standing at the top of the stairs.

"Bravo, Owen," he said. "Another one bites the dust, huh?"

Owen never asked what happened to the woman after that.

"MY MOST important lesson to you, Owen, is the one we have only touched on once or twice, and that is because it can be debilitating when you're not used to it. I call it *flooding*. When you make skin-to-skin contact, you're opening a door to the very root of a person's knowledge. Unlike reading truths, this is like opening a book and sifting through all of the contents until you find the information that you want.

"First you must clear your own mind. You don't want to muddy the waters with your own content. Then focus on one idea. Put the thought in their head, as it were, and you will find your answer. Now we'll practice on me. It will be much harder than with others because I have the skill to block you. If you can read me, you can read anyone."

Owen spent months practicing the technique. He had been blocked every which way, and when the professor let go? It was like he was reading an entire encyclopedia set all at the same time. The professor would start slowly, at first letting a little, then more and more information slip out at a time. By the time he was eighteen, Owen had it down as best as it was going to get. These thoughts were not usually very emotionally charged, so the pain in his head was less.

"Owen, I will bestow upon you a trick," the professor said one day at lunch with a wink. "If you want to read someone's heart and they're blocking you (as some people will), give them a good old-fashioned kiss."

Owen spit out his water and started laughing. "Are you filling my head with lies?"

The professor puffed out his chest. "Why of course not! I would never. Trust me, it will help you one day."

Owen rolled his eyes and went back to his sandwich.

SHORTLY AFTER Owen had turned eighteen and earned his GED, the professor became sickly. For the first time in all of the time he had lived with the professor, he discovered that the man had cancer. He had been in remission when he met Owen, but it had been detected again about two years prior.

Owen felt betrayed. How could he leave Owen in the dark for so long? They were family, weren't they?

Owen sat idly in the chair next to the professor's bed as he slept. He kept reaching out for the professor's truth, but the normally chaotic happiness was muted. Owen felt—knew—that he was going to be all alone again.

"Owen," the professor said, his voice cheery but weak. "Let me tell you some things that will make this transition easier."

"What transition? There is no transition. You're leaving me."

The professor patted his hand gently. Owen couldn't tell if it was meant to be so gentle or if he hadn't the strength.

"Owen, I don't want you to carry your past around like the burden it is to you. Your birth certificate reads that you are one Owen Hart, born and raised right here in this house. You will have no record of anything before you obtained your GED. I have set aside a trust for you to pay for school, lodging, and food. I have left you a good sum of money as well, but I am under the impression that my children, rotten as they are, will fight you tooth and nail for it."

Owen shook his head, tears spilling down his cheeks. "I don't need money. I don't *want* money. You have given me so much. I could never ask for more. I'm going to miss you," he said, the last bit merely a whisper.

For a moment, the old passionate, teasing Professor was back.

"Owen, please leave. I don't want you here when I go. I want to know that you're set up someplace."

Owen nodded, feeling hurt but understanding at the same time. He stood up to go out when a hand gripped his shirt gently.

"Owen," the professor said, waiting until Owen looked him in the eye, "you know you are like a son to me, and I love you."

Owen walked back and leaned over for a gentle hug. "Me too," he said, letting his tears dry on the professor's nightshirt for a moment before leaving with a quick smile.

That was the last time he had ever seen the professor.

CHAPTER 10

OWEN SHARED everything with Leo. Don't ask him why Leo seemed more trustworthy than his long-term friends, but here he was, sharing a part of himself that he had always kept personal. Part of it, he thought, had to do with the memory of the professor. As if, so long as he kept it buried in his own heart, the memory couldn't hurt him. Suddenly the flood gates were open, and that secret life that he led with the only person he would want to share it with, the professor, was out there.

Owen didn't realize he was crying until he felt a hand on his face, wiping the tears from his cheeks.

"Owen, truly, thank you for confiding in me with this. It's a story that I'll go to the grave with. Don't worry," Leo said gently, still brushing Owen's cheek with his thumb.

Owen experienced a swirl of his own emotions. A small part was distrust and regret, but the much larger part was relief, along with happiness that this burden was not only his to carry anymore.

And then he took a good look at Leo. His face was alert, but his body language suggested fatigue.

"Leo, I really think you need to sleep," he said.

Leo waved a hand in the air. "I'm fine. I have questions," he said, almost slurring his words.

Owen pouted at him. "Okay, Leo. I'm going to use your kitchen to make brownies. I have a request, and I would have to be blind to not notice the excessively wonderful quality of your kitchen. So I propose that I will stay here making brownies, and you sleep until I'm done. Fair?"

Leo looked at him strangely, then shook his head with a smile. "Really, I am fine."

"I'll sit here and stare at the wall, responding to none of your questions. I will say nothing, and I won't even look at you. And if that's not enough, then I'll hold my breath until you go to sleep."

"Owen, really...," Leo started.

Owen made a dramatic show of sucking in air, crossing his arms, and facing the wall over Leo's shoulder.

Leo looked at him, a little confused, although Owen didn't know if it was in response or due to lack of sleep. Finally he relented.

"You're the boss," Leo said, heading to the bedroom. "If you don't wake me up for fresh, warm brownies, you'll be sorry."

Owen snickered to himself. That's what microwaves were for.

"HEY, JACOB?" Owen asked, opening the door and recognizing his truth.

He smiled. "Did you finally get Mr. Ellis to sleep? It's always hard to get him to turn his brain off when work needs to be done."

"Oh here, look," he said, holding out a napkin with a fresh-baked brownie on it. He paused as Jacob reached out to take it, his emotions swimming with an excitement that never made it to his face. He always wore that kind, gentle smile.

Owen peered at the brownie and frowned. He took the napkin back.

"Hang on one second," he said and ran back to the kitchen. Jacob didn't follow him, and he suspected that Leo didn't invite many people into his space. A sliver of disappointment wove itself into Jacob's aura.

Owen ran back to the door, being careful to tread and speak lightly so that Leo could sleep.

"Here you go, Jacob!"

Owen presented a napkin with two of his largest brownies. Jacob's smile matched the surge of happiness and appreciation.

"Thank you, Owen."

Owen wondered how other people perceived Jacob. He was quiet and almost always seemed to run on neutral. But Owen could feel his truth. He could read the changes in his mood and thoughts even without seeing it reflected in his expression. Owen was about to close the door when he heard the ding of the elevator.

He stepped out of the apartment, curious to see who was there.

Alex stepped out and made eye contact with Jacob. He opened his mouth to speak but stopped when Jacob brought a hand up to shush him. Understanding shone in his eyes, and he put his own finger to his lips.

Owen noticed a burst of humor, comfort, and *was that arousal?* coming from Jacob.

He reached out to Alex and felt exuberant joy, all the energy that came from that small body. And infatuation?

Owen looked between the two of them as Alex walked quietly toward the door and wondered....

He pulled his glove off and touched Jacob's hand. "I'm sorry, I thought I saw something on your hand."

Before he pulled away, he focused on what was going on between them. *Only friends.* The admission was tainted with sadness and disappointment. He reached out to fist-bump Alex, who appeared surprised but happily complied. *He doesn't like me like that.* As with Jacob, Alex's thoughts were unhappy.

"Jacob, they need you down on level two," Alex said quietly once he got to the door.

"Okay. Owen has brownies," Jacob said, as if to remind Owen to share the goods.

"Score!" Alex mock-shouted, throwing one arm dramatically into the air.

Owen rolled his eyes but smiled, going back to the kitchen to retrieve two more brownies for Alex.

"Shift change, Owen. I'm out here if you need me."

Owen nodded and shut the door.

Owen wasn't much of a matchmaker. He liked to stay out of people's business. He already felt that he had an unfair advantage in the game of love because he could feel what was brewing under the surface. Well, other people's love. He was never that good at it for himself.

This brought up the question of Leo. Owen liked him. He liked the childlike side of him. He liked talking about video games, movies. He liked when they had dinner. And he liked that when Leo said that it was the best carbonara he'd had in his life, Owen believed him, even running blind. He liked being able to really learn about a person from time and affection rather than getting slapped in the face with it right from the get-go.

And Owen would be remiss if he didn't say Leo Ellis was *hot.* God knows why, but Owen was more attracted to Leo after knowing him for all of two weeks than he had been with any other partner in his life.

Owen tried to imagine what the professor would have thought of him. They were both very headstrong. Leo may not have liked him, but the professor loved a challenge.

This brought Owen back to the present. He had spilled his guts all over Leo. He'd never told *anybody* as much about himself and his childhood as he did Leo. Dozens of people had some knowledge, some half-truths, about who he was before the age of eighteen. But Leo now knew *everything*.

Owen snagged a brownie and sat on the sofa. He didn't bother turning the TV on; there was too much running around in his head. It had been so long since Owen had allowed himself to even think about the past. Tears welled up, and he tilted his head to keep them in. He wasn't about to cry. Not now.

He rubbed his eyes, then sat back, staring into space, letting his thoughts flow by with no attention. He meditated in this way for a while, then came back to himself when he heard a knock.

"What's up?" Owen asked, opening the door. He hadn't paid attention because he thought Alex was still outside. Instead, the stranger at the door had a cool, not unkind alertness about him. But wait, didn't he look familiar?

"Hello, Mr. Hart. I believe we have met briefly before. My name is Tyler, and the reason I knocked is because it is getting near dinnertime. Would you like me to get you something to eat?"

Owen thought for a moment. "Hold on, I'll be right back," he said, not bothering to close the door.

Owen walked farther into the penthouse, pausing to look into rooms until he found the one that Leo was in, sleeping soundly.

"Leo," he whispered. No response.

He went back to the door and smiled at Tyler's confused aura and cool face.

"Can I actually get a car? I want to pick up dinner."

"OWEN! IT'S been a while. Where have you been?"

"Hi, Teresa. It's been too long."

Teresa was the owner of Lola's café. She was a sweet woman in her sixties. She had opened the café about four years ago. She said it was always her dream to own her own place and, once she got the funds, she did just that. And thankfully, her dream was a success. Of course now Owen knew where those funds had come from.

"What can I get you, Owen? The usual?" She didn't even take out a pen, knowing his order.

"Actually, Teresa, I have become acquainted with another one of your customers, Leo Ellis."

Teresa's mouth dropped open, and he could see the bemusement on her face.

"Oh, lovely," she said after a moment. "You know—" She lifted her hand as if in secret. "—Leo Ellis is actually a lovely customer. He's the only reason I could afford to open this shop. Though I haven't seen him in a while. Do you know what he's been up to?"

"He's been busy. I don't know with what, though. I only met him a few weeks ago," Owen responded.

Teresa gasped. Owen jumped and looked around to see what had gotten her attention, but she was looking at him.

"Owen! You've got a crush," she exclaimed quietly, so as not to disturb her customers.

"What? No," he said, sounding juvenile even to his own ears.

"Yes. I have a keen eye for these things, and *you* have a *crush*."

Her laugh sounded like tinkling bells. There was something soothing about it, and he couldn't help but smile.

"Oh, whatever, Teresa," he said. "Can I please order my food now?"

Teresa dramatically pulled out a piece of paper and pen and positively beamed.

"What can I get you, young man?" she asked, humor still in her voice.

"I'm going to get the Lion," he said.

She looked at him for a moment. "How many?"

Owen blushed a bit, knowing what she would think. "Um, two."

Teresa walked away to make the food, laughing to herself the whole way.

CHAPTER 11

WHEN OWEN returned to the building, Tyler was waiting for him. Before Owen could say anything, Tyler gently took the bag of food from him and moved the sandwiches around, looking for what? A weapon or something?

Owen was a little insulted, but at the same time, he understood. He hadn't been here long, and he had only had regular contact with the lobby staff, Jacob, and Alex. So he brushed it off.

When he got back to the penthouse, Owen was hit with a wave of resentment. He didn't even have to look to know that Seth was the guard on shift. God, he hoped that Tyler was taking over. Owen didn't make eye contact with Seth, but he felt Seth's gaze on him and a swirl of disgust joining in.

"You all set?" Seth asked Tyler, his face and demeanor showing nothing but cool boredom. So different from his truth. Owen didn't trust him.

"Yes, I've got it from here."

To Owen's delight, Seth grunted and walked to the elevator, glaring at Owen as he passed. It took everything in Owen not to flip him off.

Owen was reaching for the handle when the door flew open. Owen stood for a moment, stunned, before he realized that Leo was leaning in the doorway.

"I thought you'd left for real this time," Leo said jokingly, but Owen heard a hint of seriousness in his tone.

"I come bearing gifts!" Owen responded, holding up his takeout bag.

Leo smiled and stood aside, gesturing into the room. Owen was pleased to see that Leo appeared much more alert than he had earlier. Owen went to the kitchen with a wave to Tyler, and Leo shut the door behind him.

Owen pulled out plates for the (extremely large) sandwiches. There was a dining room, but Owen hated formal eating. He ate his food on couches, the floor, and in his bed. Even when he lived with the professor, he had never eaten in a formal dining room.

Leo must have noticed the look he gave the dining room, because he gestured to Owen to come sit at the kitchen island. Owen sat, but now that Leo was awake and knew Owen's deepest, darkest secret, Owen felt lost.

He looked at his plate. Did he forget how to eat? Could that happen? Owen didn't know what to do with himself.

"Owen," Leo said gently, "you can trust me. Your story goes no further than this room."

Owen smiled down at his plate. Leo lifted Owen's face until they were making eye contact.

"You have *nothing* to fear."

Owen wasn't sure how to respond, so he went with his gut feeling and gave Leo a hug. Leo was stiff for a moment, confused, but then he wrapped his arms around Owen, and it felt so warm and *safe*. Tears welled again, but this time Owen let them slip down his cheeks.

When sobs threatened, catharsis after so long keeping everything bottled up inside, Owen muffled them in Leo's shirt. Leo had Owen pressed to his chest. He gently rubbed Owen's back and kissed his forehead.

"It's okay, Owen. Let it out. You're okay," Leo said gently.

OWEN WOKE up to darkness. He had fallen asleep? A little light spilled into the room from the half-opened doorway. From what he could see, this wasn't his room. The room and even the bed were bigger than his. He was startled, not remembering what had happened.

He pulled the covers off, noticing that his shirt and jeans were missing, but that he still had his underwear on. Then he remembered.

He had been in Leo's rooms, told his story, cried more than he had in *years*, and then… what?

He found his pants folded on a chair with his shirt. He slipped them on, then went back out and found Leo in an office down the hall.

"Um, hi," he said.

Leo looked up from his laptop and smiled. "Do you feel better?" he asked gently.

"Yeah," Owen responded honestly, "but what happened?"

Leo's smile was small but kind. "You were so exhausted from crying you seemed like you were going to fall asleep. I got you into bed so you could rest."

Owen nodded. "So we didn't, like, do anything, right?"

Leo laughed. "I wouldn't take advantage of you in this situation," he replied firmly.

"But you would in others," Owen said humorously.

"I make no promises," Leo said with a wink. Then Leo's demeanor suddenly became serious. "Actually, Owen, I have a favor to ask of you." He made direct eye contact. "We seem to have a mole. Someone whose tip to a business competitor of mine led to the attack on you, which was meant to be on me. With your skills, I imagine you might be able to gauge who may be behind this."

Leo paused, then continued, "I don't wish to force this on you. I simply wanted to ask if you would be willing to do this for me."

Owen thought for a moment. He'd never used his skill for anything quite like this. Still, he remembered Alex being attacked so badly that he was knocked out. That seemed pretty personal to him. No one should hurt someone so sweet.

"Okay. I'm in," he replied.

Leo looked a little surprised, but his expression quickly shifted to relief. "You cannot know how happy I am to hear you say that. I believe this has been going on quite a bit longer than I realized. I scoped out every employee who started work with the company or the building in the last year, and everyone checks out," he said, his focus shifting inward.

"So, Leo," Owen started, waiting for his attention. "What's the situation on those sandwiches?"

Leo laughed and closed his laptop, then led Owen to the kitchen. He opened the refrigerator and pulled out the two towering sandwiches.

"I figured I would wait for you for dinner. I'm glad you are awake. I'm starving."

They sat at the kitchen island and ate their food. Owen tried in vain to eat his sandwich with some kind of grace. Instead, pieces of deli meat, eggplant, and tomatoes kept slipping out, threatening to fall on his pants. He awkwardly leaned over his plate, trying to get the food to fall there instead.

He looked at Leo, who seemed to be having a much easier go of it. He was so graceful, Owen was jealous. He must have made a face, because when Leo glanced at him, he smiled.

"Having trouble?" he asked mildly.

Owen rolled his eyes. "We can't all have such grace eating a million-tiered sandwich," he said, pouting slightly.

"I've had a lot of practice eating this sandwich. It was made for me, you know."

Owen laughed in the middle of a bite of his sandwich. He coughed, and Leo patted him on the back. When Owen was able to speak, he said, "Well, your sandwich is too complicated."

"Like me, yes?" Leo asked.

Owen laughed. "Not even in the slightest."

Leo and Owen both laughed.

A FEW DAYS later, Owen stood in one of the offices on the second floor. He had been so curious as to what they looked like, but really this room was nothing special. Leo sat at a desk in the back of the large room, facing about twenty people. Owen stood behind Leo, feeling very self-conscious about the mixed response the staff was having toward him. Of course, Jacob and Alex smiled at him when he had their attention.

The problem was, their truths were only two small streams in a room of twenty. Many of them were curious, some resentful, and still more were annoyed by his presence. It was too much negativity for his head.

Suddenly he caught a stream of fear. He chased it to a woman with long red hair. She wore it in a ponytail and was dressed in a sleek gray pantsuit.

He was going to say something when he was suddenly smacked in the face with a strong stream of anger. He didn't even have to try to locate it. It was Seth.

Owen had become accustomed to his flavor of emotion.

Jacob shut the door to the office now that everyone was present in the room.

"I have brought you all here because we seem to have a mole in our midst. Someone, or someones, has been feeding information to Maxwell Balor. Now, we have footage of the incident the night of the fundraiser.

We ask that all of you report your location that night, and we will verify with the surveillance. If you don't have an alibi for a specific time, you will be vetted in a different manner."

The last bit sent a shiver down Owen's spine. Suddenly Owen felt a tidal wave of emotion. It was fury, violence, and ill intent. Before Owen could even consciously process it, he shoved Leo hard so that he toppled to the floor. Owen fell with him, but not before a gunshot rang out and Owen felt a sharp pain in his shoulder.

Leo sat up, catching Owen in his arms. Owen sat up as well and grabbed his shoulder, blood immediately covering his fingers. He heard the door open and shut.

Leo stood up, furious. A commotion began in the room. Although Owen couldn't see what was going on, he felt the rush of fury against Leo's attacker coming from the remaining employees. Owen was happy to know that they were loyal.

Owen gripped Leo's pant leg, and Leo looked down.

"It was Seth," Owen said, sure that even without him saying, they knew who tried to take Leo out, "and the red-haired woman."

Leo turned to Owen, concern mixing with the anger. "Are you okay?" he asked.

"Fine, go deal with this," Owen said, putting pressure on his wound.

"Jacob, Alex!" Leo called out. The two were right with him in a matter of moments.

"Take Owen to the hospital. I trust you with him. Don't make me regret it," he said.

Both men nodded. Leo raced away, following the crowd of men and women chasing Seth down.

"Oh my God, Owen, are you okay?" Alex asked as soon as Leo left, bending down to his level and taking over putting pressure on the wound.

He felt the back of Owen's shoulder. "It's a through and through," he said, a touch of relief curling around him.

Now that the adrenaline was fading, the pain was really starting to kick in.

"Come on, we're going to the hospital," Alex said, helping Owen up by his good arm. Owen felt a little fuzzy. He wasn't really present on the ride to the hospital and when he was admitted. Owen was under the impression that the two men realized this because their auras were tainted with worry.

"What is your level of pain?" a voice said.

Owen snapped back to reality and peered at the man in scrubs hovering over him. "What?"

"I asked for your level of pain, one through ten. One being the best and ten being the worst."

Owen thought about it. The pain was bad, but it wasn't unbearable. "Maybe an eight?" he responded.

"Okay, for now I will prescribe you something for the pain—"

"No," Owen interrupted.

"You don't want—"

"No," Owen interrupted again. "Give me some Tylenol."

The doctor looked a bit surprised but nodded. "Very well," he said before walking away.

"I'm glad you're more alert now, Owen."

Owen was startled to see Alex standing by the window. He hadn't noticed he was there, which was odd because his truth was so recognizable. He reached out and sensed Jacob at the door. When he touched his shoulder, he felt gauze underneath his hospital gown but couldn't remember them treating the wound.

"Hey, Alex, how long have we been here?" Owen asked.

"A few hours."

"Huh," Owen said. "Can we leave now?"

Alex shrugged. "Normally, no. But Mr. Ellis has arranged that no police report is going to be made. And you are tended to already, so we may go when you wish. No one will stop us."

"I'm ready to leave now," Owen answered, trying to ignore the burning pain in his shoulder.

"Okay," Alex replied. "Give me a few minutes to push them to discharge you, and then we'll be off."

CHAPTER 12

OWEN WAS positive that Leo would be occupied for quite some time. He didn't waste his time thinking about what exactly would be occupying him.

When they got back to the building and into the elevator, Jacob pressed the button for his floor. "Um, Jacob? Can we actually go…." He hesitated, not sure if it was his place to ask this. He wasn't sure why, but part of him believed he'd feel safer in Leo's penthouse. He wasn't sure if it was because he had successfully worked through such strong emotions there, or if he simply wanted to wait for Leo to come back—as pathetic as that was.

Either way, Jacob seemed to understand and pushed the button for the top floor. The door opening on his floor and then closing again made him feel silly. But Jacob wasn't saying anything, so neither would he.

They reached the top and Jacob unlocked the apartment door for him.

"Owen, we'll be right out here if you need us. Alex will be on elevator duty, and I'll be at the door."

"Can someone… come in?" He hesitated to ask. He didn't want to compromise their positions if they weren't supposed to enter.

Jacob smiled, but Owen felt the bitter taste of worry below the surface. Alex hadn't said anything yet, and when Owen looked at him, he was frowning, his whole truth warped with anger.

"I'll come in with you, Owen," Alex said, even *sounding* a bit angry. "Tyler can come up to watch the elevator. He is our alternate. Mr. Ellis won't mind."

Owen smiled and squeezed Jacob's hand with his own. The surprise reached his face.

"I am seriously fine. I simply need to distract myself."

Jacob nodded, his face relaxing again. Alex patted Jacob on the back, and Owen felt a surge of reassurance from both men. He was going to have to lock them in a room together like five-year-olds. At least then the sexual tension might boil over. He smiled to himself, imagining the scenario.

"Come on, Owen," Alex said cheerfully once the door was closed. "Should I make dinner for *you* for once?"

Owen laughed. "Alex, you don't strike me as someone who knows the way around a kitchen."

"You caught me. I'm a horrible chef. But I make pretty good spaghetti with jarred sauce."

Owen laughed again but gestured to the kitchen. Even if cooking (oh God, or baking) seemed appealing, his shoulder really hurt, so he opted to sit at the island and watch Alex fumbling to find the appropriate pots.

"I feel kind of bad for how things turned out with Seth. I knew he was a bad egg right from the get-go," Owen mused.

"What? Seth always seemed calm. Quiet, but not threatening."

Owen snorted. Alex shot him a curious look.

"Well, I tend to be a good judge of character," Owen responded, "and he rubbed me the wrong way." He paused. "Oh, Alex, by the way, who was that red-haired girl with the ponytail and the gray pantsuit?"

"Ah, that would be Lexi. She was always very quiet. She did pop up on Mr. Ellis's radar a few months ago for embezzling money from Spades."

Owen let out a laugh but quickly covered it with a cough.

"So Mr. Ellis gave her one warning, as he does with most people when the crime isn't serious. Apparently she has actually been working for Mr. Maxwell Balor. I got the call on that a while ago. I wonder how she was implicated."

Alex made a plate of spaghetti for Owen, then sat beside him with his own.

"Who is Maxwell Balor? Leo mentioned his name before too."

"Ah," said Alex, "it is not really my place to share such information. You'll have to ask Mr. Ellis."

Owen hummed, taking a bite of his pasta. "This is the best spaghetti with jarred sauce that I have ever had," he said, smiling.

Alex snorted. "It's the best I can do. Unless you want cereal."

Both men laughed, but Owen grabbed his shoulder, trying to stop because of the pain the movement caused.

"Ah, Owen, are you okay? I'm sorry, I wasn't even thinking."

Owen waved a dismissive hand. They ate the rest of their meal in comfortable silence.

"Do you play video games?" Owen asked after Alex had washed the dishes.

"Do I play video games," he said with a smirk.

"WHEN DID this... alliance... begin?" Leo asked coolly.

Seth spat on the floor. There was blood in it. More than a few teeth lay on the floor already. "I have nothing to say."

"Well, Lexi tells me you have been funneling information to Maxwell Balor about my whereabouts for quite some time now. She also tells me that he's gunning for my casino, trying to get dirt that would make me sell it."

"Well, she doesn't know what she's talking about. She's so low on the totem pole she might as well be a pebble on the ground. I don't even know why he bothered to get her involved," Seth said, his speech slurring slightly, probably a sign of a concussion.

"I'll let you live if you tell me exactly what information has been exchanged. If you don't tell me, I still have Lexi in my custody."

"Like I said, she doesn't know shit."

It was remarkable to Leo that while the words seemed to indicate that he was protecting her, the tone indicated bitterness toward her.

Leo gestured to one of his men, who handed over a revolver. Leo took aim and shot Seth in the shoulder. The man bit his lip until it bled, too stubborn to cry out.

"That's for Owen," Leo said neutrally.

"That piece of shit? After that incident a few days ago, he's been on Mr. Balor's radar. If you're not careful, he'll take him for—"

He didn't finish his sentence. A bullet lodged between his eyes. Leo wanted to unload his clip but chose not to waste the bullets.

"Um, sir?" a woman interrupted the red haze of rage filling Leo's senses. "I don't mean to interrupt, but I don't think we got the information from him that we had planned...."

Leo gazed down at his hand, then at Seth's lifeless body. "Ah shit," he said simply.

She was smart enough not to smile.

"What's going on with Lexi?" he asked her.

She frowned, and he remembered that the two of them had been friends. He probably should have left her upstairs.

"Well, she told us that Balor was looking for a weakness to exploit. As for the casino, he had very little. From what I understand, he was only starting to funnel information from you."

"Fine. That's all I need." He looked at the woman. Ella, he thought, was her name.

"Thank you for your help. I'll have someone else take care of the rest."

Her eyes welled up with tears, but she held them in. She nodded and headed back upstairs. Leo felt sorry that she was going to lose her friend. The least he could do was not have her witness it.

CHAPTER 13

LEO WAS tired when he got on the elevator. He wondered how Owen was doing. He hit the fourth-floor button. He had gotten word that he had returned from the hospital a few hours ago. When he exited the elevator, his skin went cold. No one was guarding the door.

He ran over, not worrying if it was a trap, and pushed on the door. It was locked, but Leo had a skeleton key. He got in, and no lights were on. Owen wasn't in his bedroom or his bathroom.

Leo pulled out his phone, ready to call Jacob, who had better be gone because he was dead or worse, and he saw a missed call and text message.

I know that you are busy, but Owen is waiting for you in the penthouse.

Leo's shoulders slumped in relief. He made his way back up the elevator, pleased to see Jacob at the doors and Tyler at the entrance to the penthouse. Wait.

"Jacob," he said seriously.

"I know what you are going to say, but Mr. Hart didn't wish to be alone, so Alex is sitting with him inside."

Leo nodded, not really caring about anything but Owen at this point. He burst into the room and scanned it quickly, seeing Owen and Alex both jump up from the couch. Owen looked at him nervously, probably because of the anger that he could feel in his own features.

He walked quickly to the couch. Owen froze while Alex moved smoothly out of the way and headed toward the door.

Leo went right up to Owen as the door shut and kissed him. Another moment and then Owen melted into Leo's embrace. Leo squeezed him tight for a moment before Owen let out a muffled grunt of pain.

Leo relaxed his grip, now mindful of Owen's wound.

And that was it, wasn't it? Leo didn't want anything bad to happen to Owen ever and for all eternity. But at least if Owen was hurt by his own doing, that was something Leo could deal with. But this? Leo had put Owen in a dangerous situation, and Owen had paid the price for it. This was on *him*.

Leo spun them around and sat on the sofa, gently pulling Owen on top of him. Owen straddled his waist, his lips hovering over Leo's and his breath coming in rapid pants. Leo wondered if Owen had been worried about him. Even going so far as to wait for him here.

He gripped Owen's hair and pulled his lips down onto his own. He bit Owen's lip, hard enough to draw blood. Owen gasped into his mouth, but Leo was already licking the wound. Owen went to lick the wound himself, but Leo got in the way, and Owen settled for licking Leo's tongue instead.

Leo slipped a hand under Owen's shirt, sliding it up his back. Owen leaned into the touch. Leo moved his hand all the way up to Owen's bad shoulder. He lingered there, gently feeling the gauze, anger starting to seep into his lust.

Owen twitched at the contact with his wound but didn't remove his lips from Leo's.

Content to table this issue for now, Leo slid his hand down Owen's chest, pausing to massage his nipple. Owen's breath was getting heavier now, and Leo wondered idly when Owen had done this last.

Honestly, he didn't know much about Owen's personal life. He would like to change that.

Leo used his other hand to massage Owen's back. He hooked Owen's shirt with his fingers and lifted it up and away, then threw it onto the floor. He pulled his lips away from Owen's, eliciting a disappointed moan.

He smiled as he tilted Owen's chin up, kissing and licking his way down Owen's body. Owen panted quietly, gasping at the little nips Leo took along the way. He paused at a nipple, massaging it with his tongue before making his way lower. When he could go no farther in his current position, Leo gently maneuvered Owen so that he sat on the couch with Leo kneeling on the floor bent over him.

He made it to Owen's belly button before Owen seemed to catch on. He gripped Leo's hair as Leo struggled to pull his pants off, laughing breathlessly.

"Owen, why do you wear such tight pants?"

Owen struggled to slide out of his pants, underwear and all.

Leo allowed a predatory smile to grow on his face. Owen was blushing and looking down at him with lidded eyes, fingers still curled in Leo's long hair.

Leo lightly squeezed the base of Owen's member, licking up the shaft before wrapping his lips around the head, teasing for a moment before sucking hard. Owen's body bucked, and Leo looked up to see his eyes shut, mouth hanging open.

He liked that look.

Leo removed his mouth from Owen and teased him with small licks and kisses instead. He didn't look away from Owen's face even once. He liked watching the change from ecstasy to frustration, so he leaned over and licked the inside of Owen's thigh, prolonging the teasing.

Owen opened his eyes for a moment, then closed them again quickly, his cheeks burning brighter. He grunted in frustration.

"What's wrong, Owen?" Leo asked, very much knowing the answer to that but wanting Owen to say it himself.

"Can you... can you just... uh," Owen stuttered as Leo continued to lick his inner thigh.

"Can I what?"

"Can you do... what you were doing... with your mouth." He broke off, biting his lip and staring somewhat longingly at Leo's mouth.

Leo smiled wide. "Good enough."

With one hand, Leo began to pump Owen's member in time with the movements of his lips. After a few moments, he reached into his own pants to touch himself, enchanted by the beautiful little moans Owen was making. He felt Owen release but didn't move, swallowing even as he reached his own pinnacle. Owen was panting, gazing at him in a daze, fingers still on Leo's hair but not gripping.

Leo grinned, licking the small trail of cum that had dripped out of his mouth. He moved back to the couch next to Owen and put one arm around him, hugging him to his chest. Owen didn't fight it.

"What about you?" Owen said after a dazed moment.

"Oh, I finished, don't worry," he said with a salacious smile.

Leo waited until Owen came totally back to the present. He could only imagine how Owen felt. So much had happened in such a short amount of time. He wouldn't be surprised if Owen wanted to leave him. Wait. Was he going to leave him?

Leo fretted about this for a minute before Owen spoke up. "Did everything go okay? Well, I guess not *okay*, but did you catch Seth and that woman?"

"Yes," Leo said, a trace of anger entering his voice, "I have dealt with that." He smiled. "You don't have to worry about anything. I was wrong to involve you like that. It was my fault you got hurt."

Owen frowned, pushing his way up as gently as he could using his good arm so that he sat upright next to Leo.

"I don't care, you know. If I had a problem with all your, I guess, business dealings, I would have left already. I'm not weak, and I'm not stupid."

Leo assessed him. "And you are not planning on leaving now?" he asked quietly.

"No! Why would I even be waiting for you here if—"

Leo cut him off with a gentle kiss. "I'm sorry that you were hurt. I will do my best to make it up to you."

OWEN FROWNED at Leo, not liking pity. He tried to sense what was behind Leo's expression but still got nothing. Leo's eyes looked kind, though.

"You know what frustrates me?" Owen asked after a moment.

Leo appeared curious. "What?"

"I can read everyone. I know the emotions and thoughts behind the scenes. But you? I can't read you at all. It's like a block. It infuriates me because I don't know what you are thinking."

Leo looked surprised. "So all this time…?"

"Nope. Nothing," Owen responded.

Leo positively beamed. "So it must be nice to have some excitement in your life, some mystery, huh?"

Owen did his best not to match Leo's smile. He strained to keep his expression neutral. He didn't succeed.

"On that note, I'm going to my room to get some sleep," Owen said.

"No!" Leo said. "I mean, why don't you stay here? After this whole incident, I would feel better if you stayed near me and the people I trust. I have a spare bedroom you can use. Unless you want to sleep with me." He moved his eyebrows suggestively.

Owen was bemused. Sleeping in the same bed had never dawned on him as an option.

"Okay," he said at last. "But if you take all the covers, I'm leaving." Owen let himself smile.

Leo looked so pleased to see Owen so cheerful that it almost made Owen forget what had happened that day. But then Leo glanced at the gauze across Owen's chest and frowned.

Almost.

OWEN WOKE up that first night and took a moment to remember where he was. He noticed, when he was conscious enough, that he was wrapped in the blankets like a burrito. He turned his head and saw that Leo had no covers at all. He was fast asleep anyway, but Owen felt guilty. He struggled to unravel himself, then got up and walked around the bed to cover Leo once more.

"Looks like I was the one who should have worried about a cover hog," Leo said, his eyes still closed and a smile on his face.

Owen's attempted frown curled up into a smile instead.

"I can move to the couch if you want," he said.

Leo tugged on Owen's hand until he lost his balance and landed right across Leo's torso. He didn't miss the support Leo put on his left side to keep the pressure off of his shoulder.

"Who needs blankets when I have my own personal bed warmer?"

Owen laughed. "I think we need more blankets," he said.

Leo got up and went to the closet, then came back with two throw blankets. Owen fell asleep as soon as his head hit his pillow again.

When he woke up again, he found himself in an even bigger blanket burrito.

OWEN NEVER went back to his old suite. Without him even asking, his clothing appeared in the closet next to Leo's. All of his possessions were boxed up and left in the living room one day. Owen slept with Leo at night. They had messed around, but never had sex. Owen was kind of disappointed, but at the same time he was too nervous to initiate, which is what he thought Leo was waiting for.

He couldn't say why he was so nervous. It wasn't like he'd never had sex before. The problem was that Owen felt so strongly about Leo in such a short amount of time, and it scared him. He didn't want to get hurt if this was just a passionate fling.

Owen had shared so much with Leo. His story, his abilities, he had been attacked and shot, and both times Leo had been there with him. He was scared that doing something as personal as having sex with Leo would be giving away his last chance of getting distant.

He was the problem as well. When he started to feel too much emotion, he tended to leave the situation. His past lovers never had any secrets from him. He could feel every emotion. All the bitterness, resentment, anger, frustration mixed with love, affection, humor. Owen would leave before it drove him crazy.

Leo wasn't like this. Owen couldn't feel him, and it scared him. Rather than being overwhelmed or fed up with being his lover, Owen was nervous that he didn't know what Leo was thinking. It was scary, and he wasn't sure how to deal with that.

The next few weeks were a blur. Owen had run out of his large stash of brownies and decided that next up was cookies. He opted to use the mixer, as holding the bowl steady was hurting his arm. It had healed a lot but was still sore.

Owen made four different kinds of cookies, three batches of each. Leo had returned from work that night and laughed as Owen placed the last tray of cookies onto the dining room table. He had run out of room on the island.

He had Jacob taste test, and his aura felt like that of a kid on Christmas.

CHAPTER 14

"YURI, CAN I ask you something," Owen said one day during a lull at Spades.

"Shoot, honey," she said cheerfully.

"What do you do if you like someone a lot but can't know for sure that they like you back?"

Yuri smiled. "Ah, Owen. Love troubles, huh? Well, the scary part is, you don't know. You can't read minds." She laughed to herself. She had touched on his big fear without even realizing it.

"Listen," she went on, "what you need to do is talk. If you're very serious, the only way to know if they feel the same is to outright ask. That's scary, but it's the best advice I can give. I remember telling Rebecca that I loved her. We weren't teens in love. We were both ready for a life partner. I was so nervous. I remember deciding and speaking quickly, iloveyoudoyoulovemetoo?" Yuri's smile turned gentle. "She laughed at me, and I thought I was going to cry, but then she kissed me and said, 'Of course I do.'"

"So you think I should talk to him?" Owen asked, heart sinking at the thought of being rejected.

Yuri must have seen something in his face because she ruffled his hair playfully. Owen quickly tried to fix it; it was so unruly he didn't need help messing it up.

"Honey, you have to take the risk," Yuri said. "Better to know now than find out down the line that you're not on the same page."

Owen nodded, frowning.

"So, who's the lucky man?" Yuri asked slyly.

Owen laughed. "You wouldn't believe me if I told you."

Yuri pouted and opened her mouth to say something when the bartender interrupted her.

"We've got new players sitting down. Go get orders!" he said.

"Oops," Yuri said, taking her notepad and heading over to the blackjack table.

Owen headed to the poker table, taking orders without a smile. He was too enthralled with the idea of asking Leo about... feelings. He never did—never needed to—talk about feelings.

The thought stayed in his head his whole shift. He didn't get good tips that night.

LEO SIFTED through the account book for his laundering services. Tyler had begun keeping track of the accounting since his predecessor, Jack, had run off. Tyler had informed Leo that Jack left with quite a bit of money.

Leo decided to check for himself and grew more and more frustrated. He had always thought that he knew his people. He vetted them, but this was too much betrayal at once.

He sighed and rubbed his forehead.

Things with Maxwell were escalating as well. The man was boldly poaching his clients. He'd even killed two of Leo's mules as they were doing a run for Spades. Leo continued to shift his delivery routes, but Maxwell was still persisting. Leo needed to deal with this.

He had no choice but to call Maxwell out on it. This was a risky move, because although they were not involved directly in business, they shared contacts, and if this went wrong, one of them was going to make enemies.

"Tyler," Leo called. Tyler had been waiting patiently as Leo looked things over. "I need you to go back over the data and give a full and detailed report about exactly what was taken and by whom. I would also like you to have Devon find Jack's trail. Send people out and bring him back here to me."

Tyler nodded. "Yes, sir. Sir, may I make an observation?"

Leo looked at him curiously. Tyler was usually all business. He didn't usually say or do anything beyond his job description.

"Sure, Tyler."

"Mr. Ellis, there is a lot going on. You have not left the building for anything more than business. I think it's taking a toll on you."

Leo waited, but Tyler said nothing further.

"So you are saying that I need to get out?" he asked humorously.

Tyler merely nodded, his cool demeanor showing a touch of nerves.

Leo smiled. "You know what, Tyler? I think that you're right."

OWEN HAD the day off. It was a Saturday, and he was alone and bored. He wanted to go visit Aiden, but Leo had told him to stay put unless he was with him. Owen had gathered that this Maxwell Balor fellow who had sent people to kill Leo was still a threat.

He had spoken to his friend a few times, but he was still bored stiff. Even with Jacob and Alex nearby. He needed to get out.

At around 5:00 p.m., the door opened and Leo walked in, looking cheerful. Owen was lying on the floor with his feet up on the sofa, reading a magazine.

"What's up?" Owen greeted him without making a move to get up.

"Owen, we're going out," Leo said.

Dramatically, Owen stretched his arms above his head on the floor. "Finally," he exclaimed.

Leo laughed. "I guess you have cabin fever too."

"Where are we going?" Owen asked.

"Dinner at Primavera."

Owen was torn. Primavera was an amazing Italian restaurant. On the other hand, it was the type of place that didn't list the meal prices. Which spoke volumes.

"Is this a date?" he asked playfully.

"Yes," Leo said. "I am trying to woo you."

Owen laughed, getting up from the floor and heading to the bedroom.

"I'm putting nicer clothes on. That is a classy place," he said.

Owen went through his clothes in the closet, frowning. He really didn't have a lot of options he had chosen for himself. He had money, of course. Leo paid for everything for him, so his five-thousand-dollar-a-month salary was piling up. He could even afford brand names!

"Leo, can we go clothes shopping after dinner?"

"Of course," Leo called from the other room.

"I'm paying. I don't want to be your sugar baby," he responded.

He heard Leo's laugh but got no answer. Well, he was putting his foot down on this one. He had a credit card, but he never received a bill. He was using his debit card instead.

Owen picked a pair of tight black suede pants and a nice maroon shirt. He went to the floor-length mirror to check his outfit. He paused as he looked himself up and down, settling on his eyes. He thought for a moment before taking out his contacts and heading to the living room.

Leo turned around when he heard Owen come out.

"You look…." He started fading off when his gaze landed on Owen's eyes. "Oh, you finally decided to listen to me."

"Know that I am only doing this for you. You owe me," Owen said, still feeling self-conscious.

Leo must have seen something in Owen's body language because he walked over and cupped his cheeks.

"If anyone asks, you're starting a fashion trend. You look beautiful."

Leo placed a soft kiss on Owen's lips before pulling his hands away and gesturing for Owen to precede him to the door.

Something occurred to Owen. "What's the guard situation?" he asked.

"There will be people waiting in the car and four plainclothes guards inside."

"Are they just going to be standing there? Isn't that awkward?"

"I usually have them in sets of two strategically sat for dinner."

"So, a two-person dinner? May I make a suggestion?"

ALEX WAS nervous. He was thrilled to be taken on guard duty at the Primavera. Mr. Ellis always covered their food, encouraging his people to eat whatever they wanted. Of course, he never took advantage of that. He usually ordered chicken parmesan.

But no, today he was nervous.

He had been shocked when Owen happily informed him that he would be dining with Jacob. He had been partnered with Jacob lately guarding Owen, but that was probably because Owen liked him.

Alex knew that this was only work and that Jacob probably would not even be *thinking* about the implications that Alex saw. But he still felt like it was a parody of a date.

They left the building in two separate cars. Owen and Mr. Ellis in one with a driver and guard, and a second one with his four diners and another guard and driver. Mr. Ellis didn't go anywhere without a second car. He liked an alternate escape route should it be necessary.

Alex sat next to Jacob, only a whisper of air between them. Alex's face was burning, and he tried to think of something, anything, other than the close proximity of his hopeless crush.

He didn't want Jacob to find out how he felt. Ever. He was sure Jacob would see nothing in him. His smile was always so pleasant and calm; he was like that with everyone. But with Alex his smile was a little different. It wasn't as gentle. Alex feared that he was an annoyance. He was used to people being short-tempered with him because he knew he was too much for some.

He wished Jacob wasn't one of those people.

He shook his head, trying to dislodge his thoughts. The disappointment that settled in dulled the excitement of the night.

JACOB WAS very surprised to be paired with Alex on guard duty. Especially in this situation. He knew that Mr. Ellis was aware of how he felt about Alex, even without his ever saying it. He had noticed the gleam in his eye when he saw them together, or when Jacob even mentioned Alex.

Jacob liked to think that he had a good poker face, but he must let something slip around Alex. It wouldn't surprise him. Alex had a way of throwing him off balance. He was the most genuine person that Jacob had ever met.

Alex wore his heart on his sleeve. He saw the positive in everything, and no one who had spoken to him walked away without a smile. Despite his open demeanor, he could be pretty serious as well. He was in Mr. Ellis's inner circle, as Jacob was. This was probably why Mr. Ellis put them in charge of Owen.

But today, despite everything, Mr. Ellis was pairing him with Alex. For dinner. At a fancy restaurant.

He tried to quell the anxiety he worried would leak into his façade.

They arrived at Primavera and parked one car down the road and the other across the street from the restaurant. Two guards and two drivers hung back for surveillance.

The tables were reserved strategically so that they could keep an eye on all the exits and still be close enough to defuse any situation that might arise.

Jacob walked behind Alex, going for their seats first. The other pair would enter a few minutes later to keep from arousing suspicion.

When they sat down and got their menus, Alex closed his and put it down on the table. Jacob smiled slightly, holding down a bubble of laughter.

"Chicken parm?" he asked.

"Of course," Alex replied. He looked a little nervous.

Why was he nervous? Had Jacob said or done something? Maybe Alex didn't want to do this with him. Jacob already knew Alex was not particularly fond of working with him. He always seemed so uncomfortable. It hurt Jacob, but it was what it was.

So maybe he really didn't like the idea of having dinner. Or maybe it seemed like a date. Jacob wanted to imagine that it was. That Alex returned his feelings. But that was probably too much to ask for.

Jacob scanned the room, looking for threats. No one in the restaurant seemed off. They spoke, not even looking in the direction of Owen and Mr. Ellis. One woman was crying, probably being dumped.

Jacob turned back to Alex, seeing him doing the same thing. He took advantage of the moment to take Alex in. His beautiful black hair. His smooth, pale skin. His presence, strong for someone so petite. The mild look on his face, hiding that ever-present cheerful smile. Jacob didn't understand how no one had scooped him up yet.

OWEN WATCHED Jacob and Alex as he idly twirled his fork in his food. He saw that they were doing their job, watching for danger, but that they kept sneaking glances at each other when one would be discreetly looking around.

"Owen, you are making me very lonely."

"Sorry, but do you see those two? They're hopeless!"

"Why, can you get a read on them?" Leo asked curiously.

"It's hard to pick apart because it's all a jumble. I'm getting nerves, but they also give off some excitement. Can you order people to kiss?" Owen asked Leo.

Leo laughed.

"I actually keep them apart on purpose. You are the only reason they work together now. If you get them together and they break up, then it's on you." Leo sounded firm, but he smiled as he took a sip of his wine.

"Okay, whatever. I'll make it happen if it kills me," Owen said. "Look, not to bring up business, but when can I go out on my own again? I feel like I'm on house arrest."

Leo swirled the wine in his glass, frowning.

"Well, you pretty much *are* on house arrest. I'm sorting some things out, and you will not be safe by yourself right now."

"Is this about that Maxwell guy? What if I left with guards?"

Leo shook his head. "I'm weeding out my people. I seem to have several leaks that need fixing. Until I'm sure that it will be safe, you will not go anywhere but work. Unless you're with me."

"Leo, you are always working. I am so bored. Do you at least have some kind of giant library like in *Beauty and the Beast*?" Owen joked.

"Who's a beast?" Leo asked, laughing.

"Well, I am obviously the beauty, so...."

"That you are, Owen. That you are."

Owen let the matter drop. He wasn't on social media, which he was sure Leo knew. But the downside of this was that he couldn't check on his friends. Though he could call when he was bored.

Suddenly Owen felt a wave of curiosity in the atmosphere. He looked around but couldn't pinpoint where it was coming from. Usually when an emotion was that strong, it was aimed directly at him. Owen shrugged it off but felt the emotion like a fly buzzing in his ear. He was so preoccupied he didn't notice the man approaching until he was standing over the table.

"Hello! My name's Marcus. May I sit?" he asked as he pulled up a chair anyway. He had dark skin and brilliant blond hair. Owen wondered if he dyed it.

Marcus smiled brightly, focusing all of his attention on Owen. Leo wore an annoyed expression, but Owen was more curious than anything. Oh. That's where the feeling was coming from. He could sense it clearly now. But why?

"Is there something I can help you with?" Owen asked.

Marcus looked thoughtful. "You look like someone who can really read a room, am I right?" he asked.

Owen was confused.

"You know," Marcus continued, "you are a very empathic person. Like you really understand how other people feel."

Owen hesitated. Did this man know about his abilities? But how was that even possible? As far as he knew they had never met before. Marcus's face lit up, as if Owen's hesitation was all the answer he needed. Which it probably was.

"So we're kindred spirits!" Marcus said, excitement in his voice. Owen could feel the excitement in his aura as well. He brushed a hand over the man's wrist. Yes, it seemed they were the same.

"You can feel emotions?" Owen asked.

"I can see them, yes. But I can't see yours for some reason. Can you see mine?" Marcus asked.

"Loud and clear," Owen responded, although he had never thought of his ability as a form of "seeing" before.

"If you've satisfied your curiosity, Owen and I are trying to have dinner," Leo said. Owen felt guilty because he'd almost forgotten Leo was there.

"Marcus." A woman had approached them and stood over Marcus.

"Oh, forgive me. Owen, Mr. Ellis, this is my friend Maribelle," Marcus said, "I think you and she are acquainted, Mr. Ellis."

"Yes, how are you doing this evening?" Leo said, standing up to shake her hand.

"Excellent. I hope you have a wonderful dinner. I'll be taking this one with me," she said, tugging on the back of Marcus's jacket.

"Well, that's all the time I have. Owen, I would love to hang out. Maybe we can swap tricks! Here, give me your phone," he said.

Owen handed his phone over immediately. He had never met anyone with abilities like his before. He had so many questions, but now was not the time. Marcus jotted in his number, then handed the phone back.

"Enjoy your dinner. I hear this place has amazing cheesecake," Marcus said before obediently following Maribelle out of the restaurant.

Owen watched them go, and when he turned back, Leo was staring at him with a look that Owen couldn't read.

"What was that?" he asked.

Owen shrugged. "I'm guessing he's like me. I've never met anyone like me before," Owen said, smiling slightly. This could be interesting.

"Well, he was very off-putting, if you ask me," Leo said, frowning.

If Owen didn't know better, he would almost think that Leo was jealous.

"Come on. Let's go get dessert somewhere else. There's this really awesome gourmet ice-cream shop down the road that I've wanted to try out," Owen said.

He paused, halfway standing, then sat back down and pulled out his phone.

"What's wrong?" Leo asked.

"I'm taking care of something that should have been dealt with a long time ago," he said, sending a text.

Then he stood up and held out his hand to Leo. Leo took it with a smile and followed Owen to the exit. No one bothered them for the check, so Owen assumed that had been dealt with already.

ALEX WAS thrown for a loop. He had started to get up when the stranger approached Owen, but Jacob had ordered him to sit down. Alex saw that Mr. Ellis hadn't given any signal and relaxed back down in his seat, still watching nervously, ready to jump in.

Apparently, he needn't have worried.

What he *was* worried about was Jacob. He seemed quieter than usual, which was really saying something as he was the calmest man Alex had ever known. They were about to leave when he got a text from Owen.

Alex, you and Jacob are hereby ordered to finish dinner and dessert. I suggest you take a walk in the park before calling a car, because if you get back before I do, I will not cook or bake for you two for a month.

Alex laughed and sat back down. Jacob followed suit, curiosity in his face.

"It looks like we have to continue our date." Alex laughed before realizing what he'd said, then blushed a little.

Jacob's face shifted. Alex couldn't read it, but then Jacob smiled.

"Our date, huh." He looked like something had clicked for him, a sly smile on his face.

"Well, yeah, I mean, that's what Owen said," Alex lied.

Again, Jacob had that strange look.

"I was told that we need to get dessert."

The same wide smile that popped up when sweet treats were inevitable spread across Jacob's face.

"I GUESS WE'RE ordered to walk through the park?" Alex said, laughing nervously as, dessert done, they crossed the street and entered the pleasant city commons, trying to allow himself to make like it was a joke.

Jacob smiled, but something was different. His smile seemed playful, but his eyes seemed intense. It was a little unsettling. It made Alex's heart beat faster.

"Is this still a date, then?" Jacob asked, smile firmly in place.

Alex couldn't tell if he was making fun of him. "Well, it's a nice night, so it doesn't matter," he brushed it off. "I'm more concerned we're going to get jumped."

Jacob waved a dismissive hand. "This park is safe enough. Plus, you have me." He winked.

"I wish," he mumbled, freezing when he realized that he had said it out loud. "Wait, I don't mean that like—"

Alex's words were silenced when Jacob's lips met his. They stood, lips lightly pressed together. Then Alex stepped back. He went to wipe away the kiss, but froze with his hand touching his lips.

He looked up at Jacob. He had that same look on his face that Alex had always thought meant he was getting annoyed with him. But if he was annoyed, then why did he...?

"Alex, do you like working with me?" Jacob asked, a surprisingly childlike tone coloring his words.

"Why wouldn't I like working with you?"

"Do you like *me*?"

"Do I like you? I mean, you didn't know that?" Alex asked, floored. He had thought Jacob didn't like *him*.

Jacob pulled Alex in for a much harder kiss. Alex's lip smacked into his teeth.

"Do you like *this*?" Jacob asked, his voice husky.

Alex *liked* that sound. "Yes," he answered dreamily. He realized what he had said and panicked. He opened his mouth, but before he could get any words out, Jacob put a finger to his lip.

"Don't worry too much about it. What do you say we head back to the apartments. I'm sure they're done shopping by now. I still have a room for myself if you want to stay there after our shift."

Alex nodded dumbly. He felt like he'd been hit by a Mack Truck. His emotions were all over the place, but he mostly felt happy. Excited. Jacob liked him? Liked *him*? He thought of Owen. It looked as if they would no longer both be with him at the same time.

He didn't really care so long as he worked with Owen during some of his shifts. Owen was taking him on a culinary trip around the world, and next up in the order was paella. He had been looking forward to that.

OWEN HAD begged Leo to have Jacob and Alex check in when they got back. Leo acted like that was a chore, but he could tell that Leo was as curious as he was.

As asked, Jacob and Alex came up to the penthouse as soon as they got to the apartment building. Owen had to contain himself. Their truths were on the same wavelength. Happiness, excitement, shock.

They were totally going to bang.

Leo looked at Owen, who nodded with a smile.

"I see you both had a good time," Leo said with a smile.

Alex blushed, but Jacob smiled. Owen mused that it was somewhat predatory, but he wasn't sure if he was only seeing that because of the wave of lust he felt coming off him.

"So we're dating now, hmm?" Leo mused.

Alex blushed and opened his mouth but was silenced when Jacob wrapped an arm around him.

"Yes," Jacob said.

Owen could feel the embarrassment coming off of Alex, but he also sensed joy and a little confusion. He smiled slightly, looking dazed.

"Well, I expect that you only stay with Owen one at a time. I will allow you to alternate duties because I know that Owen is fond of you both. Tyler will cover the other position."

Owen felt the relief wash over Alex. He was happy to know that Alex liked Owen as much as Owen liked him. Well, he liked his cooking at least. Just as Jacob liked his baking. He thought for a moment. Did these two men only like him for his food?

Owen laughed out loud before covering his mouth. He had clearly missed something because they were all looking at him.

"Sorry, I had a funny thought."

"Well, for tonight we have guard duty covered, and anything else can wait until the morning. So you two are free for the rest of the night. You are dismissed…." Leo paused. "Have fun."

Alex flushed right down to his collar. Jacob merely nodded, excitement behind the gentle smile Jacob always wore. God, no wonder Alex couldn't read him.

"I'M GLAD YOU called," Marcus said the next day, sitting across from Owen in the back of Lola's café. Lately, it almost seemed like that seat was reserved for his and Leo's use, although the waitress had given Marcus an odd look.

"Well, I have a lot of questions," Owen replied. So much had been going on that was out of his control, Owen wanted to try something that he could handle.

He paused as Teresa came by the table, balancing two coffees with two croissants.

"Here you go, boys. On the house," she said. Her eyes lingered on Marcus. Owen felt a harmless curiosity emanating from her. The moment was over as quickly as it started, and she was back off to the counter.

"So. Questions?" Marcus asked.

"Yes. How long have you been able to read people?" Owen asked.

"Gosh, as long as I can remember. My father taught me how to control it so I didn't burst from sensory overload," Marcus said.

"Is that your real hair color?" Owen asked.

Marcus stared at him for a moment before bursting out laughing.

"Really? That's really important enough to be your second question?" he asked, still trying to control the laughter.

"Well, this is my natural eye color." Owen blinked to call attention to his contact-free violet eyes. "So, I was just curious if you had a quirk like that."

Marcus finally stifled his laughter and looked at Owen with a big smile. "Yes, this is my natural hair color. I got lucky, though. My father's natural hair color was a deep blue. It was gorgeous, but he had to dye it to get the kind of job he wanted," he said. "Okay, what's next?"

Owen studied him thoughtfully. "You said that you couldn't read me, right?" he asked.

"Correct," Marcus replied. "That's why I approached you in the restaurant. Hasn't happened to me before."

"You know, I can't read Leo," Owen said.

"That's probably why you two get along, I should think," Marcus replied.

"Do you know why I can't?" Owen asked.

"No clue," Marcus said.

"Wait, so you said that you could *see* feelings?" Owen asked.

Marcus took a sip of his coffee. "Yeah, no one ever showed you how?" he asked.

"No. I don't think my guardian knew you could do that," Owen said.

"Well, I can show you sometime. I actually started only being able to see auras. I had to learn to dial it down so that I could see people without a whole cloud of emotions blocking their face," Marcus said.

Owen stopped talking and tried to absorb these thoughts.

"While I'm here, I have a question for you as well," Marcus said after a long moment.

"Shoot," Owen said, still in his own head.

"I thought I recognized one of the guards at the restaurant. Was there a man named Tyler there?" Marcus asked, sounding more serious than Owen had heard him thus far.

"Why?" Owen asked, worried about giving out personal information.

"Because we used to be friends. I haven't seen him in years, and when I saw him there, I was too nervous to see if he remembered me," Marcus said.

Owen couldn't imagine anyone forgetting Marcus. He had such a big personality. Kind of in-your-face.

"There is a man named Tyler working for Leo, yes," Owen admitted.

"Tall, dark hair, pale, kind of serious?" Marcus asked.

"Yes," Owen replied.

Marcus pursed his lips. "Tell me his number! Wait, no. Give him my number. No, he won't call me, but wait, he won't take my call either. Huh. I have to think about this," he said in a fit of energy.

Owen watched him talk it out in stunned silence.

"Okay. Don't give me his number yet. I have to prepare for this," Marcus said.

"I don't even have his number," Owen admitted.

"That's fine. It's fine. Let's just eat breakfast," Marcus said.

CHAPTER 15

OWEN WAITED as the bartender made his drinks.

"God, Yuri. I've only left the house twice for anything other than work in, like, three months," Owen bemoaned.

"Why are you cooped up? Go see that mystery person of yours. Go shopping. Oh! Come to my place. Me and Rebecca and the munchkin have a small house about a twenty-minute bus ride from here," Yuri exclaimed.

"Unfortunately, there's been some stuff going on, and I had to vow to stay close to home. I'm so *bored*."

"Well, honey, I don't know what to tell you. If you ever feel like sneaking out, you are formally invited to my home," Yuri said, positively beaming.

"Thanks, Yuri. As soon as I get the green light, I'm going straight to you." He paused for a moment. "Do you like empanadas?"

"Who doesn't?" she responded, picking up her tray of drinks and walking away gracefully.

Owen truly wished he could achieve that level of elegance. He was about to pick up his drink orders from the bar when he felt a tap on the shoulder. He turned around to see a man he didn't recognize.

"Hello, sir. How can I help you?" He frowned in confusion when he realized that this man's truth wasn't floating freely. It was unusual enough to set him on guard.

"Mr. Ellis has sent me to pick you up."

Owen looked hard at the man's face. "I don't recognize you," he said curiously. Owen glanced around to see if Jacob was still waiting for him but didn't see him.

"You've only been here a few months. You wouldn't have been able to meet everyone." The man smiled mildly. From outward appearance, Owen was getting honesty.

"Come with me, Mr. Hart. Your work can wait."

Owen nodded and headed toward the exit with the man behind him. As soon as he walked out the door, arms wrapped around him and a cloth was pressed to his face. He went to claw the man in the eyes, but his hand was pushed away.

In that brief moment of physical contact, the man's truth came out. It was calm, cool, and detached, but with a strong flavor of ill intent. Not that this helped him now. He struggled as much as he could before he began seeing dark spots in his vision. The last thought he had before being pulled under was the hope that Leo wasn't in the same danger as him.

"WHAT DO you mean he's gone?" Leo bellowed, standing up from his desk at the casino.

The woman in front of him didn't flinch. Her face remained neutral.

"The bartender said that Owen left with a man who claimed to be one of yours. The bouncer was nowhere to be seen. We suspect that he was paid off."

"Well, go find the bouncer and bring him in for questioning."

As Leo was about to leave, he got a phone call.

"Maxwell," Leo answered coolly.

"Leo," a sinuous voice responded.

"What have you done with Owen?"

"Ah, so impatient. Don't you have any time to talk to an old friend?"

"What do you want? I am not in the mood for games."

"Leo, really. Now you are just being rude."

Leo didn't respond. He tried not to lose his composure.

"Spoilsport. Leo, I have your paramour. What happens to him now is entirely up to you. As of right now, he is relatively comfortable."

"Get on with it!" Leo said with frustration.

"We are going to have a little chat. I'll tell you what I want from you only once we meet in person. I invite you to my office. Of course, it would be rude of me to tell you to come alone. You may bring two guards with you, no more. Shall we meet, say, Saturday?"

Leo was furious. That was three days away. He had to sit on his hands for three days while Owen was in danger?

"Tomorrow," Leo snapped.

"Saturday," Maxwell responded firmly. "Remember, I hold all the cards. If you try to send someone to break your boy toy out, I will kill him."

"Fine," Leo said and hung up the phone.

Someone was going to pay for this. Maxwell was going to pay for this. While Maxwell had sent moles into his organization, Leo had sent a mole in himself. She had been there for about two years, and as far as he knew no one suspected her. She could confirm that Owen was safe.

Leo had some idea of what Maxwell wanted. The question was really *how much* he wanted. Leo was unwilling to give everything up, but the other option was getting Owen killed. Personal feelings aside, Leo didn't like being the reason one of his people lost their lives.

It had happened a few times before. Thankfully, those who got caught by other organizations chose to go to the grave with his secrets. He made absolutely sure that they were loyal before sending them in, and they were all aware that he would take care of their families.

Leo knew what he ought to do. He should go to this meeting, turn down whatever ridiculous offer Maxwell was presenting, and let Owen.... He couldn't even bring himself to think the word.

Leo wasn't worried for himself. Maxwell wasn't stupid enough to go after him personally when they met. He thought for a moment about who he wanted to take with him. His first choice brought up a question that chilled Leo's heart.

"Where is Jacob?"

The woman frowned.

"We located him in the employee bathroom. He had been knocked out with chloroform. He should be rousing by now. Shall I send him in?"

"Yes." Leo was relieved that Jacob hadn't betrayed him but still couldn't suppress the anger in his tone.

Leo waited alone in his office, pacing back and forth. When he heard the knock at the door, he sat down and called for Jacob to enter. He walked in, a bruise starting around his right eye.

"Sit," Leo said.

Jacob hesitated, then sat on one of the chairs across the desk.

"Sir, I take personal responsibility for my failure to keep Owen safe." Leo noted that he didn't correct himself for using Owen's first name. He was probably as frazzled as Leo was.

"I don't tolerate mistakes like these. But as I know you're loyal to me and that you are personally connected to Owen, I'd like to give you a second chance to make this right."

Jacob looked almost disappointed by this response. Leo suspected that it was because he wanted a harsher punishment for his mistake.

"Jacob, do you remember Annabella?"

Jacob perked up. He smiled slightly as he realized what Leo was getting at.

"Our woman on the inside. I almost forgot her assignment."

"Yes," Leo said, calmer now as he formed a plan. "She's due to check in every month, but she'll know to reach out sooner in this situation. We contact with burner phones. I want you in charge of taking her call and getting every bit of information from her that you can. You won't have a lot of time, but you must find Owen's exact location. I have the layout of Maxwell's building already, and I'll be ready to have Owen retrieved."

Leo handed him a phone, and Jacob's brief smile twisted back into a frown.

"You and Alex will not be accompanying me on Saturday to that bastard's office," Leo went on, "but you will be on hand to help Annabella rescue Owen. So prepare."

"I will make it happen, sir," Jacob said, standing up and nodding before leaving the office.

CHAPTER 16

JACOB HAD to rein himself in to avoid slamming the door behind him. He had failed horrendously. His one job was to protect Owen. He stayed day in and day out watching him and making sure nothing bad happened.

Of course, nothing had seemed threatening for some time, so maybe he'd grown lax in his duty. He didn't remember clearly what happened. He had been walking down the hallway toward the bathroom. He opened the door and was smacked in the face by a fist. He ducked out of the way before he could be hit with another blow. The stranger dove behind him and pressed a cloth to his face.

Next thing he knew, he was looking up at Jessica, one of the employees at the casino. It took him a moment to work out what had happened, and then he was struck with a thought. If he was out, then what happened to...?

He shot up, immediately regretting it as the world swam around him. Jessica filled him in on what had transpired, and he had gone with shame and fury warring within him to see Mr. Ellis.

And still after this audacious event, Mr. Ellis had trusted him to deal with the situation. He wasn't sure if this was because he trusted Jacob as an employee, or because he trusted him to do right by Owen.

Jacob stared at the phone in his hand. He willed it to ring, although he knew it would be too soon. He kept his cool as best he could. He nodded to those he passed on the way out of the casino, keeping his face as neutral as he could, but he must have not covered his feelings well enough, because a few people looked at him nervously and hurried by quickly.

Jacob didn't say a word from Mr. Ellis's office in Spades to the apartment. He opted to take the forty-minute walk, phone in his hands the whole time, but even the fresh air couldn't soothe his emotions. He had failed Owen; that was the beginning and end of it.

He took the elevator up to the penthouse with a jolt of anxiety. Informing Alex felt wrong on two levels. First, he would be devastated to hear what had happened. And would he be angry at Jacob? He should be.

The elevator door opened, and Jacob stepped out to meet Alex.

"Jacob. What's up? I thought you were at the casino."

Jacob frowned, searching for the words.

"Jacob? What's going on? What happened?"

Jacob rubbed his face with his hands. "Owen is gone. Balor took him right under my watch."

He covered his face, waiting for whatever reaction Alex was going to have. He lifted his hands in surprise when he felt arms wrap around his chest.

"Alex," he said brokenly.

"I can tell what you are thinking, you idiot. It's not your fault." He stepped back to look Jacob in the eye. Jacob almost turned away from the intensity in Alex's gaze. He had never seen so much anger from this man in his whole life.

"What do we need to do?" Alex asked calmly, which sounded so odd to Jacob's ears.

"First, we wait for a call."

OWEN WOKE with a horrible headache. He covered his face with his hands before even opening his eyes. What happened? He thought that he was working. Did he faint? What...? Then it came back to him. He shot up in the bed he was in, immediately regretting it as his head began to spin.

He paused for a moment to let the nausea settle. He opened his eyes slowly and took in his surroundings. The room he was in was plain and small. No windows, no pictures. The walls were a calming blue color. The bed he lay on was a twin. The sheets were actually pretty comfortable.

He pulled his legs across the bed to stand up but stopped when he heard a clink. He glanced down and rolled his eyes. A cuff on his leg? Really? Was this a movie?

Owen reached over and tugged on it. It was attached to the floor by a chain, and it didn't give way. He got out of the bed and walked across the room, but he came up short of the door and frowned. He looked around again and saw a toilet and sink against the wall. Classy.

So, Owen had made a stupid mistake. For some reason in his time spent with Leo, Alex, and Jacob, Owen had let some of his defenses down.

Obviously he had made a careless error. It was sad that this had to happen for him to remember that most people are out for their own benefit.

Owen wasn't sure where he was, or why. He knew he was going to find out sooner or later, but first he needed to take stock of the position he was in. He took a turn around the room, holding the chain up so that it wouldn't make noise as he moved.

The room was bare except for the bed, sink, and toilet. He tried to tug the sink off the floor, doing the same with the toilet seat, all to no avail. He ducked under the bed and found nothing useful.

He tried to raise the legs of the bed, but they were bolted down as well.

Tugging on the chain as he stepped back to the middle of the room, Owen got as close to the door as he could. Carefully holding the chain and stepping lightly, Owen reached out.

He read only one truth. Although since he hadn't been able to read the man at the casino easily, maybe he was there as well. The stream that *was* there felt bored. Whoever it was didn't seem very alert, but with Owen restrained by the cuff on his leg, that wasn't surprising.

Disappointed but done scoping out the room, Owen took stock.

Okay, so this happened while Leo had him staying close to home because of this guy, Maxwell Balor. Logically, that was who took him. Although who knows? It could be random.

But probably not.

Owen shook his head. So, what now. Was Leo looking for him? Owen knew that Leo genuinely cared for him, but part of Owen worried that he would leave him behind. This Balor man seemed to be a bitter rival. Maybe he would ask for more than Owen was worth?

What exactly was Owen worth to Leo?

Wow, Owen. Way to get yourself depressed.

He shook the feeling off. Owen weighed the pros and cons of getting his guard's attention. The chain didn't even make it as far as the door, so the element of surprise was out. Maybe he could find out why he was here? Or where he was?

Or he could tip off that he was conscious, and then worst-case scenario, he got a beating. Best case scenario they realize they've made a mistake and get him a cab.

He snorted, muting the noise with his hands. No. He needed to be serious here. His best bet was probably to wait it out. Maybe even feign unconsciousness when someone did come for him. At least they would get close enough for Owen to have a go at them.

"Go for the eyes!" the professor had always said.

Go for the eyes, Owen thought, lying back on the bed.

Owen must have fallen asleep at some point because he came to when he heard the door creaking open. He lay on his back with his eyes closed. Someone was walking toward the bed.

"Mr. Hart," a voice came from right beside him. Owen sensed the same boredom from before. "Mr. Har—"

Owen silenced the man with a punch to the stomach. He doubled over in pain, and Owen quickly searched him for keys. There were none. Crap.

He picked up the slack chain and wrapped it around the goon's neck. No one was in the room with them, but he felt more people coming.

"Unlock these shackles," he said quietly, pulling on the chain until the man gagged.

"Fuck you, whore."

Owen swallowed the fury that came with that comment. People had said the same thing about him and the professor. They thought he was some twink of a sex worker who'd charmed his way into a sugar daddy. Well, fuck all of them.

Owen ducked so that the choking man was between him and the door in case… yes. The people who crashed through the door had guns.

"Unlock these chains, assholes!" he shouted. The first man stopped gagging as his airway was completely blocked. No one responded either to help Owen or their comrade.

"I said—" Owen was cut off by a gunshot. The man he was choking slumped down to the ground, dead.

Owen's eyes widened to what he imagined were comic proportions. He dropped the chain but stayed low with the body in front of him in case they wanted to send a bullet his way.

"So you're not as stupid as you look," one man said. His voice was weirdly calming. Owen looked over the body and locked eyes with him as he lowered his gun. He stood in the doorway with about five other people.

He had short deep red hair and burning eyes that were almost golden brown. His truth reeked of quiet sadism.

"Are you that guy who's obsessed with Leo?" Owen asked.

The man appeared surprised for a moment, then burst out laughing. It sounded lighthearted. His truth swirled with unkind humor. Owen sensed a huge disconnect between what the man meant and what he presented.

"I can already see that you are more interesting than Ellis's other escorts. I've heard that your relationship goes farther than that, though."

Owen frowned.

"Ah, I apologize. I'm being rude. My name is Maxwell Balor. You may call me Mr. Balor. Or sir, if you prefer," he said, smiling.

"Mr. Balor, what the fuck am I here for?" Owen asked, completely ignoring the last comment.

"Right to the point? It's kind of tedious that way." He frowned slightly. "You're here because, as I assume you know, I am blackmailing Leo Ellis. I want to make a deal with him, and it will go much easier so long as you are my guest."

Owen snorted. Maxwell's face changed to quiet curiosity.

"We have been...." Dating? Were they dating? "We have only been together for a few months. What makes you think he would do anything for me?"

Balor beamed. "You know Leo and I have a history. Do you know how we met?"

Owen was suddenly very curious. Plus the longer they spoke, the longer he could put off a beating, if that was where they were going with this. Maybe. He hoped so. When Owen didn't answer, Balor went ahead.

"We both worked for the same company. This is going back at least ten years." He waved a dismissive hand. "We both started around the same time, similar age, similar minds. We were fast friends. I was in charge of accounting, and I admit that I was... supplementing my payment. He discovered this, and instead of keeping my secret, he had me booted from the organization. Thank goodness he got me fired without letting anyone know about the money. I took my money and the contacts that I had made and started my own loan company."

Balor paused as if to make sure that Owen was paying attention.

"You can drop the body now, Owen. I am a good shot. If I wanted it, you would be dead already."

Owen sighed, pushing the corpse as far away from him as he could manage. He sat cross-legged on the ground, looking up at Balor.

"Please, continue," he said, feeling weary as the adrenaline faded from his system.

"Well, years go by, and I come to find that my old friend Leo has grown into his own business. He had acquired a casino and started a money-laundering operation."

Maxwell paused as if waiting for a reaction.

"And?" Owen asked when Balor did not continue.

"*And* we became competitors. See, I never forgave Leo for his betrayal. Had he stayed in his lane, I would have ignored it. But witnessing that man who tried to ruin me making a name for himself as *my* competitor? No."

Owen frowned. "So you think that Leo is going to hand over everything you ask for in exchange for his 'whore'?"

"About that...." Balor's smile grew wicked. Owen felt that wave of sadism again. "I wasn't planning on getting anything out of this other than a discussion and a warning. But after hearing Ellis's reaction? I'm asking a lot more. That or you die. I don't really care which. I get satisfaction either way." He paused significantly. "And now I'll let you get aquatinted with your new friends, Shiloh and Jeff."

He waved as he left. All the guards but two walked away as well. The two remaining guards, who must be Shiloh and Jeff, approached Owen, guns drawn.

"Come with us," one said mildly, coldness coming off of him.

Owen waited while the other unlocked his shackle and pulled him up by his arm. They guided him toward the door, and Owen's heart sank. If they were moving locations, it was either to kill him or to beat him somewhere they could clean the blood easier.

As he thought about the situation, he realized it was probably the latter.

"WHAT DID Annabella have to say?" Leo asked coolly, sitting at his desk with his head resting on his hands.

"She says that he's alive," Jacob said.

"He's alive? Is that all?" Leo tried to keep it together. He was no good in this situation, being so emotionally charged up. Jacob was no better. Honestly, if he trusted someone, *anyone*, else with this, he would be better off. He needed cool heads for this.

Jacob gritted his teeth. "It appears that he has sustained some injuries in the past two days."

"Can she extract him?" Leo asked, barely managing to keep his cool.

"No. There won't be an opportunity until everyone is busy preparing for your arrival. That will divert enough men to make it possible to get him out."

Leo rubbed his face with both hands. He had barely eaten or slept in these past two days. He was so worried. Although he knew in his heart that Owen was strong, inside and out, he couldn't help fearing that an experience like this would take that special spark out of him.

Or if he survived, would he leave? Leo wouldn't blame him.

No matter what happened, though, Maxwell was going to pay. He had many clients who would be willing to sanction moves against his organization for such dirty dealings. There was an unspoken rule against using outsiders as pawns in the admittedly odd morality of this illegal business. And Owen was an outsider. Yes, Maxwell Balor was going to pay, hopefully at Leo's own hand.

"Jacob, please contact Gregor Musk. I believe that now is the time for action."

Jacob nodded. His posture appeared more confident as he walked out of the office, leaving Leo to fantasize about how Balor was going to meet his end.

OWEN COUGHED and spat out a tooth. Crap. He hated the dentist.

As another blow landed to his stomach, he curled into a ball to try to defend himself from the barrage of kicks. His attackers backed away for a moment, and Owen almost cried with relief. When the blows didn't start up again, he opened his eyes. His right eye was swollen shut, but he could still see out of his left.

He tried to sit up when he saw Maxwell Balor enter the room, but he didn't have the energy. Instead, he lay on his back and stared up at him. He tried to muster an angry expression, but from the satisfied look on Balor's face, Owen must have looked as scared and helpless as he felt.

"Owen, my meeting with Ellis is tomorrow, and I've been trying to think of what exactly I should do for him. So I thought and thought, and then it hit me!"

He paused for drama, but Owen was so fuzzy he could hardly follow along.

"Spades!"

Owen waited for more. Balor said nothing else.

"What?" Owen finally asked.

The sadistic aura spiked enough to make Owen wince.

"You work for Leo's casino, Spades, right?" Balor said. "Well, what would he like better than to have a brand to show the world that you are his. Then he wouldn't need to worry about this sort of thing happening again. I really am such a good friend."

Owen shifted his gaze to the ceiling, not really following what Balor was saying.

"Hey, Owen," Balor kicked his side. Owen moaned.

"Pick a side, left or right." He waited for Owen to catch up, then asked again, "Left or right?"

"Le… ft?" Owen could tell he had a concussion. It was making him dizzy.

"Left it is."

Balor went out of Owen's view for a moment. Then a hand turned Owen's head and moved his hair to reveal his neck. Owen cried out as searing pain went through him. His screams sounded pathetic to his own ears.

Blessed black spots that indicated he was going to lose consciousness danced behind his eyes. Then darkness.

When he woke up, Owen was back in his room. He looked down at his legs and noted that he wore no shackle. It didn't really matter. Owen was in too much pain to get up and walk around anyway. He was scared. More so than he had ever been in his life. He had no concept of how long he had been here or how long he would have to wait to be rescued.

Would he be rescued? Part of him feared Leo wouldn't take him home if Balor asked for too much. *Which he probably would*, Owen thought hopelessly.

Owen lifted his arms and looked down at his legs. All he had on was a pair of pants; the rest of his exposed skin was either covered with blood-soaked gauze or bruises. He sighed. At least he was alone for now.

Owen attempted to brush his hair out of his eyes and swallowed a shout of pain. He gently touched the left side of his neck, and the mere touch of his fingers felt like fire. The wound was raised. It didn't feel big. The textured contour was about half the size of his palm, but the pain radiated until it felt like the whole left side of his neck was on fire.

Owen was thirsty. He braced himself for the pain and sat up on the bed. He immediately regretted doing it so fast when the vertigo hit, and he closed his eyes and held his head in his hands until the feeling subsided.

Groaning, he threw his legs over the side of the bed and stood up. He wobbled to the sink and turned the faucet. The water ran brown and murky, but fuck if he cared. He drank as much as he could without feeling sick.

He wasn't stupid. Days. *Had it been days?* He had been in and out of consciousness several times. With no windows he couldn't track time by the light, but he had woken up in the bed twice, so it must have been at least two days.

Queasy from standing up, Owen lay back on the bed and stared at the ceiling for a while. He had tried a few times to determine who was at the door, but his head was too fuzzy to get a read.

A few minutes, or hours, later, Owen heard a commotion from outside the door. He sat up, slowly this time, and once more reached out to the door. Someone was muted, likely unconscious. He wasn't sure if this was a good sign or a bad one.

Keys jangled, and a woman entered the room. She was tall, with black hair tied up in a ponytail. Her energy didn't feel aggressive, so he relaxed a bit.

"Who are you?" he asked, his voice cracking.

She came to the bed and looked him over. "My name is Annabella. I work for Mr. Ellis, and I only have a small window of opportunity to get you out of here, so you're going to have come with me now."

She grabbed Owen's arm and hefted him to his feet. He winced and jerked his head as the motion sent a shaft of pain through his neck. She peered at him curiously and then brushed his hair to the side, freezing at what she saw.

Shaking off her obvious shock, Annabella threw Owen's arm over her shoulder and took some of the weight off his body. He heard her mumbling to herself. Something about doing something to a child. He didn't care. He wanted to leave.

The pain faded to the background as adrenaline kicked in. He moved so fast that Annabella, even with her long legs, had to pick up the pace. She took him to a room right down the hall and closed and locked the door behind them.

Owen was nervous. Maybe he should stop trusting people just because they dropped Leo's name. He needn't have worried. She crossed the room to a small window. Owen followed her and looked out and down. He was on the second floor.

He scanned the area to find something that could break his fall, then froze and stared. Jacob and Alex were right across the street, sitting on a bench in front of a bus station. He was going to call to them but realized how stupid that would be.

Annabella pulled out a phone and held it to her ear. Owen only heard mumbling. He glanced down the building and decided he could shimmy his way down the pipe running next to the window. It didn't go all the way to the ground, but he could probably jump the last bit.

Not that it would be a graceful or painless drop. Owen looked back at the bus station and was pained to see the bench was now empty. He peered around, saw no one, and felt tears pricking at his eye. Then he spotted his friends again. They must have separated and walked around the building because there they were, meeting below the window.

Annabella started to say something, but Owen didn't give a shit. He pulled himself out the window and onto the pipe, not even pausing at the wave of pain the movement caused. He shimmied down as far as he could go. Jacob stood underneath him, waving for him to jump.

Without a second thought, he did, landing in Jacob's outstretched arms. Owen's emotions were so high that it numbed the pain. He got to his feet but didn't let go of Jacob. Owen tried hard to hold back, but he was so overwhelmed by truly feeling safe that he cried on Jacob's shoulder. He didn't make a sound, not wanting anyone to notice him, but he could feel a wet mark growing on Jacob's shirt. Jacob didn't push him away, instead rubbing his back and hair. It felt like a century but was probably only a few minutes before a black car pulled up next to them.

Jacob gently ushered Owen into the car. It was only when his skin hit the leather that Owen realized he had no shirt on. Looking down at himself, Owen was suddenly self-conscious. Some small part of him didn't want anyone to know how badly he was injured—almost out of a sense of pride.

Jacob pulled a blanket from under his seat and wrapped it gently around Owen's shoulders, and he quickly hid his wounds behind it.

Jacob looked odd. Owen was still too fuzzy to get a good read. Jacob's truth was negative, though. His smile was gone. The frown he wore was intimidating. Owen read anger. He didn't even know that Jacob could *be* so angry.

After a few moments, Alex climbed into the car next to Owen and they began moving. Neither of the men said anything, and Owen was happy that he could feel *safe*. Alex gently pulled Owen's head onto his shoulder and petted his hair, and Owen realized that he had started crying again. Embarrassed, he wiped his eyes and struggled to sit up, but Alex instead turned in his seat to hug him.

"You are safe now, Owen. I'm not going to ask if you are okay, because the answer is obvious. Relax. We'll be home soon."

"What happened to Leo? And what is going to happen to Annabella?" Owen asked.

Alex was quick to answer. "Don't worry about Mr. Ellis. He has the situation totally under control. As for Annabella, she is leaving immediately before anyone finds anything amiss. She'll be fine."

Owen frowned.

"They *both* will be fine, Owen," Jacob agreed, as Alex once again let Owen lay his head on his shoulder. Owen slumped into him and closed his eyes.

CHAPTER 17

LEO WAS antsy as the car pulled up to Balor's office. From the outside it was an ordinary historic building. Leo always thought the rough stone façade appeared somewhat eerie.

He waited in the car for as long as he could, staring at his phone, willing it to ring. He sighed and finally got out. He hadn't reached the door when his phone rang. Leo picked it up before the first ring even ended. He said nothing.

"It's done. We're halfway home."

Leo let out a breath he didn't realize he was holding.

"Is he okay?" he asked warily.

Jacob didn't immediately answer. "He's safe. He'll be home when you finish your business," he said finally.

Jacob hung up. Leo stood for a moment, still holding the phone in his hand. He took a deep breath, then shut down his face. It would do no one any good for him to walk into this meeting with his heart on his sleeve.

Knowing that Owen would be rescued—well, praying—Leo had brought five guards with him rather than the two Balor had sanctioned. He wasn't stupid. It went against every code he had learned growing up in his sort of business to attack someone during a meeting.

But then, it was also against the code to involve a civilian with no direct ties. So to take an innocent person and put them through hell, all to spite a rival, was definitely a no-go.

Leo entered the building. Two guards preceded him, and the other three followed close behind. The men at the door looked nervous. Obviously they hadn't expected so much man power. Leo observed the men displaying so much emotion. He took pride in employing men and women who could maintain their composure under pressure.

"Leo," a voice sang out.

His guards moved aside, and Leo saw Maxwell Balor waving at him as if they were old friends catching up. Which, well, maybe they were.

"Leo, it's been too long."

Leo judged by the overly sweet tone that he had not yet realized Owen was gone.

"Maxwell, I am not here to retrieve Owen."

Balor looked stunned for a moment. His smile tightened. "Giving up so soon? I will happily kill him for you if he means so little."

"How much he means to me is irrelevant. He is long gone."

Maxwell's face pinched. "Go find him." He sent one of his guards out.

"You won't find him," Leo said. "No, I am here to formally warn you. I have contacted Musk. He finds your dealings as deplorable as I do. He, along with several other of your clients, is backing me up now. So here is the deal that I will make *you*. You are done laundering money. You can keep your little loan company, and I will even take you as a client of my own, if you wish. But if you choose not to sell me your laundering companies, I will poach every single one of your clients." With allies like Musk on Leo's side, this was no idle threat, and Maxwell knew it.

By the time Leo finished speaking, the guards Maxwell had sent out returned and whispered something in his ear. Maxwell's face grew enraged. Leo wasn't sure if it was because of his declaration or because Owen was missing. He didn't care either way. He was simply glad to see the expression.

"Leo," Maxwell bit out, "I have no choice but to acquiesce to your demands. But know this. The day will come when I will make you pay for this. I will not go down quietly."

Leo hid his anger at the audacity of Maxwell even trying to threaten him in his position.

"We are signing the contract at Gregor Musk's office on Tuesday. It will be us and Lilith Planton, Anders Wintip, and Holly Creay. Surely you will not snub your long-held clients."

Leo was delighted by the shock that crossed Maxwell's face.

"Until Tuesday," Leo said, mock bowing before turning to leave. Of course, his guards covered his back. He was smart enough to realize that Maxwell *would* be stupid enough to shoot him in the back if he thought he could.

Leo got into the car. He settled back as it pulled onto the street. He smiled to himself. Maxwell would be crippled by losing these clients. Short of beating and killing Maxwell himself, this contract was the second-best form of revenge that Leo could hope for.

What about Owen?

Leo had forgotten him momentarily, distracted by seeing Maxwell brought so low. But now he was heading home, and Owen was going to be there. How he hoped that he was okay. He had known that he was hurt. Probably more than Annabella had time to say. Or more than Jacob was willing to tell him.

Either way, if this incident had scared Owen enough to drive him away... he wouldn't blame him. Leo sighed. Maybe Owen would be better off going back to his old life. Leo wouldn't allow him to live like he did before, of course. He would give him all the money in the world if it would make him happy. Although he didn't think that Owen was the type to take a handout.

But no. Owen didn't deserve to be put in danger because of *him.*

Leo rubbed his face with his hands. It was no use thinking of such things even before he saw him.

OWEN WOKE up with a start. He panicked for a moment, waiting for guards to come take him into that small, damp basement of a room. He closed his eyes and prayed that they would leave him alone.

"Owen?"

Wait. Owen opened his eyes and saw the canopy above the bed he was in. His bed. Owen turned his head to the doorway, where light was spilling in. It was Alex.

"Owen, the doctor is here."

Alex turned on the lights, and Owen had to squint until his eyes adjusted. A woman walked into the room, followed by a man dragging an IV and a tray with various nefarious-looking tools.

"Owen, I am Dr. Neuva. I'm going to remove these bandages and your clothing so I can see what needs to be treated, okay? If you feel nervous or unsafe, please stop me." She smiled.

Owen smiled back, feeling warmth and kindness coming from her.

She marked where his wounds were on a drawing of a male body. She cleaned all of his wounds and covered up those that needed it. A few cuts needed stitching, and she accomplished that quickly and with minimum pain. She checked a few broken ribs. Finally, she made note of the mark on Owen's neck. He had forgotten about it because his pain was distributed all over, but now it burned. He didn't know what it was, and honestly, he wasn't looking forward to finding out.

Dr. Neuva said nothing about it, and indicated it on the picture.

"Does any place hurt significantly more?" she asked.

Owen shook his head, freezing as the burning sensation sharpened.

She noticed and frowned at him. "Owen, I am going to put you on an IV drip. It's just fluids. Can you tell me how much pain you are in? One to ten with one being the best and ten being the worst."

Owen laughed lightly. "Ten."

Owen heard a disgusted grunt. He felt bad for a minute. He'd forgotten Alex was there.

"Okay, well, I will give you something for the pain...."

"No, thank you," he responded quickly.

"What?"

"No drugs, please. Just give me Tylenol."

"But your injuries—"

"Nope. No pain meds."

The doctor stared at him for a minute, then shrugged. "Tylenol it is, then. If you lie down, we can put some ice packs on you. That might also help with the pain."

"Sure thing, Doc," Owen said. His voice sounded scratchy.

Dr. Neuva nodded to the nurse and left, and the nurse hooked Owen up to the IV.

"I'll send some Tylenol up," he said, "but you're going to have to eat something first."

Owen nodded, and the nurse left the room.

The second the nurse was gone, Alex sat on the bed and held Owen's hand.

"Owen, do you have any injuries in, you know, where we can't see?"

Owen shook his head. Thank God for small miracles. "Alex, can I have some water?"

Alex shot up from the bed, looking angry at himself for not thinking of that. He dashed out and back in record time.

"Can you hold it yourself?" he asked, handing a water bottle to Owen.

"Yes," he responded, accepting the bottle. He wanted to down it all, but he paused when it reached his lips. If he guzzled the water, he was going to throw up.

"Go slow, okay?" Alex said.

Owen nodded. He tried to sip the water as slowly as he could, warring with his thirst.

A commotion began outside the door. Owen could hear a slam. He wasn't sure if the door was closing or opening. He figured the latter when Alex left his side to go to the living room. There were murmurs, and Owen could sense at least three truths milling about in the air.

Suddenly Leo appeared in the doorway. He came in, and Owen was stunned. He didn't know why he was surprised, because this was his room after all. Leo looked like he was going to slam the door shut but then reined it in at the last minute.

He gently closed the door behind him, walked over to the bed, and sat down on the end beside Owen.

"I'm sorry," they said in unison. They shared looks of surprise.

"But it's my fault for being caught to begin with," Owen said. "I made all this trouble for you."

Leo actually growled. "*You're* sorry? I let you get *kidnapped by a psychopath*! And then I didn't come for you…." He bit his lip, blood droplets forming.

Owen looked at him for a long time. He didn't want to ask. He did not want to sound weak or entitled. He wasn't sure he wanted to *know*.

"Why?" he finally asked, pausing. Leo waited for him to continue. "Why *didn't* you come for me?"

Leo stared into his eyes, scowling. "We had to wait until it was safe. Until it was guaranteed to be successful. Had I known the extent—" Leo's words cut off.

He brushed Owen's hair behind his ear, pausing when Owen twitched in pain. He gently touched the bandage on Owen's neck.

"What is this?" he asked, somewhat ominously.

Owen frowned. "I'm not thinking about it right now."

Leo's face shut down. Owen had never seen him look so serious, so intense. Leo started to unravel the gauze. Owen tried to stop him, but Leo shoved his hands aside. When he got to the skin, Owen realized that he'd been wrong.

This was the most serious face he had ever seen. Owen got the sense that Leo was holding his full reaction back. After a moment, a calm control returned to Leo's face.

"Is it bad? I haven't seen it yet. What is it?" Owen was torn between curiosity and the feeling that if he didn't know, then it wasn't real.

"It's… a spade."

"Like the casino? Well, that's a low blow," Owen said calmly.

"A low blow?" Leo asked.

"I remember him saying that it was a present for you or something. I mean, I guess if I'm going to have a brand on my neck, I can pass it off as a fashion statement."

Leo looked at him oddly. "You're not mad?" he asked.

"Oh, fuck yeah, I'm mad! But it's there now… forever, I guess. I'm glad it's not, like, initials or something. At least a spade could be a fashion statement. I'm not going to think about it now."

Leo shook his head. "What do you need, Owen? Can I get you food?"

Owen hadn't eaten anything in the last few days, but he wasn't even a bit hungry.

Leo got up and opened the door. "Alex, what did the doctor say about food?" Leo called.

"She said chicken broth and bread. I'm already heating up the broth."

Leo left the room, and Owen swallowed his desire to beg him not to leave. He was coming back.

Owen shut his eyes for a minute.

WHEN HE woke up, the room was dark again. The only light came from a laptop Leo held on the chair where he sat at Owen's side.

"How long was I out?" Owen asked, his voice textured by sleep.

"Oh, only an hour or so. I didn't want to wake you. You need to rest."

"Can I get more water?" he asked. "Oh, and turn on the light. I need to get food in me."

That was what the professor always said to him when he was sick. "You need to get some food in you. The less you want, the more you need."

Owen's eyes teared up. In moments like this, he missed the professor the most. Owen wiped his eyes before Leo returned. He held a water bottle and a piece of bread. He sat back down beside the bed and handed Owen the water first. Owen accepted it gratefully and took a few small sips before putting it down.

Next he took the bread. Just the smell of it turned Owen's stomach. Still, he took a few small bites before giving himself a break. It stayed down. Owen considered that a win.

He looked over at Leo, who was staring at Owen's chest with anger. "Leo," he said.

Leo glanced up, and the anger dissipated. "Yes," he said.

"Leo, I don't want this to affect how you see me. I'm not some damsel in distress. I can take care of myself."

Leo stared at him in surprise. "Owen, you are the strongest person I know! That's why this hurts me so, to see you so wounded."

Owen looked at him suspiciously. As bad a shape as he was in, he really didn't want to think about what had happened. It did make him feel weak.

Putting it aside, Owen leaned back into the pillow and closed his eyes.

Just like before, Owen woke up to a dark room, lit only by the small sliver coming from the curtains on the window.

Also like before, Leo sat next to him, laptop in hand.

"What time is it?" Owen asked sleepily.

Leo glanced up and smiled. "I was waiting for you to wake up. It seems that there has been a casino employee harassing her supervisor for your information. They finally came to me, and it turns out that Yuri, lovely woman, has been trying to contact you since the day you were taken at the casino. She swore up and down that something had happened because you would never up and leave during a shift. Her calls and texts have not gone through as your phone is nowhere to be found."

Leo handed Owen a brand-new phone. It had eighty-seven messages. Figuring that it would be best, Owen called Yuri's number first. She answered on the second ring.

"Owen? Owen, is that you?" she said quickly. It was like getting hit in the face by a wave.

"Yes, Yuri. I heard you were worried—"

"Worried? I'm about ten levels above worried. Are you okay? What happened?"

Owen smiled. He couldn't read her over the phone, but her voice sounded so genuine.

"I've been sick. It started in the middle of the shift, and as you can see, I misplaced my phone, so I did not even know you were trying to reach me."

There was a long pause. "Owen, I'm gonna tell you right now that I know you are lying. But I am going to let that slide. I'm just glad you are okay. You are okay, right?" she added.

"Yes, Yuri, I'm the best that I could be."

Yuri didn't say anything. Owen imagined that she must have nodded her head.

"Okay, Yuri, I won't be working for a bit, but I promise not to lose this phone. Okay?"

"Good," Yuri said. Her voice turned sly. "Say hello to Mr. Ellis for me."

Owen didn't know if she knew about their relationship or was guessing. She was rather astute.

Leo looked at him curiously.

"Yuri says hi," Owen said, smiling.

Leo touched his finger to Owen's lips and smiled as well.

"A good friend, huh?"

"That she is," Owen said. "I'm lucky to have her."

"OWEN! I HEARD what happened. Do you need me to murder someone?" Marcus asked, his emotions matching the worry in his voice.

Owen blinked up at him from where he sat on the couch. He was sick of being in bed.

"Marcus, how the hell did you get in here?" he asked incredulously.

"Easy! I snuck in the delivery entrance, took the old servants' staircase, broke into an empty bedroom on the third floor, and took the fire escape up to the penthouse. The window was open," Marcus said, his emotions swirling with pride.

"Glossing over that.... Marcus, I'm fine. I don't want to talk about it," Owen said, repositioning himself on the couch to take pressure off his back.

Leo was working, which was probably a good thing, as Leo hadn't yet come to terms with Marcus. Owen had only met Marcus a few times himself, but it didn't feel at all out of place to have him there.

"Look, I'm not going to ask any questions, but I will give you cookies," Marcus exclaimed.

"Cookies?" Owen asked, knowing that he could make cookies better than any bakery.

"Yeah, they're those rainbow cookies. I don't remember what they're called. You know, the boxy ones? There's a bakery downtown that makes them, and they're so good!" Marcus said cheerfully.

Owen accepted the box, but opted to leave the cookies on the couch with him. He still felt sore enough that he didn't like getting up and down too much. If Marcus realized this, he didn't show it.

"So the real reason I came here, aside from checking on you of course, is that... I've been thinking...," Marcus started. He frowned and stopped talking, looking out into space.

After a long pause, Owen spoke up. "You've been thinking about what?" he asked.

Marcus snapped back to reality. "Yeah, so I've been thinking about Tyler, and I really want to apologize to him," he said, then stopped once again and looked thoughtful.

"Okay," Owen said, not wanting to pry.

Marcus frowned at him. Owen could feel that he was conflicted. His emotions were all jumbled up to the point that Owen couldn't separate them.

"Okay, Owen. I'll give you the backstory. Maybe you can help me figure out what to do," Marcus finally said, then plunged on in typical Marcus fashion. "When we were growing up, we were very close. At that time, I was struggling to learn how to control all the background feelings. I hung out with Tyler because I could only read him about half the time.

"The feelings came and went, and his emotions were usually calm and soothing. Of course, after a few years, I had come to think of him as my best friend. The person I cared most about in the world. We were inseparable.

"I knew that I loved Tyler when I began to get jealous of the girls who would flirt with him. I didn't understand my feelings, but I couldn't control them either. Then one day—we were probably about sixteen—Tyler told me he was moving away. I was so surprised and overwhelmed. I didn't know how to react, and so I went with my gut and kissed him." Marcus put his face in his hands.

"He immediately rejected me, which I should have expected. Then he moved without saying another word to me. I didn't reach out to him. I felt that he must have hated me for breaking up our friendship like that. I still miss him. I mean, I still...." Marcus looked wistfully at the table. "Well, anyway. I want to apologize and find out once and for all if Tyler still hates me."

Owen absorbed this. He couldn't picture the Tyler he knew as someone who would hold a grudge. He would have to ask Tyler about this when he saw him, but he didn't want to tell Marcus this in case it went badly.

CHAPTER 18

A MONTH WENT by and Owen was feeling much better. He wasn't working yet, but he was well enough to go to the pool. Which was good enough for him.

"Owen, I had an awesome idea," Alex said, approaching Owen where he floated in the pool.

"What idea?" he asked.

"You're going on vacation!" Alex said happily.

"What vacation?"

"Well. You've been cooped up in here for so long, and you are well enough for it, so I suggested to Mr. Ellis that you go to a resort."

"Where?"

"I don't know. Somewhere on a beach."

Owen stiffened. "By that do you mean in walking distance of the ocean?"

Alex frowned for a moment. "Is that bad?" he asked.

"Alex, I would give you my left arm if it meant that I could *walk* to the *ocean*."

Alex laughed.

Everything was planned extremely quickly. Owen couldn't tell if Leo had that much influence or if this had been in the works already, but the very next day found Owen's belongings already packed and waiting for a car to the airport.

Owen had never been on an airplane before. He wasn't too nervous; he was more curious. Owen had always heard what a headache airports could be, but he and Leo were rushed along in record time. They breezed right through the security checks, got right to their gate, and were the first ones on the plane.

Takeoff was kind of cool. It reminded him of that feeling you get when a roller coaster is going up the tracks. He watched the ground get farther and farther away. The buildings began to look like little bugs.

Leo had them in first class seating. Owen felt kind of guilty because he knew Leo had the guards accompanying them sitting in economy.

Still, he got free food, free beer, and a little screen he could watch movies on.

When they landed, Owen was almost disappointed. The ride there alone was basically the best vacation he had ever been on.

When the plane landed, Owen was ushered out of the port and into another car. The car in turn brought them to a ferry.

"So, we are going to your friend's private island?" Owen asked as they waited for the boat to dock.

"Yes. More of a business associate than a friend," Leo responded.

"Whatever. And you promise that we can walk to the beach?"

Leo laughed. "For the fourth time, yes, Owen."

Owen went to get his bags but was waved away by one of Leo's guards.

"I can still carry my own bags, you know."

Leo frowned. "You know you have a ten-pound limit right now. If you push yourself too hard, you could rebreak a rib."

"I would be rolling it on the ground," he pointed out.

Leo's response was to take his hand and walk him onto the boat himself.

"Everyone's treating me like a friggin' baby," Owen mumbled to himself.

Leo must have heard him because he gently poked Owen's cheek and kissed him when he tried to respond.

"Who's treating you like a baby?" Leo said sweetly.

Owen blushed, painfully aware of the four plainclothes guards walking behind them. Which reminded him.

"Why didn't Jacob and Alex come along?"

Leo smiled. "Well, first off they would be way too distracted to work. Secondly, I need Jacob to take charge in my absence. He's the head honcho when I am gone."

Owen frowned. "When was the last time you took a vacation anyway?"

"Well, if you don't include charity events, which feel like work, it has probably been about five years."

"All that money and no vacation, huh?" Owen mused.

"How about you, Owen?"

Owen laughed. "When I was younger, the professor used to take me up to the countryside a few times a year to hang out and practice shooting. The cabin—I don't remember if he owned it or rented—was small and only had one bedroom. We fought every single time over who got the bed and who got the couch. He was stronger than me, so he always managed to strong-arm me off the couch and into the bedroom. It was only a few times that I managed to take over the couch so he could sleep in the bedroom."

"That's a lovely memory," Leo said.

"Yeah. But anyway, I've never been on a vacation like this before," he finished. "I've never seen the ocean in person."

Leo looked surprised. "You of all people have never been to the ocean?"

"Nope," Owen said happily.

The boat docked on the island, and Owen was ushered off by Leo. They took a small shuttle bus across the island to a huge mansion set on a hill. By the time they got there, the sun had gone down. Owen didn't pay the accommodations much mind; he was too enthralled by the vastness of water before him. He reveled in the breeze, which smelled slightly of salt. The waves sounded so soothing. He could see why some people liked to sleep to the sound of the sea.

"Leo, can we go to the beach?" Owen asked in a rush.

Leo eyed Owen with a knowing smile. "Owen, it's dark."

"But we can have a moonlit stroll?" he asked hopefully.

Leo laughed. "Get settled in first. Then we can go for a walk."

"Yes!" Owen exclaimed.

When he got inside the building, though, Owen almost forgot about the ocean. Almost.

The whole building was lit in a warm glow. Sconces lined the walls with beautiful antique patterns. The entry was spacious, and two grand staircases wound up to the bedrooms.

Owen looked around. He couldn't see the kitchen from where they stood. Curiosity was killing him. "Are we cooking our own meals?" Owen asked excitedly.

Leo shook his head, a small smile on his lips. "Hate to break it to you, but no, Owen."

Owen pouted.

Leo's guards preceded them, scoping out all the rooms, upstairs and down. When they finally came back, they nodded at Leo.

"Okay, let's get you settled."

Owen walked ahead of Leo, taking in all the lights and wondering how much they paid for electricity.

Leo stopped Owen at one ornate door. "This is our bedroom," he said.

Owen went in and was stunned. The room looked like one of those roped-off rooms at historical mansion tours. Everything was stunning but had that aged quality that made Owen too nervous to touch anything.

Their bags had been dropped at the entrance, and Leo brought them into the room, then closed the door behind him.

Excitement bubbled up in Owen. "Okay, I'm settled. Let's take a walk!"

Leo rolled his eyes but gestured for Owen to lead the way. Which he did happily.

OWEN STOOD on the sand, letting the waves wash over his feet as they moved back and forth from shore to sea. He closed his eyes, feeling a light spray of salty water and hearing that beautiful sound.

When he opened his eyes, it was to a full moon in a clear sky. It truly was the perfect night. Owen turned his head to look back at Leo. "It's a lot nicer if you take your shoes off," he said.

Leo shrugged. "This has never really been my thing."

"This is everyone's thing," Owen exclaimed.

Leo went to Owen and pulled him away from the water. He held Owen against his chest, gently kissing Owen's eyes, nose, and then lips.

"This is my thing," he said quietly.

Owen smiled. That was so cheesy, but it was sweet.

Leo pulled away, but Owen grabbed his shirt and dragged him in for a *real* kiss. Their lips met gently; then Owen increased the pressure and pushed his tongue past Leo's lips to lick at his teeth.

Leo tried to step back, but Owen gripped his shirt harder. "Leo, for God's sake, I'm fine!"

Leo shook his head. "The doctor said to take it easy," he said.

"Fuck the doctor. I'm fine!"

"But Owen—"

"First off, that was over a month ago."

Leo frowned.

"Second off, I'm frustrated. I am so sexually frustrated, and it's all because you think I am too weak to mess around!"

Owen regretted saying that almost immediately. The smile that grew on Leo's face was absolutely devious.

"That's why you're frustrated, huh?"

"Yes, for fuck's sake," he said, starting to feel embarrassed. He hoped the darkness hid the flush burning his cheeks.

"Okay," Leo said, turning around and walking toward the manor. Owen was stunned. Leo kept going without looking back. Owen half followed, half struggled to slip his sandals back on. When he caught up, Leo took his hand without even looking at him.

Owen's heart beat faster, the simple touch of Leo's hand warming him.

They passed the guard standing outside and entered the dimly lit house. It was kind of romantic lighting, Owen thought.

Hand in hand they climbed the stairs, passing no one. Leo still didn't look at Owen. They made it to the room, and Leo ushered Owen in and shut the door.

"So you're frustrated, huh?" he repeated slyly. Leo put his hands on Owen's shoulders, guiding him to sit down on the bed.

Owen frowned. "This is what I mean. I don't need to be treated like a porcelain doll. It's been weeks. I'm fine."

Leo frowned. "You're not fine, though."

"Yes. Yes, I am. I'm tired of feeling weak." Tears welled in Owen's eyes. He had never felt so weak in his life as he had those few days in Maxwell Balor's custody. Leo was making it worse by driving that point home.

Leo frowned as Owen wiped his eyes. He leaned over and pushed Owen onto the bed gently. Owen rolled his eyes. Leo could have been rougher with fine china.

Owen pulled himself up and flipped Leo onto the bed beneath him. Leo hooked Owen's shirt with his thumbs, then ran his hands along his body to get the shirt up and over Owen's head. Owen shivered at the contact.

Owen made short work of Leo's shirt, then kissed his way from Leo's stomach all the way up his chest until he settled with a gentle kiss on Leo's lips. They kissed lazily; then Owen pulled up and off of Leo.

Leo looked confused and disappointed.

"One sec," Owen said, stumbling over to his suitcase. He fumbled around, finally coming up with a bottle of lube. "They say those who fail to prepare...."

Leo laughed, sitting up.

"No! Stay there," Owen admonished.

Leo lifted his hands and obediently lay back down.

Owen hopped back over Leo. He noted the look Leo gave him, as if to say he was being too rough for his injuries. Owen stuck out his tongue at him.

Quick as anything, Leo leaned up and sucked Owen's tongue into his mouth. Owen moaned, feeling the sensation run down his body. Leo took that moment to shimmy Owen's pants down to his knees.

He must have dropped the lube because in the next moment he heard a click and felt cool, wet fingers teasing him.

He pushed his body down on the sensation, his bare member pressing against Leo's pants. Owen frowned at him.

"What?" Leo asked.

Owen sat up from Leo, missing the fingers as they fell away. He stood next to the bed and fought to get his pants off. Maybe Leo was right. Maybe his pants were too tight.

Then he went to work removing Leo's pants and underwear and throwing them away like they had the plague. Much better.

He hopped back over Leo to lie gently on top of him. He stole the lube, poured some out into his hand, then took Leo's impressive erection next to his own and stroked both of them gently. Owen's back arched at the lazy pleasure. It was so pervasive. It was like... wait.

Owen stopped for a moment, disappointed. The sensation wasn't his. He started again and felt pure pleasure swimming in both his head and body. Of course. He was sensing Leo!

Chasing the high of Leo's pleasure, Owen pulled his hand away and guided one of Leo's hands back to his opening. Owen felt satisfaction mixed with anticipation. Then he sensed Leo's.... Or was it his? He wasn't sure. But *someone* was on the precipice of climax, so he stopped the motion of his hand and instead squeezed the base of both their cocks.

Leo hissed in disappointment. Ah, it was him.

Owen smacked Leo's hand away and received a look of disoriented confusion. Owen was satisfied to have put that look on Leo's face.

With one hand, Owen held Leo's member steady, lifting himself up by his other hand on Leo's chest. Confused surprise radiated from him. They hadn't done this yet, but Owen could feel Leo's arousal swimming around in his head.

Owen sat back, his spine tingling. He could feel Leo inside of him physically as well as he could sense Leo's pleasure as a ghostly touch on his own cock. He went slow—arching up, then easing back down. He did his best to tease, moving slowly, stopping, until finally Leo shot up and flipped him over onto the mattress, just as he'd hoped.

Owen's hunger grew deep in his gut. He pushed his hands against the headboard as Leo's thrusts rocked his whole body. He didn't have to use too much energy to feel the pure and simple lust radiating from Leo with each thrust.

Owen wasn't sure whose release he felt first. He felt that heady rush of satisfaction, amplified by two.

Leo dropped his weight onto him, and Owen grunted. Leo froze at that and completely lifted himself off of Owen. Owen reached for that sense of him, but the connection was lost. He frowned.

"Owen, are you okay? I am so sorry. I don't know what happened."

Owen rolled his eyes. "I'm fine. Again, I do not need babying!"

But Leo frowned like he was still disappointed in himself.

Owen pouted, not liking his attitude. "I'm taking a shower if you care to join me, Mr. Grumpy Pants."

"COME ON, Leo. We're at the *ocean*. Who doesn't swim in the ocean?"

Owen bobbed up and down with the cresting waves. Leo stood where the sea met the shore, wearing loose white muslin pants and a matching long-sleeved shirt. Owen always thought half the fun of the beach was wearing *less* clothing than normal. Well, no. Who was he kidding. The whole fun of the beach was swimming in the water.

"Come oooon! It's not even cold," he shouted.

Leo shook his head, moving farther away and sitting in the sand.

"I'm fine here. I'm not a strong swimmer, so if you get swept out, I can't help you. And the guards are watching the access to the island and the house since you insisted we have the beach to ourselves. So you need to be careful, Owen."

Even covered up as he was, the wind blew the light material against his slender body, framing his torso, then his legs.

Owen wished he would take the ponytail out. It would be hella annoying for Leo but hella hot for Owen.

Owen was so distracted that he didn't notice a particularly large wave coming his way. It smacked his back, then went right over his head. Unafraid of water, he kept his calm and drew himself down and away from the pull of the wave's crest. He made sure that the water had passed before popping back up, gasping for air.

"Owen!"

Owen looked toward the shore and saw Leo standing up to his knees in water. How had he even moved that quickly?

"Leo, I'm fine. It caught me by surprise," he said, laughing.

"Only you would laugh when you nearly drowned." Owen could tell that Leo was trying to sound flippant, but his tone read more as anxious.

In any other aquatic situation, Owen would have felt bad and gone back inside. But this was the ocean they were talking about here. This was a once-in-a-lifetime event for Owen.

Owen sat down on the ocean floor. He held his breath as the waves gently rocked him back and forth. He stayed down as long as he could. Finally he let himself float back up. He looked at the shore and saw that Leo had come halfway toward him. He appeared frantic.

"Owen, my God," Leo said, sounding slightly out of breath.

Owen shrugged. "Hey, you got in the water, right?"

For a moment Leo didn't seem to know how to react to this. Finally he smiled and shook his head.

"Right, so I'll play in the water with you, and you'll stop making me think you are drowning."

Owen grinned, running (as fast as you can through water) to where Leo stood, about waist-deep before the waves came.

"So you want to jump waves with me?" Owen asked excitedly.

Leo smiled and shook his head. "I was thinking of something a bit different."

Leo pulled at Owen's arm until he lost his balance and fell against Leo's chest. He took the opportunity to press his lips against Owen's. A wave washed over Owen's waist. The combination of Leo and the waves at his back excited Owen from his head to his toes. The kiss tasted salty.

Owen laughed into Leo's mouth as a strong wave pushed them tightly together, almost knocking them both down.

The next wave did knock them down.

Owen surfaced first, tugging Leo up by his shoulder. Leo frowned, lifting his arms as if to see how wet his sleeves were. Owen cupped Leo's head and kissed his eye.

"Don't tell me this isn't fun," Owen said gleefully.

Leo shook his head. "I'm going back to the sand where it's safe."

Owen shrugged, patted Leo on his shoulder, then turned around and dove under the next wave. He was too busy splashing around to see the fond smile on Leo's face.

"LEO," OWEN said, stretching out the name. He lay on the floor. Its coolness was nice in the heat. And fuck if he gave a shit what those weirdly uptight guards thought.

Owen had been getting wave after wave of "better-than-thou" attitude. They didn't show it, but they sure felt it. Owen made a note to tell Leo about it. After they got back. Owen didn't want to ruin the vacation.

Leo sat with his glasses on in front of a laptop. "Owen," he responded with quiet humor.

"Why are you working? We're on vacation."

Leo lifted his glasses and rubbed his eyes. "I'm almost done. Why don't you go get yourself something to drink."

Owen rolled his eyes. Leo was looking at the computer again.

"I don't want a drink. Can I at least cook dinner, please?" he asked, hearing the whine in his voice.

"Owen, what is the point of a vacation if you have to make yourself dinner every night?"

"But I *like* cooking. It beats sitting around here. What about swimming?"

"It's dark, and you are not going into that water alone," Leo admonished.

"I'll sit on the sand," Owen compromised.

Leo looked up from his computer and stared Owen in the eyes.

"If you put even one toe in that water without me there, you are not going to be allowed to bake for a whole month." The threat was undercut by his smile.

Owen stretched out on the floor before jumping to his feet. He walked over and gave Leo a kiss on his head.

"I will not put a toe in the water," Owen said, holding a hand up as if to swear to it.

He put his legs in the water.

Leo *had* said toe....

Owen sat on the cool sand, waves breaking over his legs, never quite making it to his hip. It felt nice.

He was surprised at how cool it had gotten after the sun went down. He kind of wanted a jacket but was too happy to walk away from the water.

Owen shut his eyes and listened to the wind and the waves.

"No baking was your choice, huh?"

Owen lay back in the sand and stared up at a smiling Leo.

"You tell Jacob that I won't be making those blondies I promised him," Owen responded.

Leo laughed. "I could never do that to such a loyal employee," he said.

"I can only imagine the disappointment he would exude," Owen said. He suddenly had a thought. "I sensed you the other night. You know, when we were doing the dirty?"

"Doing the dirty? Really?" Leo responded.

"Yeah, it was weird. I kind of wonder if the intimacy triggered it. I mean, this whole situation is still new to me. I'm not used to having to find out who another person is without, I guess, cheating."

"You'll have to see if the same thing happens next time," Leo said.

Owen looked up and stretched his body out.

"Wanna find out right now?" he suggested.

Leo's hungry smile was answer enough.

CHAPTER 19

"OWEN! OWEN, Owen, Owen, Owen." Yuri practically dropped the (thankfully empty) tray she was carrying as she barreled into Owen, hugging him tighter than he would think possible for her petite form.

"Yuri! I'm sorry I worried you. I had a nasty virus."

"You should be sorry. Here I was thinking my poor Owen was dead in a ditch somewhere. No one seemed to know, or care, about what happened. And I was... Owen, what happened to your neck?" she asked, brushing his hair aside and making the gauze visible.

Owen touched it gently, feeling self-conscious. The brand was pretty much healed up, and as much as he tried to shake it off, he wasn't totally ready for anyone to see it yet. He had decided to make it a fashion statement, but the truth was, seeing it there made him remember his brief stint as a crash test dummy.

"Don't worry, Yuri, it's nothing," he said, gently patting her shoulder.

She looked at him hard for a moment. The seriousness of her face and truth was a shocking disconnect to what Owen was used to from her.

"If you ever need help, a place to stay, a shoulder to cry on, or a crazyass lady to make some heads roll, I am always here."

Owen was touched. "Thank you, I appreciate it so much."

She stared into his eyes as if searching to see if he was being truthful. Finally she lifted her tray over to the bar, put in the drink orders, and looked back at Owen. She smiled playfully.

"I don't know what made you decide to go purple in the eyes, but I bet you will get more tips," she said, laughing.

Owen smiled.

And she was right. He made a killing that night.

A FEW MONTHS went by, and Owen returned to a feeling of normalcy. He made three bowls of a ramen recipe that Yuri swore by. Jacob and Alex were both on break. They tended to spend that time with Owen, and he would make them lunch or dinner. Leo was kind enough to schedule their breaks together for precisely that reason.

"So, Owen, are you excited for the fundraiser next week?" Alex asked.

"Fundraiser?" he asked curiously.

"Mr. Ellis didn't tell you? Um...." Alex trailed off, suddenly looking guilty.

"There is a fundraiser?" He frowned. "Jacob"—Owen looked the man square in the face—"did you know about this?"

Jacob slurped some noodles. "My mouth is full. I can't talk," he said, clearly able to talk.

"Okay. Someone is going to tell me what is going on or I am taking away the ramen."

Alex and Jacob exchanged a look before eating faster.

Unable to follow through on his threat, Owen subsided.

LEO UNLOCKED the door and stepped inside.

"Leo." Owen was sitting beside the door. He jumped up as Leo gazed at him, bemused. "What is this I hear about a fundraiser?" he asked.

Leo rolled his eyes. His men were becoming more loyal to Owen than they were to him. It was why he trusted them.

Leo'd had no intention of even asking Owen to come. He had been through too much, too many times, and all because of him. He had been attacked the last time they went to an event, he had gotten shot, and he had been beaten to within an inch of his life.

Why Owen chose to stay with him was beyond his comprehension. He didn't want to put Owen into a position of danger.

"It's not really a big deal."

"But I want to go. You're paying me for that," Owen said, frowning.

"I am paying you for your work at the casino."

Owen snorted. "Yeah, five thousand dollars a month for a part-time waiter position."

Leo shook his head. "I'm not going to put you at risk," he said firmly.

"I see. Well, not only am I going with you for free fancy food and a chance to play dress-up, I am also packing a knife. So it'll be totally fine," Owen said confidently.

Leo wasn't convinced.

"Leo, I don't want to be a victim. I'm not letting other people put me down."

Leo looked hard at Owen. It was true that it wasn't in Owen's nature to back down. He knew that much. He also had a feeling that Owen wanted independence and self-reliance.

"Okay. But you will be by my side the whole time," he acquiesced.

"Leo, that makes no sense. I'm supposed to be representing you, not following you around like a whore."

Leo scoffed. "You are far from a whore," he said.

"Which is why I'm fine. I'll have a guard, I'm sure. Plus I only have so much bad luck, and I hope it's run out," Owen said, smiling.

Leo really wanted to tell Owen no. He wanted to forbid Owen from going. But he could tell that Owen needed this. Something normal. He sighed.

"Okay, Owen. You will accompany me. I'll retrieve some basic information for you."

Owen looked curious. "What is the fundraiser for?"

"I believe it's invisible... something?"

Smiling, Owen asked, "Invisible children?"

Leo was surprised. "Yes, why, you know of it?"

"Better than that, I know the hostess." Owen winked at him.

But Leo couldn't get rid of his feeling of dread. On one hand, he was thrilled that Owen's spirit wasn't broken. He was only now realizing exactly how strong Owen truly was.

On the other hand, he felt so protective of him. After everything, Leo was well and truly scared that he would lose Owen. He didn't want Owen to leave him.

Sure, when he'd initiated this relationship, it was out of curiosity, pure and simple. Those gorgeous violet eyes, that strange awareness, that fearlessness. But the more he knew about Owen, the more he saw to love.

Owen was caring to a fault. He loved life, and he lived without remorse. He could certainly stand up for himself. He was incredibly independent. Almost to the point that Leo wished that Owen would rely on him a bit more.

"Owen, I formally invite you to a fundraiser next weekend," Leo finally said.

"I formally accept," Owen said with a nod.

CHAPTER 20

"HI, OWEN! We're fundraiser buddies again," Alex said cheerfully, walking into the living room of the penthouse.

He turned to Alex and smiled. "Just how I wanted it," he said. "Wait here a minute while I go change."

Owen entered the bedroom to find his fashion-forward maroon suit lying across the bed. Leo's suit had been there too, but a woman had come in and taken it with her. Owen asked her where Leo was.

"See you in car," she said with a thick Asian accent.

Owen waved, but she was gone.

He got himself dressed and studied himself in the floor-length mirror. God, he loved having nice clothes. It was the one thing that he truly thought was worth spending excess money on. Well, it was really Leo spending the money.

He frowned. He really didn't want Leo paying for everything. It seemed too much like a sugar-daddy situation. Anyone who knew Owen would have expected him to leave if he wasn't relying on himself, his funds, and his actions.

Owen returned to the living room. Alex stood patiently by the door.

"Wow, that looks amazing on you," he exclaimed.

Owen bowed dramatically. "How much time do we have?" he asked.

"About an hour before we leave," Alex responded.

"I have leftovers if you want some."

Alex smiled. As if Owen even had to ask.

An hour later Alex brought Owen to the car. Leo was waiting for him.

They got in and the car pulled away.

"Leo, why did you even bother to give me this?" Owen asked, handing over a small file titled Owen Thing: The Sequel.

"I figured I would give you more information so you would know what to expect."

Owen sighed. "I will admit the map of the grounds and the house was useful. But the rest? There's nothing worth even mentioning."

"Well, I know you'll mostly be using your gift anyway, so I didn't put in a lot of effort."

Owen smiled. "I'm keeping the map on me," he said.

"As you should."

They pulled up to a large house on a quiet street. Unlike the last time, this mansion was almost rustic in style (if you could believe it) and was set on a hill with a steep drop at one end of the house. A wooden porch connected the house with the drop-off. It was all quite beautiful.

They once again had to walk to the house on a long dirt driveway.

As soon as they entered the house, Owen was smacked in the face by warring emotions. He knew that in reality it was fairly quiet, but all Owen could feel was fifty truths coming at him all at once. He immediately put a hand to his head.

Leo looked worried. "Owen, are you okay?" he asked.

Owen rubbed his eyes, then grimaced.

"I'm fine. Just have to take a minute to adjust."

"You can leave whenever you want to," Leo reminded him.

"I know. I'm fine. Now shoo! Go do dirty dealings and such."

Leo laughed. A stout man spotted them and waved.

"Goddammit," Leo said under his breath. "Interrupt me at any time if you need to, you hear?" Leo said sternly.

"Yes, yes, goodbye" was Owen's response.

Owen wandered around for a bit. He greeted a few people who stopped him. He chatted a bit, using handshakes as an opportunity to get some talking points.

He didn't drink. He stuck to soda and the little hors d'oeuvres that were being passed around. They had one shrimp scampi appetizer in the rotation that he kept going back to. One of the waitresses went straight to him now each time she refilled the tray.

"Owen!"

Owen looked behind him and spied Marcus in a smart gray suit walking up to him. He patted Owen's back.

"Are you here to save the whales?" Marcus asked playfully.

"That's not what this is about," Owen said, the tightness in his head lessening with Marcus's insanely positive energy.

Marcus laughed. Owen extended a hand as Maribelle approached.

"Marcus, you need to stick close to me. What else is the point of being here?" she asked quietly, but not so quietly that Owen couldn't hear.

"What does that mean?" Owen asked curiously.

Maribelle giggled. "You're like Marcus, right? You can see emotions?" she asked.

"Um...." Owen was caught off guard. Why would he tell her that?

"Maribelle is not the real owner of Sunrise, Inc.," Marcus said, naming the company Leo had told him she owned. "It's me," he said.

Owen was confused. "So why would...?"

"Well, I don't care to be in the public eye. I can work way better when I'm not the face of the company. People tend to tell you more when they think you're one of them," Marcus said with a childish grin that did not at all match the tone of his voice.

"Talk if you want, I'm going to mingle," Maribelle said. "When you're done, Marcus, come find me."

Owen watched her walk away. Leo made a beeline for her. Owen wondered what that was about. But more pressing....

"Huh. Well, how do you make decisions in meetings, then?" Owen asked, curious.

"Oh, easy. I can give her my thoughts so she can act on them."

Owen stared at him silently.

After a moment, Marcus laughed. "You can do it too! You have to really focus on it, though. Give your whole self up to the thought, then guide it through your arm and into their skin," he said.

"Their skin?" Owen asked skeptically.

"Yeah, you need to make physical contact," Marcus said.

Owen thought on it. "That sounds interesting. Will you teach me?" he asked.

"Of course," Marcus said, "Are you working Friday? You can come over, and we can get takeout!"

"Marcus, do you only eat takeout? You want it every time I see you. Don't you have a private chef?" Owen asked.

Marcus pouted. "Maribelle only lets me eat takeout when you come over," he said sadly.

Owen was floored that Marcus was older than him because he acted like a child in so many ways.

"Takeout tomorrow at my house!" Marcus said, way too loudly. People turned to look at them, but Owen didn't care. He liked Marcus. They had become good friends over the months.

As Owen got himself ready to go out on Friday, Leo came into the room with a big frown.

"Owen, you know I don't trust Marcus," Leo said firmly.

Owen stared at him in confusion. "Well, I do. Are you saying that I'm a bad judge of character?" Owen countered, genuinely annoyed.

Leo looked frustrated. "No, I'm not. I don't want you to see him anymore," he said.

Owen was taken aback. "You what? Since when could you dictate my life?" Owen exclaimed.

He might have been overreacting, but he had been growing more and more frustrated about this lack of freedom Leo was pressing on him. He paid for everything, had someone accompany Owen everywhere he went, and put obstacles up when he wanted to go visit friends. He wanted to do his own thing for once without Leo interfering.

"I'm going over to Marcus's house. I am a grown man. If you try to force me to stay, then I'm going to be gone for good. Have Alex take me—at least he treats me like I can take care of myself," Owen practically shouted, storming out the door and to the elevator.

He waited a few minutes before a car pulled up to the entrance and Alex came out to join him. If he knew about his and Leo's fight, Alex said nothing.

Owen was getting frustrated. No matter how hard he tried to master "transfer of thoughts," as Marcus put it, he couldn't get the hang of it. He sat on the floor of Marcus's spacious living room, eating chicken with broccoli and doubting himself.

"Oh, come on, Owen. You'll figure it out in your own time. It's not easy at first," Marcus said loudly.

Owen chewed his food, trying to think about anything other than being a failure. "Oh, Marcus," he said, putting his food onto the floor.

"What's up?" Marcus asked, looking confused at Owen's changed mood.

"Did you call Tyler yet?" he asked.

Marcus shoved a huge piece of chicken into his mouth and started chewing very slowly. He gestured at his mouth, indicating that he had to chew. Owen shook his head.

"If you don't want to talk about it, you can say so," he said.

Marcus stopped chewing and gazed at Owen like he was trying to decide whether to confide in him. He nodded, then began chewing faster, washing his food down with a huge gulp of water and almost choking.

"Okay," Marcus said between coughs, "so I haven't."

Owen waited. A few moments went by and Marcus looked uncomfortable.

"I don't know what to say," he said. "I mean, I know what I want to say, but I know that I'm going to choke. I don't want to humiliate myself after all these years. Especially when it was all my fault!" Marcus said, with raw, honest emotion.

"Listen, it can be scary to look into the past. But that's it. It's past. What's the worst that can happen? He says he doesn't want to talk to you? Well, you're not talking to him now, so it's not like it makes a big difference," Owen said.

Marcus sniffed, and Owen was shocked to see genuine tears in his eyes.

"But what if he tells me that he can't forgive me? I don't think that I can live with that," Marcus said quietly.

Owen scooched himself over to Marcus and gave him a side hug.

"Do what you think is best. I will only say this once, but I think you should go for it," Owen said, pulling away. Marcus smiled at him and wiped a stray tear from his cheek.

"Since you're my friend and you obviously care for me, can you do me a favor?" Marcus asked, the cheerfulness starting to take its usual place in his eyes.

"What do you need?" Owen asked, ready for anything.

"Can you get my eggroll from the kitchen?" Marcus asked.

Owen rolled his eyes but stood up.

"Yay!" Marcus cheered.

"I'm only doing this because I want to get more soup anyway," Owen said.

"I don't care about the 'why.' I'm still grateful that it's happening!" Marcus said, smiling brightly.

Owen was amazed at how quickly Marcus seemed to shift between emotions. It made him wonder what his friend was really thinking.

OWEN AND Marcus moved their two-person party onto the patio.

"Do it this way," Marcus said, touching Owen's wrist. *Feel the sensations. Now see them. See the connection. Look....*

Owen was suddenly seeing what Marcus saw. Individual truths swirled around everyone, and he could see it.

Marcus took his hand away and the vision was gone.

"Cool, right? It makes it easier to separate the buzzing," Marcus said cheerfully.

"I call it the truth," Owen said.

"Oh, I like that! I'm stealing it from you." Marcus laughed.

"So how do you manage it all?" Owen asked, leaning into his Adirondack chair.

"Manage what?" Marcus asked, shielding his face from the sun. He stood up and turned his chair around until he was out of the sun and facing Owen.

"You know, running an organization that no one knows is yours?"

"Ah, that. Well, some people do know the situation. Only if they have proven to be well and truly loyal. It's easy when you can read someone," Marcus responded.

"Yeah, I get that, but how does Maribelle always know how to respond?" Owen questioned.

"Well, you know, I insert thoughts. For example, Maribelle might be going over a contract, and I will maintain contact with her and funnel my thoughts and opinions straight into her own mind. It's a pretty useful trick."

"Hmm," Owen mused. "I think I'm going to go home now, Marcus. I have things to take care of." Owen was thinking of Leo.

"Do you want to do something this weekend? Oh, do you want to go to a club with me and Maribelle?" Marcus said loudly.

"Um," Owen mused.

"Oh, come on. I know the comedown is bad, but it's so worth it! Please," Marcus urged.

Owen had a love-hate relationship with dance clubs. On one hand, being in a sea of happy drunk people was so heady and intoxicating. It felt better than actually being drunk. The hate came in with the "hangover." The headache he experienced the next day was of biblical proportions.

But if Marcus could handle it….

"Okay. I'll come. But I'm bringing Leo." Well, he hoped Leo would come. Who knew after that earlier outburst.

"Tomorrow? It's Saturday, so it's perfect timing!" Marcus looked (and felt) excited enough to jump out of his own skin.

"All right, I'm leaving now, though," Owen said.

"Next time I'll show you how to share thoughts. Keep practicing the visuals! I'll text you where we're going," Marcus said cheerfully.

Alex walked over to the two of them, obviously having been welcomed inside.

"Mr. Hart, the car is still outside if you are ready to go," he said.

"Goodbye, Owen," Marcus said, happily waving.

THEY PULLED up to the apartment building, and before Owen could even turn away from Alex to open the door, it flew open. Leo leaned into the car, his hands resting on the top of the door.

"I'm sorry, Owen," he said frantically.

"It's fine. Leo, I need to speak to you privately, so if you will excuse me," Owen said, pushing his way past Leo and out of the car. He walked silently into the building, Leo so close behind him that he could feel the body heat.

He didn't need to read Leo in order to sense his impatience as they stepped into the elevator. With only him, Alex, and Owen in the elevator, Leo once again tried to speak. Owen lifted a hand.

"Wait until we are in private," he said firmly. He could almost feel Leo's frown.

The elevator dinged, and Leo led Owen swiftly to the apartment. He shut the door behind him and froze. Owen fancied that he wasn't sure what to say.

"Here, sit down." Owen gestured to the couch. Leo complied, and Owen sat on the floor across from him.

Owen waited. After a pause, Leo unleashed the floodgates.

"Owen, I'm so sorry. I do think of you as a smart, capable man, but I get so worried! So many people that I've cared about have been hurt because of me, including you, and I've become so afraid that it will happen with you again," Leo said.

Owen shook his head. "Let me be my own person. I want to be able to go out on my own. I will concede that you can send someone with me when I'm alone, but I should be able to decide where I want to go and who I want to go with. Feel free to argue, but leave it at that. I *need* to be my own person," Owen said.

Leo looked thoughtful. "No, I think I will have to earn your forgiveness for how I behaved today."

"Well, you can start by going out to dance with me, Marcus, and Maribelle tomorrow," Owen said.

Leo appeared stunned. "You want to go clubbing with them?"

"No. I want to go clubbing with you, and also with him and Maribelle," Owen responded.

Leo was quiet for a good minute. Likely he was trying to decide whether he could get out of the situation without Owen being hurt.

"Oh," he said at last, "after our fight, I wanted to do something for you, so...."

Leo stood up and went to the kitchen, where he picked up a plate from the island. He walked over and handed it to Owen.

Owen looked down at... burned cookies. He laughed.

"Did you make these?" he asked.

Leo frowned. "Well, I tried. I don't know if you really want to eat those," Leo said, sounding disappointed.

Owen picked one up and bit into it. Yes. That was a very burned cookie. He managed to chew and swallow it, immediately getting up for water because it dried his whole mouth out.

"I tell you, though, Leo, I could see this as a step toward forgiveness," he said when he returned.

Leo beamed.

"Now I'm going to make more cookies because you put me in the mood. Both to bake and to eat," Owen said.

"Wait!" Leo said, running out of the room. He came back a minute later holding up a black-and-red apron.

"I forgot that I bought this for you. So you can stop ruining clothing," Leo said.

Now it was Owen's turn to smile. "That's two steps toward forgiveness."

CHAPTER 21

"JACOB, I'M telling you this Marcus guy is strange. I don't trust him," Alex said, sipping his coffee.

Jacob nodded. "He seems quirky, but I have always found Owen to be a good judge of character. He seems to have a knack for sensing honesty. I mean, he likes you, doesn't he?"

They sat in the back of the small coffee shop across the street from the apartments. Leo always arranged that their breaks were at the same time. This was the easiest place to go. Plus, Alex knew that Jacob liked the sweets here. He usually ordered one for Jacob and one for himself.

Alex had sworn to Jacob that the fact that he bought a pastry every single day and every single day was too full of coffee to eat it was a coincidence. Not that Jacob pushed him on that. Alex mused that the man could eat his weight in cookies.

"I know, I know that Owen is good at reading people. I don't want to think that he's being taken advantage of. He said they had a similar upbringing. That could affect how he is viewing the situation," Alex said.

Jacob took a bite of his danish, taking a moment to think.

"Do you even know anything about Owen's life? Has he ever said anything?" he asked.

Alex looked up in thought. "No, nothing. Is that a bad sign?"

"Probably," Jacob said. "Not our business, though."

Alex wrapped his fingers around his coffee, focusing on the warmth. "I think we should go," he said.

"Go where?" Jacob asked, licking the remnants of his pastry off his fingers.

Alex was momentarily distracted.

"Go where?" Jacob repeated, smiling slyly as he licked his already clean fingers.

"Stop it!" Alex hissed, not wanting a public erection. He could swear Jacob liked tormenting him.

"I hear that Owen and Mr. Ellis are going clubbing with this guy tonight. And his boss, Maribelle. We should go with them.! We both have off, don't we?" Alex said.

"Yes," Jacob said thoughtfully, "but I don't dance."

Alex frowned. "I don't think Mr. Ellis does either. You can sit with him and keep him company."

"Yes, sitting in a loud club, drinking with my boss. That's living the dream, isn't it?" Jacob said.

"Oh hush, it'll be fun!" Alex replied.

Jacob sighed. "You're the boss."

WITH THE okay from Owen, Alex readied himself for a night of clubbing. Well, Alex was thinking of himself as more of a chaperone. He wanted to make sure that Marcus didn't do wrong by Owen.

Owen was one of the nicest people Alex had ever met. People often said the same about him. But he wasn't sure this was as true as they thought.

Jacob was a patient man.

Jacob had a permanent room at the apartment building. It was one of the benefits of being high up on the corporate ladder. It did mean that he was on call basically twenty-four seven. So Alex had been living with him the last few months.

It was so... domestic. Something Alex had never had before. He came from an essentially empty household. His parents were often away on business or affairs or whatever else they did without him. Half the time he didn't even think they knew they were leaving him alone, each convinced that the other was home.

Alex learned quickly to pocket money he found around the house in purses, briefcases, set aside on tables. He needed it for food for when he was alone. No one seemed to notice. Sometimes Alex wondered if they even remembered that they had a child.

But for the first time in his life, Alex had the sensation of really having a home. Not just a roof over his head; Alex felt loved and *seen*. He was happy and excited and a little bit scared. Scared that this was all some practical joke and he was going to end up back in his tight little studio apartment, alone.

"Is that what you're wearing?"

Alex turned around and saw Jacob walking into the room. "Of course!"

Alex wore a pair of black skinny jeans and a sky-blue shirt that hung off one shoulder.

"Is that what *you're* wearing?" he asked.

Jacob wore a pair of slacks and a long-sleeved white shirt.

"You're going to roast in there," Alex said.

Jacob shrugged. "Like I said, I won't be dancing."

Alex tried to frown, but he couldn't help but return Jacob's smile.

"Okay. Come on, we should be going now," he said.

They went down to the lobby and waited for Owen and Leo to meet them. When they finally did, Alex was surprised to see Owen in a long-sleeved maroon shirt covered by a mesh T-shirt, and wearing gloves. It wasn't cold out to begin with, and the club was bound to be steaming. What was with those gloves anyway?

"Alex. Jacob. Are you ready to go?" Owen asked.

"Ready as ever," Jacob replied. Alex poked him in his side.

The four of them hopped into a black car. An identical car with guards pulled up behind them. The drive was short, only about ten minutes. The club was called Queen of Hearts and was apparently owned by a friend of Marcus's.

Too soon, the car stopped and let them out. Alex was nervous. He hoped that he didn't show it. He looked over at Jacob. Cool as a cucumber, as always. They were greeted at the door by none other than Maribelle herself. Alex tried to squash his feeling of unease.

"OWEN!" A VOICE shouted.

"Marcus," Owen returned calmly.

Marcus rushed up with arms outstretched to hug Owen. Leo stepped in front of him. Without missing a beat, Marcus grabbed hold of Leo's right hand, cradling it between his own.

"Mr. Ellis! So nice to see you again. Can I call you Leo?" he asked, "I'll call you Leo, and you can call me Marcus," he said, not even waiting for an answer.

"You've met Maribelle a few times also, right?" he continued, gesturing as she extended a hand.

Leo shook it, smiling slightly. "I'm happy to see you, as always," he said kindly.

Maribelle laughed. "I think you'll be happy to know that I am here to babysit Marcus. He's too wild to let out on his own." She shot him a long-suffering look. Marcus shrugged.

"Oh, you brought backup in case I try to steal Owen away from you?" Marcus asked, gesturing to Alex and Jacob.

Owen could feel the humor behind it, but clearly Leo couldn't. He tensed up and put a hand on Owen's back. Owen tried not to laugh.

"Will you stop winding Mr. Ellis up?" Maribelle scolded.

"Leo," Leo corrected her.

"Ah, Leo," she mimicked.

"Come on, Owen and company. We get VIP seats and free booze. The benefits of working with the boss!" Marcus said.

They followed Marcus into the club. The music was loud and the dance floor was packed. Owen could already feel the waves of excited, drunken joy pulsating from the crowd. It was absolutely heady. They passed the bar and the floor and were ushered into a back corner to a large, round table with comfortable seats lined up in a semicircle.

"You wore gloves?" Marcus spoke quietly into Owen's ear, "That's smart. Oh, hang on. I'm pissing off your boyfriend again."

Owen turned around, and sure enough Leo was sitting at the table frowning at the two of them.

He looked like he was going to say something when a man walked into their section. Owen almost mistook him for a bouncer because he was so big, but he smiled at them cheerfully, and his air of authority ruled that out.

"Welcome, friends. My name is Lucas Black, and I would like to welcome you all to my club. We don't serve food, but your drinks are free. You'll be in good hands with our bartender, Ian."

"Excuse me. Jack, please move. I can't…. Oh, hi! I'm Ian. I'll be serving you tonight." Ian was a well-dressed man with dirty-blond hair, a full face of makeup, and a broad smile. Owen thought that Ian might be a few years older than him, but it was hard to tell with the makeup.

"Hi, Ian," Marcus said. "Owen, he makes the best cocktails. Ian, can you make me that coconut cocktail, please," Marcus said loudly.

Ian smiled. "Sure. Would you like one also, sir?" he asked Owen.

"It's Owen. And sure, I like coconut," he said.

"Cocktails for anyone else?" Ian asked.

"A bottle of your best wine," Leo said.

"We have a lovely chardonnay. Is that all right?" asked Ian.

"Chardonnay is fine," Leo said.

Ian turned his attention to Jacob and Alex. Owen got a bit of trepidation from Alex. He imagined that he was nervous being out with the boss.

"He'll take one of those coconut cocktails, and I'll have a scotch," Jacob responded for him.

Alex looked and felt relieved, and also kind of excited.

Owen waved and pointed to the dance floor. Marcus took Owen's hand and dragged him that way.

They moved with the beat. Owen wasn't particularly good at dancing, but neither were many of the people he was smushed between. Thank God he had worn the long-sleeved shirt. Marcus had opted to do the same thing. He wore a long-sleeved pink top with stylishly ripped jeans.

Owen completely lost himself in the music and the truths. He was flying high, particularly getting a blast of giddiness from the woman at his back. Marcus pushed Owen's hair aside and pressed two fingers to his neck.

Do you want a drink? It might dull some of the buzzing.

Owen willed his thought into Marcus, who looked confused and didn't respond.

Sighing, Owen said, "Yes." He had to shout over the music.

Marcus nodded and wormed his way over to the bar. Owen stood still for a minute, suddenly feeling choked by the crowd. The emotions were almost too much without the grounding he got from Marcus's presence.

He followed the path that Marcus took. When he reached the bar, Marcus was already waiting for the drinks.

"Did you two like my cocktail?" Ian shouted over the music with a knowing smile.

"We didn't even taste them. But we'll take another, please," Marcus responded cheerfully.

"I'll bring them over," Ian shouted. "Go have fun."

"Marcus, can we sit for a few minutes?" Owen asked.

"Heck yeah. Let's go bother the party poopers!" Marcus responded.

They walked over to the VIP section. The music was still loud in that corner, but it wasn't as deafening.

"Hi, Leo," Owen said happily as he slid into the seat next to him. He was completely aware of the slight slur in his speech, but Leo didn't comment.

"Where did Jacob and Alex go?" he asked.

"They went to the bar," Leo responded, brushing hair out of Owen's face.

"Why would they go to the bar if they could have ordered drinks here?" Owen asked, frowning.

"For a change of setting, I suppose," Leo said mildly.

Owen stared at him for a few seconds. He couldn't read Leo's mind, but he imagined that Leo had encouraged them out of the section to keep an eye on him. Leo's smile never left as he took a sip of his drink.

Owen took a big gulp of his cocktail. He could feel the knowing humor from Marcus.

"So much better," Owen said. Even with that amount, his slur began to lessen. He glanced over at Leo, who gazed at him like he was a puzzle that needed solving.

"Ah, so another case of the reverse drunk," Maribelle said, laughing lightly.

Leo wrinkled his forehead, and Marcus quickly touched Maribelle's hand. She looked confused and then slightly embarrassed.

"What does that mean?" Leo asked curiously.

"What Maribelle is saying is that I've always been an odd duck. When I go out to the club or a concert, I get more sober with one or two drinks in me than if I have nothing. Owen seems to be the same way as me. These are our first drinks," Marcus said.

"It's all the chaos floating around," Owen added, gesturing in a circle.

"Ah," Leo said after a pause, "emotions run high here, yeah?"

Owen smiled, taking another sip of his drink.

"Is there a VIP bathroom?" he asked after a moment. "I don't want to brave the public restroom here." He made a face.

"Yeah, definitely. It's down that hallway to the left," Maribelle said.

Owen was already up and moving before she finished. He didn't have to use the bathroom, but he needed a minute to calm down. He was so wound up. The bathroom was single-person use, and he didn't bother to lock the door.

He went right to the sink and splashed water on his face. He leaned into the mirror, inspecting his eyes. It was still new to him, seeing his eyes with their natural color. He idly wondered at the quirks he and Marcus had.

A knock came at the door.

"Yes!" Owen extended the word.

Leo walked in.

"Owen, I wanted to make sure you were okay," he said.

"I'm fine. I'm probably going to have another drink, then go dance again," Owen responded. "You know, you shouldn't have followed me. People are going to *talk*."

Leo laughed. "Do you really care?"

"Ah, fuck no. Come here." Owen held his hands out to receive a hug.

Leo happily delivered.

Owen gripped Leo, one fistful of hair in each hand, and pulled his lips down on his own. Leo tasted like wine. The quiet of the restroom, mixed with the radio silence he usually got from Leo, did a lot to sober him up.

Owen licked the inside of Leo's teeth, bumping into his tongue as he went along. He loosened his grip on Leo's hair.

Leo took hold of Owen's shoulders and shoved his back against the wall. Owen let out a huff of breath, momentarily stunned, and Leo took the opportunity to tilt Owen's head to the side. He paused.

Owen felt like he'd been hit with a bucket of cold water when he realized what had stopped Leo. It always did. And every time he thought he was over it, he was painfully reminded that he wasn't.

Leo tilted Owen's face until he was looking him in the eye. With all the emotions running through him from the club and from the reminder, Owen could feel tears spilling from his eyes.

"No matter where this came from, know that you are mine. Let me take those memories away. This—" Leo brushed his fingers across the nearly healed brand. "—does not mean anything. Because I will always be here for you. Bear this mark as a sign that I will always come back for you."

Owen sniffled and quickly wiped his face with his sleeve. Leo looked him in the eye for a few moments, then frowned. Owen wished he could read him. It only ever seemed to work in desperation. Or during sex. He waited for Leo to reassure him again, as he assumed he would.

Instead, Leo brushed the mark gently with his finger and then his lips. The wound wasn't completely healed, so that made it itchy, but Owen didn't care. He could feel warmth there too. Owen was lost in the sensation until he realized that Leo was once again upright and looking down on him with a soft smile.

"So you'll always come back for me, huh?" Owen said it as a joke, and maybe it was because he was out of sorts, but he felt a sort of hysterical desperation as he said it.

Leo must have noticed because he gently cupped Owen's face, drawing it toward him.

"I will *always* come back for you. You have my word, and my heart," he said, kissing Owen gently.

They lingered in the kiss until Owen heard a banging at the door.

"Owen! Stop fucking your boyfriend. I want to dance," Marcus shouted way too loudly.

Owen rushed to the door and pulled it open. Marcus was standing there smiling.

"I'm kidding. I could feel that you were having some kind of moment, but it was basically over, right?" he said.

Owen rolled his eyes, but he wasn't mad. Not really. In a way he was kind of happy Marcus had interrupted them, because he was about to lose it. Did Leo basically say that he loved him?

Sure, Owen loved Leo, but neither of them had ever said it out loud. It was kind of scary that his first "I love you" was almost in a bathroom at a nightclub.

"Dance time?" Marcus said hopefully, crossing his fingers dramatically.

"Let's recruit one or two more," Owen responded.

Owen found Jacob at the bar. He was sitting with his back to the bar, assessing the crowd.

"Hey, Jacob. Where's Alex?" Owen said, walking up from behind where he was looking.

Jacob turned his body around and smiled. "Ah, we were wondering where you were. Alex braved the dance floor looking for you."

"What happened to a night off?" Owen said with a frown.

Jacob laughed. "Alex doesn't consider watching your back to be work," he said fondly.

Owen could feel the affection and joy Jacob was experiencing swirling around him. And could he…? He focused. Yes, he could see it. A delicate, translucent rose color.

God, that was a cool trick.

"Well, now I'm off to rescue Alex. Shall I send him back here?" Owen asked.

Jacob brushed him off with the wave of a hand. "You let him dance with you. I know he's been itching to all night. He just didn't want to leave me. Tell him I'll be with the big bosses." Jacob winked.

Owen noted that he didn't get up to leave. He figured Jacob wanted to make sure they united with Alex first.

Owen waded through the crowd, holding Marcus by the hand so they wouldn't be separated.

"I got it!" Marcus shouted over the music, pulling Owen behind him and moving purposefully. "I can see his trail."

A few feet more and Marcus ran straight into Alex.

"Sorry, man. I came in too hot," Marcus said, laughing.

Alex looked past him. "Owen. I was worried when I didn't see you," he said.

Owen grimaced. Not liking the sense of worry mingled with all the excitement and joy.

"We went to get a drink. We must have not seen you at the bar. Do you want to dance?"

"Uh," Alex said, looking across the dance floor to the bar.

"He gave us orders to make you dance," Marcus said cheerfully.

Alex glanced at Owen, as if to make sure.

"That he did, Alex," Owen responded.

A smile grew on Alex's face. "I mean, if you insist," he said.

"We do," Marcus and Owen said in tandem.

CHAPTER 22

"BYE, OWEN and friends!" Marcus waved as Maribelle dragged him to the car. "Oh, hang on." He tapped her arm, and she let go.

As Marcus ran up to him, Owen could feel the manic energy coming off of him in huge waves.

"A trick I learned: lie in the dark and listen to some soothing classical music. It sponges some of the excess buzzing out. Enjoy your massive headache." He shouted the last part.

Owen felt Leo looking at him.

"What?" he asked.

"How are you going to have a headache? You only had one drink," he said.

"You'll find out later. Let's get going before Marcus's prediction comes true."

And it did. About halfway home.

Leo, Jacob, Alex, and he all sat in the same car. All three men were looking at him in concern. Owen held his head in his hands, eyes closed. He could feel the blood vessels in his head pulsing. And the wave of concern coming from the three men was overstimulating him.

"Please stop feeling things," Owen said. He could hear the slur in his voice again, this time in a bad way.

Jacob and Alex were confused, but Leo covered for him.

"He means his head. Since we're here, can you update me on the recent hire at Spades?" he said.

Jacob immediately shifted to work mode. Alex's attention remained on Owen for a minute, then transferred to Leo and the ongoing conversation. Owen didn't care at all about their discussion. He was just happy that no one was throwing their emotions at him.

They got to the apartments, and Owen kept his cool all the way up to the penthouse. The second he stepped into the room, he hissed and turned off the lights.

"Owen, how are we going to find our way to the bedroom?" Leo asked.

Owen stared at him, wondering if that was a double entendre. "They say when one sense goes, the others get stronger," he said.

Leo laughed. Owen wrapped his arms around him. The lack of any thought or emotion coming from him was so intensely soothing.

"Okay," Owen said as he flipped on the light, "move quickly."

When Owen rested his head on the pillow and light turned into blessed darkness, he sighed. Why did he always do this? Every time he went to a club, he swore it was the last. And yet here he was, more hungover than that man at the bar doing seven shots likely would be.

He felt the other side of the bed dip down as Leo lay in it.

"Can I get you anything, Owen? Do painkillers help?" he asked.

"No. It's my brain being overstimulated by hundreds of drunken emotions. It'll be better tomorrow. You know what you could do...."

Owen rolled over until his body pressed up against Leo's and he could hug him. Leo did not even hesitate to scoop Owen into his arms.

"That's better," Owen said, using the contact and warmth to ground himself.

He fell asleep with a smile on his face.

OWEN WOKE up the next morning. His head had settled into a dull ache. He looked around. Light filtered in through the curtains. He stretched and rubbed his eyes, got up, threw on some sweatpants and a T-shirt, and went to look for Leo.

He glanced in the rooms that he passed on the way to the main living area.

"Leo?" he called out to no response.

In the kitchen, he noticed a note on the refrigerator.

Owen, I am called away on urgent business. Dinner reservations at seven. See you then.

Owen tossed his phone onto the bed and flopped down. He rubbed his eyes against the ache in his head. And he knew what would help.

"PIES?" JACOB asked as if simply clarifying. Owen felt a burst of excitement, carefully masked by a straight face.

"Yes. I made apple, blueberry, lemon meringue, Boston cream, pecan, and cheesecake. Well, I mean, cheesecake isn't a pie. I was in the mood," Owen responded.

"Is this what you've been doing all day? Mr. Ellis gave us strict instructions to leave you to rest. I'm happy to see that wasn't necessary," Jacob said.

"Okay, Jacob, I'm going to do a magic trick. You give me your hand and I will read your palm to find out what kind of pie you want to taste first."

Mildly amused, Jacob offered his hand. Owen made a show of going over his palm, running his fingers over the patterned lines.

Blueberry.

"You want to try the blueberry first, right?"

Jacob's expression shifted to surprise. "How did you know that?" he asked.

"I told you, it's here in your palm." Owen laughed as he sensed Jacob's total bewilderment.

"Are you going to get dinner tonight with us?" Owen asked.

"Sadly, no. I'm working the casino, and Alex is teaching a self-defense class to female employees of Spades," Jacob said.

"Oh! That's so cool. I hope Yuri signed up," Owen responded.

"Yuri signs up for every free class or seminar we offer." Jacob smiled slightly.

Yuri knew everyone, and everyone knew her. It was her bold personality.

"Where will you two be going?" Jacob asked.

"Hell if I know. Leo is on a big seafood kick. I kinda hope he picks one of those crappy side-of-the-road places by the water. They always have the best food. But he also likes the fine-dining atmosphere. So I probably won't be getting lobster mac and cheese at Crab Shack."

Owen pouted. Now he was in the mood for lobster mac and cheese.

"You always like it when you go out in the end," Jacob reminded him.

"One of these days I'm going to make Leo eat at McDonald's." Owen suddenly remembered. "Jacob, is Tyler working today? I keep forgetting, I have to convey a message."

Curiosity filled the air, but Jacob asked him nothing.

"He's with Mr. Ellis right now. Would you like me to send him here when they get back?" Jacob asked.

"Yeah, that would be good, thanks," Owen said.

Jacob let the subject drop and returned to his post outside the penthouse door.

Owen sat with his headphones on, listening to music. He played calming classical music as Marcus had suggested. It actually helped. It turned his focus away from the now-dull pain.

Alone with his thoughts, Owen thought back on what had happened last night. He knew that one day his nonconsensual body modification wouldn't make him feel so self-conscious. But that day was not today.

Leo always knew how to make him feel better, though. And then he had almost said he loved him. In a roundabout way. It had been more than six months since they started living together, and neither of them had actually said the words.

It's not that Owen wasn't in love with Leo; he defiantly was, inside and out. The problem was Owen had never told a partner that he loved them. It had rarely ever gotten this far. It got boring always knowing exactly how the other person was feeling and thinking. And he had always been afraid of intimacy.

But Leo? He was a force of nature. He made Owen feel safe. And seen. And Owen wasn't thinking for two with him. So should he say it? When? Where? How?

God, this seemed more complicated than it should be.

Owen walked to the door.

"Hey, Jacob? Can I ask you a question?" Owen asked.

"Shoot," Jacob said.

"Have you ever told someone you love them?" he asked.

Jacob looked surprised, and then understanding crossed his features. "I have," he replied.

"So how do you know when it is appropriate to say that to someone?"

"There is no 'appropriate' time. The truest confessions are unplanned. You'll know. It's always scary to be the first to say it, but if it's not reciprocated, you'll know where you stand," Jacob said.

That made Owen nervous. What if Leo didn't love him back? No, that was ridiculous. Leo had said it, hadn't he? Had he meant it?

"You know, Alex has told me that he loves me," Jacob said mildly.

Owen's attention shot back to Jacob. His inner gossip popped out. "What? When?"

Jacob smiled. He was clearly aiming for that reaction.

"We were sitting in the park, feeding bread to the koi fish. I made some stupid joke, and Alex laughed like it was the funniest thing he had ever heard, as he usually does, and then right when his laughter was beginning to die down, he said, 'God, I love you.'" Jacob said.

Owen's excitement meter went up. That was so frickin' cute. And so like Alex.

"So what happened after that?" Owen asked, excitedly.

"After that I hugged him tight, kissed him, and said, 'I love you too.'"

"You know, you made me more worried with that cute story. I feel like I'm going to just… do it wrong. Or something," Owen said.

Jacob shook his head and tousled Owen's hair. Owen quickly fixed it. Why did people like touching his hair?

"Like I said, there are no wrong answers in love," Jacob concluded.

It didn't make Owen any less anxious.

"SO WHY are we eating at a… can you even call it a restaurant?" Leo asked, looking suspiciously at the nautical-themed decorations.

"It's good! The food is what matters."

Owen had won a lengthy argument about where they were going to eat. He cited that he never had a choice. And that he would abstain from any physical contact even as small as a handhold should he not get what he wanted.

"But the word 'shack' is in the name." Leo looked disgusted.

"Oh, come on. The food is good here. And I know the owner, so we got a table that doesn't tilt."

Owen was having fun with Leo's reaction. That alone was reason enough to get him here. Who knew when Leo would allow him to do this again. He was such a food snob.

"What am I supposed to order?" Leo asked, squinting at the menu. He was too lazy to bring and use his glasses.

"They have awesome crab cakes, stuffed clams, linguini in white clam sauce, and any of the fresh-caught fish," Owen suggested.

"What are you getting?" Leo asked.

"The lobster mac and cheese."

Leo scrutinized him. "I'll get the same thing, and if it is not good, you can eat mine also."

Suddenly Owen hoped that Leo wouldn't like it.

Sadly, he did like it. A lot.

"I told you some of these small places have the best food," Owen said on the way home.

"I concede that the food was good. But you'll have to drag me if you want to go somewhere like that again. I would rather order out." He flipped his hair behind his back.

Owen stared at Leo as he poured himself a scotch. He was too focused on not spilling the liquid in the moving car to notice Owen's attention. He wanted to say it. Should he say it? It didn't feel right. Should he have said it over dinner? God, why was saying "I love you" so hard?

Leo looked up, and Owen turned his head to stare out the window. Owen could feel Leo's gaze, but he was unable to tell what he was thinking. This attribute that he loved suddenly seemed a hindrance.

They sat in silence. It felt heavy to Owen, but when he glanced at Leo, who was now looking out of the window on his side, he seemed normal.

They exited the car and headed into the building. Owen always marveled at how elegantly Leo held himself in public. His posture demanded respect.

They took the elevator up. When they reached the top, Tyler was there, and Owen suddenly remembered Marcus's request.

"Hey, Leo, I'm going to meet you inside, okay? I have to talk to Tyler about something," he said.

Leo looked confused but didn't push it. He shrugged and went inside. Owen shut the door gently behind him. He gestured for Tyler to move with him toward the elevator. He didn't want Leo to overhear, since he still disliked Marcus for some reason.

Confusion and a little concern permeated the air.

"Hey, Tyler. So I met a man named Marcus," he said.

He paused when an intense wave of shock and hope hit him. He waited for the initial reaction to die down.

"I honestly don't know his last name, come to think of it. I've known him for a few months and probably should have asked. Anyway, he told me you used to be friends but had a falling out, and he wants to apologize. So can I give you his number? You can choose to call or not." Owen was getting nervous himself as Tyler's anxiety skyrocketed.

But Tyler's face was blank.

"Is he about thirty-four, tall, dark skin, blond hair?" Tyler asked after a pause.

"Yes," Owen said.

Tyler radiated confusion. And excitement. And anger. It was like a mosaic of emotions.

"Apologize? Why?" Tyler said under his breath.

"So do you want his number?" Owen asked.

Tyler jumped slightly, as if he'd forgotten Owen was there.

"Ah, yes. Please."

Tyler's emotions finally settled to an even match between anxiety and hope.

Owen was really curious. But he wasn't close enough to Tyler to ask.

TYLER GLANCED at his phone again. He was too nervous to even enter Marcus as a contact. He probably only wanted to remind Tyler how much he was hated. And he deserved it too. Marcus had grown up with him. They were neighbors; they went to the same school; they were inseparable.

Marcus was popular. He always had been. He had so much personality and an air of authority. Tyler half expected to see him with his own talk show when he grew up. Yet for all that, he always had time for Tyler, who was so quiet people often overlooked him.

But Marcus didn't. He would drop everything he was doing if Tyler needed anything. One time, Tyler had simply waved at Marcus, who was playing soccer with the other kids, and he left the field and ran right over to him.

"What's up?" he asked, catching his breath.

Tyler was stunned. "I was just waving hello," he replied.

Marcus looked at him funny. "But you're feeling sad, right? Did something happen?"

Tyler had no idea how, but Marcus could always see right through him. Sometimes it was like he could read his mind. Other times he didn't seem to be as intuitive with Tyler as he was with others. It kind of made him a bit jealous.

"Nothing happened. Go play soccer."

He wasn't going to admit that he wanted Marcus to pay attention to him instead of playing soccer with his other friends.

Marcus stared him down for a moment before putting a hand on Tyler's shoulder.

"Well, why don't we ditch and go to the park. That always cheers you up," he said.

"I told you, I'm not sad," Tyler lied.

"Yeah, okay," Marcus said, sounding like he was placating a child. "We're still going."

Tyler simply nodded and followed Marcus away from the school.

And Marcus was right. He did cheer up. But it wasn't because of the park; it was because he was with *him.*

Tyler's feelings for Marcus scared him to the core. His whole life his parents had told him how evil and sinful homosexuality was. It would be a curse upon the family should anyone have a same-sex partner, yada, yada, yada.

Tyler had been harboring these feelings for Marcus for years. Ever since they were young, he always had this warm feeling in his chest when Marcus was around. He felt so safe. But he knew that it was wrong. Well, he thought so at the time, but that was enough to ruin a relationship.

Tyler's parents decided to move out of state when he was around sixteen, in pursuit of a better job opportunity. Tyler was devastated by the news. He didn't have a lot of friends, forget about lovers, but he had Marcus.

When he couldn't wait to break the news to Marcus any longer, Tyler took him to the park so they would have some privacy. They sat on a bench among towering old trees. Tyler didn't know how else to put it. "Marcus, I'm moving," he said, trying to hide the devastation in his tone.

Marcus did nothing for a few moments. He was eyeing Tyler closely. It felt like he was trying to read his mind. And failing, based on his look of frustration. Marcus gave him this look a lot. He could never figure out what it meant.

"When?" Marcus finally asked calmly.

"In a week."

"What? How long have you known?" Marcus shouted.

"A few months," Tyler admitted. "I was trying to find the right time to tell you."

Marcus was fuming. He stood up and paced back and forth in front of the bench.

"A few months! Tyler, what the fuck?"

Tyler hadn't seen Marcus this upset since he'd beat up a kid who was bullying him.

"I'm sorry," Tyler said quietly. A tear escaped his eye. He quickly wiped it away.

Marcus must have seen it because he was giving Tyler one of those funny looks again. Tyler was about to open his mouth to say… something. He wasn't sure what. But he was saved the effort when Marcus walked right up to where Tyler was sitting, tilted his head back, and kissed him.

The kiss sent fire down Tyler's spine. He felt immediate comfort and happiness. And then it sunk in, and he felt like he had been doused in cold water.

Tyler pushed Marcus away hard enough that he fell backward, butt to the ground. He had a stunned look on his face that quickly shifted to panic.

"Tyler, I'm sorry! I just… I mean… I…." For the first time since Tyler had known him, Marcus was at a loss for words.

Tyler was angry. He was angry at himself for wanting to reciprocate. He was angry at Marcus for even *doing* that. He was angry that he was leaving. And he was angry that this friendship was now over.

Tyler turned and ran off before Marcus could even pick himself back up. He didn't stop until he got home and into his room. He quietly closed the door, sat on the floor, and cried. He did all he could to suppress sobs.

When Tyler thought of Marcus, his feelings were always jumbled. Marcus always caught him off guard. Maybe it was for the best that he was leaving.

He feigned ill for the next week so he wouldn't see Marcus before the move. He didn't know how he would react if he saw him again.

By the time Tyler figured himself out, got kicked out of the house for it, moved back to the city, and found a position working for Leo Ellis, he had no idea how to reach Marcus. Assuming he had the guts in the first place.

Which, he thought, looking down at the number scrawled on scrap paper, he may not have.

CHAPTER 23

OWEN SAT on the sofa, completely distracted.

"Owen, what's wrong?" Leo asked.

He got up from his chair and sat on the sofa next to Owen.

"It's seriously nothing."

Should he feel it out? Somehow ask him how he feels first? Or should he blurt it out? No, that would be stupid. What if Leo wasn't as attached as he was? He knew that Leo cared, but what if he wasn't as invested as Owen was? He'd had so many other men and women in this position as his escort. And it was safe to assume that he'd had an intimate relationship with some of them.

Owen's train of thought was interrupted when Leo poked him between his eyes.

"What?" he asked.

"Stop stressing over whatever you are stressing about," Leo said. "Want to talk about it?"

"No," Owen said too quickly.

Leo gave him a look of frustration. "It's been like this since we went to the club. Does this have anything to do with Marcus?" he asked.

Owen laughed quickly, then covered his mouth. Leo seemed too serious.

"No, really, it's got nothing to do with him. I'm fine. I don't want to talk about it yet," he said.

Leo looked unconvinced, but dropped it.

"YURI, I REALLY truly don't know what to do," Owen moaned.

The bartender was swamped, so he and Yuri were stuck waiting.

"Oh, come on, there is no perfect moment. Blurt it out like I did." she said.

"But what if it's one-sided?" Owen said.

Yuri gave him a strange look. He could feel suspicion and some giddiness.

"Level with me, Owen. Is this person you are pining for by any chance Mr. Ellis?"

Owen's eyes widened. He was stunned. He didn't answer, but Yuri seemed to find what she was looking for. That giddiness became her predominate emotion.

"Aha! I knew it. I had a small bet going with Rebecca. You made me suspicious when you got sick and dropped off the grid. Mr. Ellis dealt with my questions personally. And he seemed really bent out of shape at the time," Yuri said.

She tapped her fingernails on the bar for a moment. "Ah, young love," she said with a sigh. "Okay, look. One of us is telling Mr. Ellis that you love him by the end of this week," she said, looking entirely serious. Her mood spoke differently.

"Ah, come on, Yuri, you would never do that to me," he said confidently.

"So, you called my bluff." She laughed. "But in all honesty, the next time you get that warm, happy glow in the pit of your stomach, say it. Say it straight out: 'I love you.'"

"Who loves who?"

Owen almost jumped out of his skin.

"I didn't know my employees had so much downtime," Leo said, curiosity in his voice.

Owen took a breath and let it out. He couldn't read Leo's feelings, but he could tell from his tone that he wasn't on to what they were speaking about. Well, or who.

"I'm waiting on drinks, Mr. Ellis. And as for who loves who—" She leaned in conspiratorially. "—I suspect that nice man Jacob and his coworker Alex are a happy item."

Leo smiled, and Owen was once again stunned by how intuitive Yuri was.

"Well, it's not polite to gossip," Leo said. "Your drinks are done. Get them out to the tables."

Yuri didn't seem at all perturbed. "Will do, Mr. Ellis!" she said, grabbing her tray and leaving the bar.

"That woman is something, right?" Owen said.

"That she is. One of my best employees on the floor," Leo replied. "Oh, I almost forgot. The reason I came here was to give you your phone. You left it in the apartment, and *someone* won't stop texting and calling." He rolled his eyes and handed over the phone.

Owen was glad that Leo had shifted his opinion on Marcus from unlikeable to exhausting but tolerable. That was probably how people normally saw Marcus. Owen found him exhausting too, sometimes, but he liked his personality. For all that he behaved like a child most of the time, he truly had a kind heart and a lot of love to give. He opened his phone and saw quite a few missed texts and calls.

Owen, I'm going to call Tyler.

Answer your phone!

I need your help!

What am I gonna say??

Answer the phoooone!!!

Answer me or I'll hold my breath!

Ok that was childish.

But I will do it!

Come on, Owen, call me back!

OK. Let's meet for dinner.

I will pick you up at 7.

We are going to Junipers.

You can wait outside the building. Or hide. That's ok because I will find you! (;

Owen shook his head. *I'm working tonight. Let's get lunch tomorrow.* He'd barely hit Send when he got a response.

12 pm. In front of the building, or I WILL FIND YOU!

Owen laughed, shutting the phone and putting it away. He jumped at the sound of the bartender calling his name.

"Owen," she said, "Your drinks are ready."

"Oh sorry, Leanne. I was distracted."

"You kids are so wrapped up in your phones," she said, gesturing him along.

He picked up the tray and went to hand out drinks.

He passed Yuri a few times, and every single time they made eye contact, she mouthed "Say it."

Owen needed love advice from someone less bold. But who could he ask?

Marcus wasn't helpful. He'd asked Jacob already, but he was so cool and collected.

Ah! Alex. He was that perfect medium. Both bold and shy.

Planning on finding Alex tomorrow, he got back into the lulling rhythm of repetitive working.

"OWEN, YOU have to help me!" Marcus whined.

They met for lunch but went to Juniper's anyway. It was quiet at this time, which was nice.

"Why don't you tell him you are sorry?" Owen asked.

"Owen, I have no idea what I should say! And I'm scared if I don't plan it, I'm going to say something stupid," Marcus said.

"You're getting yourself worked up over nothing. While granted you can come off as overwhelming, Tyler always put up with it, right?" Owen asked.

Marcus nodded slightly, apparently lost in thought.

"Anyway, Tyler doesn't seem mad," Owen added.

Marcus's attention completely focused on Owen. "Are you sure? How can you be sure?"

"How do you think?"

Marcus laughed lightly, but there was still a touch of sadness there.

"Marcus, can I see your phone?"

Marcus looked confused but handed it over. It was times like these that Owen was glad he was a dead zone to Marcus.

He typed quickly, before Marcus could stop him, and sent a message.

"There. Now if Tyler agrees, which I am so sure he will, you are meeting him in the park this afternoon. I checked his schedule because I thought something like this would happen," Owen said cheerfully. "You're welcome."

The look of shock on Marcus's face was priceless. Owen handed back the phone, and he took it, opening the message as if to verify that Owen had indeed sent it.

"Come on, Owen. That was a low blow!"

"If I'm reading this situation right, as I know I am, you are both a pair of idiots. I can feel how you both react, remember? If I didn't think Tyler was as open to meeting as you, then I wouldn't get involved. As it is, you have a meeting to prepare for."

Marcus shook his head. His mood shifted from fear to nervous anticipation.

"I would have done it either way," Marcus said quietly.

Owen was almost shocked by the lack of energy in his tone. "I know. I made it easier for you, right?"

Marcus smiled, and that bright happiness that Owen was used to returned.

"Thanks, Owen."

"Don't thank me. Take me out for drinks tonight. We can celebrate or wallow. Whichever is appropriate."

Marcus simply laughed. Owen could feel his anxiety increase. He probably shouldn't have joked like that. This wasn't the Marcus that Owen had known until now.

Still, he looked forward to seeing what happened.

MARCUS DID his best to stop bouncing his leg as he sat on the bench, waiting for Tyler. Every time he stopped, his mind would drift to why he was here, and it started again. He was nervous, but he didn't want to appear nervous to Tyler.

Why had he agreed to meet? Marcus was sure that Tyler hated him for ending their friendship. He'd broken all ties, so why did he agree to come here? Maybe he really was willing to accept Marcus's apology.

God, he wished he could get a do-over.

"Marcus?"

Marcus jumped. He hadn't noticed the man approaching him. He looked at him and his mouth went dry.

"Tyler?" he asked. Suddenly all those words he had carefully planned on saying flew out the window. He was drawing a blank. He stood to… to what? Oh right, to apologize.

He noticed that Tyler was fidgeting with his hands. Marcus tried to read Tyler, but as always, it was the worst times when he drew a blank.

He opened his mouth to speak and stopped when Tyler held up a hand.

"I know what you are going to say—" he started.

Marcus interrupted him before he could finish the thought. "Imsosorryikissedyou! I wasn't thinking, and I know that you never felt that way about me, but I loved you so much I didn't know what to do with myself. I should never have done that, I completely ruined our friendship, and I know you hate me, but—"

Tyler pressed the palm of his hand over Marcus's mouth. Marcus didn't move. He was so confused.

"Marcus, I came here to apologize to *you*. I always loved you. I was scared and selfish, and I was brought up to hate that side of me. I was too ashamed to contact you. I never blamed you for anything."

Marcus mumbled against Tyler's hand, "Ru ruv me?"

Tyler smiled and kissed his hand where it connected to Marcus.

"I'm glad you aren't angry at me. This whole thing was my fault," Tyler said.

He removed his hand from Marcus's mouth.

"You're right," Marcus said, getting back to his usual flow, "this is all your fault. So how are you going to repay me?"

"IT WENT well?" Owen asked, sipping his gin and tonic.

"Tyler is coming to work for me," Marcus said cheerfully.

"So I'm assuming everything worked out for you, then?" Owen asked.

"Fuck yeah! Did you know that he declared his love for me? With such passion and romance."

"Passion and romance? Tyler?" Owen asked doubtfully.

"Okay, well, I may be embellishing, but he really did profess his love for me!" Marcus said.

"And now you've poached him from Leo?" Owen asked.

"Well, I wouldn't put it like that. That makes me sound like the bad guy," Marcus said, frowning into his drink. He perked up pretty quickly. "And I'll be working more closely with your organization too! I'll be… let's say investing… my money into more businesses, including the casino. That way I don't lose everything if one group gets busted," Marcus said.

"Busted?" Owen asked, being purposefully obtuse.

"Ha, ha," Marcus said, flagging down the bartender. "Just know that you'll be seeing more of me."

With perfect timing, Leo walked up to the bar where they sat and put a hand on Owen's back.

"What did you say to Tyler?" he asked Marcus, more with curiosity than malice. "He handed me his resignation a few hours ago. I tell you, poaching one of my best men is not much endearing you to me, Marcus."

"I think it's kind of cute," Owen mused.

"Yeah, yeah," Leo replied, but his tone was light.

Owen suspected that he felt the same.

A FEW DAYS later found Owen in his favorite place: the kitchen.

Leo walked in, making a show of smelling the air.

"What did you bake this time?" he asked with a smile.

"I made coconut macaroons, but I promised Jacob that he could be the first to taste test."

Leo frowned. "Will you at least cook me something? I'm thinking burrito," he said.

Owen smiled. Leo had gotten bolder with his orders. What he wanted, Owen made. Not that this wasn't totally Owen's fault, because it was. He always gave Leo the dinner choice, never realizing how demanding he would become. When Owen refused to make exactly what he wanted, he pouted until he got his way.

Some gangster, huh?

"Leo, I have something I want to talk about," Owen said, messing with his hair.

Leo looked curious. "What's on your mind?" he asked.

"Do you remember the night at the club. In the bathroom?"

"Yes." His look turned playful.

Owen lost his momentum. He couldn't get the words out. It didn't feel right asking about it right now.

When Owen said nothing, Leo's expression grew concerned. "Owen, are you all right? Is this about your neck?"

Owen froze. No, it wasn't. And being reminded was like a punch in the gut. God, but he hoped that he could learn to live with it.

Leo closed the space between them, and like the night at the club, he pushed Owen's hair aside and brushed his lips against the mark.

"Owen, no one owns you. When you think of this, think of *me*. I am the only one who can claim you," Leo said quietly against his neck.

Shivers ran down Owen's spine. That woke a heat in his belly. Leo must have noticed because he swept him up into his arms and headed toward the bedroom.

"Leo, put me down. Goddammit, I can walk!" He couldn't control the breathy sound of his voice.

Damn Leo for being so sexy.

Leo tossed Owen onto the bed. He briskly removed all clothing between them. Owen shifted so his whole body was on the bed. Leo crawled on top of him, then leaned back. He held himself over Owen so that the weight of his groin rested on Owen's stomach.

Owen reached up for him, but Leo pushed his hands away. He loomed over Owen without making any more contact.

"What do you want me to do, Owen?" he almost purred.

Owen's face burned. He didn't really know what to say. It was embarrassing.

Leo leaned in and bit the tip of Owen's ear, hard, then licked it lingeringly.

"How is that?" Leo asked.

Owen was shocked by how aroused he became.

"I don't need a play-by-play, Leo. Just—"

Owen sputtered to a stop as Leo licked from his ear down to his neck. It was feeling good when suddenly he felt an ache.

He froze, much of his arousal dying down.

"Leo, stop…." He could hear desperation in his own voice.

Leo avoided the brand, instead licking around it. Owen felt some of his arousal returning. Leo pressed two fingers against Owen's lips, and he happily drew them in, running his tongue along the digits and sucking them. The sensation pooled in his belly.

Leo kissed his way from Owen's neck to his stomach. Owen gripped Leo's hair, wanting desperately to feel him. Obliging, Leo stroked Owen's hard cock gently. There was barely any pressure, and Owen squirmed in impatience.

Leo pressed Owen's body into the bed with one hand, that touch of dominance doing wonders for Owen's libido.

He held Owen and licked one long, slow stripe up his member. Owen found the teasing erotic but frustrating, and both reactions grew as Leo licked his way back up Owen's body to his neck.

This time it took Owen longer to notice that twinge in his neck. He sobered again, but Leo took his member in hand and gently stroked it. The feeling was stronger than before. The arousal he felt almost completely distracted him. Almost.

"Leo, stop that," he whined, sounding pathetic to his own ears.

Leo murmured, but Owen could not hear him.

"What?"

"Owen, you are mine from head to foot and everywhere in between. Including your neck," he said, somehow making it sound sexy.

He left Owen's neck alone and instead focused his attention on Owen's nipple, which caused Owen to involuntarily suck harder on the fingers inside his mouth.

Leo continued to lazily stroke his dick. His spine tingled, and it was as perfect as it was frustrating.

"Okay, can you just…," Owen said around the fingers.

Leo withdrew them and replaced them with his lips. Owen explored the plush flesh of Leo's mouth. Without parting their lips, Leo managed to get the bottle of lube out and open.

He sat back, completely off of Owen, and tossed the bottle on the bed.

"Do it yourself," Leo said, a growl in his voice.

Too excited to care, Owen took the bottle and poured a generous amount onto his fingers. He was lazy with the process. He used two, then three fingers. Not putting on a show but not rushing through it either.

He slowed down more when he noticed Leo's hungry gaze. He smirked and dragged the process out further, caressing his skin whenever he moved his fingers. When Leo was about as frustrated as he could get, a look on Leo that Owen loved, Leo leaned on top of him and kissed him even as he pushed inside of him.

Ah, there it was. Owen could *feel* Leo. His excitement, his satisfaction, his affection. So good. Like he had Leo well and truly inside of him, literally and figuratively.

Leo rocked into Owen's body. Owen began to feel the excitement growing. Leo moaned with every thrust, and Owen was fully aware of the pleasure that Leo experienced as well.

Suddenly Leo was leaning farther over him, whispering in his ear.

"This is mine," he said into Owen's ear before kissing his way from the lobe to his neck. This time it took a little longer for Owen to process what was happening. He was so focused on both of their emotions.

When he felt it, his arousal began to dampen once more. But at the same moment, Leo pushed into Owen so hard that their bodies shoved up the bed. Owen forgot what the problem was.

Leo was back at Owen's ear.

Owen felt the first stirrings of climax—in one or both of them—and at that moment, Leo licked and sucked on the mark. Owen couldn't find any energy or desire to care as he spent himself. Leo came right behind him.

Leo plopped onto the bed next to Owen. They looked at each other for a moment, then Leo reached out and rested his fingers against the scar on Owen's neck. Owen didn't flinch this time.

"I'll keep reminding you that you belong to me," he said, "so long as you wish."

Owen was back to radio silence, but he could feel the truth in Leo's words. Leo always knew what Owen truly needed.

"Leo Ellis, I love you," he blurted out before he could think about it.

Leo's grin turned devastating.

"It took you long enough," he said, laughing when Owen pouted. "Owen Hart, I love you from now until eternity," he said confidently.

It was so dramatic, and so like Leo, that Owen found himself laughing.

Between the brand, the fear, and the doubt, Owen had been on edge. Now hearing those words made his whole heart and soul leap for joy.

CHAPTER 24

"DID YOU say it?" Marcus asked enthusiastically.

They had gone for lunch at a local burger place that Leo refused to go to with Owen.

Owen lifted his burger awkwardly, trying to find a reasonable place to take a bite.

"I don't see how that's any of your business," Owen teased.

"I take that as a yes. It's about time! I declared my passionate, undying love to Tyler, and I haven't seen him in over ten years. I even nabbed him from Ellis!" Marcus laughed, and Owen sensed pure and simple joy.

Owen gave up on his burger and picked up a fry.

"You know, now that I think about it, you told me that you two had been together for almost a year, right?" Marcus asked between bites of his food.

"Yeah," Owen responded curiously.

"Well, when is your anniversary?"

Owen froze, french fry halfway to his open mouth. He set it down and frowned. Why hadn't he thought of that? They hadn't actually celebrated any anniversaries. Being together for that long hadn't even registered with Owen. So much had happened, and he'd never kept track of how much time had passed.

Did Leo know? When did they even start seeing each other? Would he count the day they met? Because that wasn't super romantic. But he supposed that would work. That would mean that their one-year anniversary would be... a few weeks? Crap, what was he going to do?

Marcus was looking at Owen curiously.

"You know, I don't think I enjoy not feeling your feelings. It makes things unpredictable. I only want that with Tyler. Hey, can you ever read Leo?"

Owen looked up in surprise.

"Well, I can read him," Marcus said lightly. "I can find out what's what about your anniversary if I see him."

"No," Owen said quickly, "*please* do not get involved. I don't need the headache."

"If you don't want a headache, don't hang out with me." Marcus laughed at his own joke.

Owen was too preoccupied.

"MR. ELLIS, your two o'clock appointment cancelled," Jacob said, entering Leo's office and shutting the door behind him.

"Jacob, can you hold down the fort Friday night? I have a meeting with a new client." He made a look of disgust.

"So I assume it's with Marcus?" Jacob was well aware Marcus was not Leo's favorite person, although he seemed to have softened toward him a bit recently.

Leo nodded, running his fingers through his hair.

"You know," Jacob said after a pause, "it may not be my place to say, but Alex pointed out to me how long it's been since you and Owen have been together."

He stopped. Leo looked at him curiously. What did that matter?

"It's been almost a.... Crap," Leo cursed. How could he have overlooked this. Neither he nor Owen were particularly romantic, but a one-year anniversary seemed important.

"Why didn't you remind me sooner?" Leo said, more frustrated with himself than Jacob.

Either his tone was not serious enough or Jacob had become accustomed to it, because Jacob gave him a small smile. It actually put Leo at ease. In another life, Jacob would have made a very good therapist.

"As I said, it was Alex who realized it first. He is a romantic at heart," Jacob replied calmly, still smiling.

"So this gives me... what... two weeks?" Leo said, counting the days on his fingers.

Jacob didn't answer. He didn't really need to.

"Crap. Okay. Let me think. Go get me the account balances for the casino."

Jacob bowed his head slightly and exited the office, gently closing the door behind him.

What was Leo thinking? He had never been one to observe things like anniversaries. In his entire adult life, he had never been in a relationship that even made it to a year.

It didn't really matter to Leo. He'd never stayed interested in anyone. Owen, on the other hand.... Leo couldn't see himself in a future without him. Being with Owen felt like being home. Safe and warm. He wouldn't say that he'd loved Owen from the moment he laid eyes on him. At first he'd been curious. But once he really got to know Owen, he had somehow wormed his way under Leo's skin. Not that he was complaining.

So, what would Owen even want?

OWEN WAS pleased when he found out that Alex had graduated, once again, from guard to babysitter. Jacob was more and more involved in business dealings, so usually Alex was around the apartment with him.

"Alex, what the hell am I going to do? What do you do for a one-year anniversary?" Owen moaned. "Does Leo even know about it?"

"I had Jacob give him a friendly reminder," Alex said, grinning.

"I've never even made it eight months into a relationship. I am not equipped for romance."

Owen picked up his bowl of dry ingredients and slowly combined it with the wet ingredients, whisking with all of his strength. Quite a bit was getting onto his clothing.

Alex moved from his seat, away from the splash zone.

"Do what makes you both happy. Romance doesn't have to be flashy. Hell, sitting around and watching horror movies can be just as romantic as a candlelit dinner," he said.

Owen paused in his ministrations.

"Horror movies? You like horror movies?"

"The bloodier the better," Alex said cheerfully.

Owen stared. It didn't seem to fit with his personality.

"Well, I at least want to get him a nice gift. God knows I have the money since Leo won't let me pay for anything," he said.

Owen poured the batter into a donut mold and popped it in one of the ovens.

"We can go shopping after you're finished, if you want," Alex said.

Owen stared at the oven. "I think I'll make another batch first," he said, dreading even thinking about presents.

Alex laughed knowingly. At this point everyone who hung around the apartment knew about Owen's baking habit.

"WHAT ABOUT clothes?" Alex asked.

"That doesn't seem personal enough. And besides, I think he owns more clothing than he could ever hope to wear. He has two closets!" Owen responded.

"What about something kinky?" Alex said, poking him in the side.

Owen laughed as he swatted the hand away.

"Why don't you think of something that you would give Jacob?" he asked.

"I just did," Alex responded. His tone was playful, but Owen could feel that he was only half joking.

"Hmm," Owen skimmed the directory of the mall, trying to figure out where to look first.

"What about jewelry? Does Leo even wear jewelry?" Owen asked.

Alex shrugged. "I know he used to wear a chain, but he lost it and never replaced it," he said.

"Hmm...." Owen always used to wear jewelry. Earrings, chains, bracelets. He hadn't bought any since he'd arrived, and he had never gotten his things when he moved into the apartment building. He didn't have anything special enough to go back for.

"This may turn into a me thing, I think," Owen said aloud.

Alex radiated confusion.

"Come on," he said, "we're going to spend big bucks on nice jewelry."

They got to the jewelry store, and immediately the frugality of Owen's old life flared into being. The prices listed were astronomical! And the pieces with no price tag worried him more.

He closed his eyes and took a deep breath. He'd earned five thousand dollars a month for almost twelve months and barely dipped into it. He could afford to spend an excessive amount.

As soon as he started looking, he spied one item he desperately needed.

"Is that malachite?" he asked the saleswoman, pointing at a bracelet.

She immediately took the piece out and set down a pad to rest it on. "And it's broken up with four hematite beads," she said.

The price on that one wasn't bad. At thirty dollars it was worth it.

"I'll take that. Also, do you have any flat anchor chains in silver?" he asked.

The woman set the bracelet aside and led him to another display case. "What length are you looking for?"

"Eighteen inches should do it."

She nodded and pulled one out for him to inspect.

"And these are sterling silver? Do you have another one?" he asked.

"Yes to both," she said.

"I'll take both of them," he said.

He hadn't meant to get the same thing for both of them. He wanted the nicest style for Leo, but it was also, obviously, his own favorite. So it could be a couple's thing. He could play it off like that was the plan the whole time.

The woman led him to the cash register. Owen only realized then that Alex wasn't behind him. He turned back and saw him eyeing a braided leather bracelet. He walked over to him before paying.

"You know, if you like that I can get it for you. I owe you for everything you've done for me."

Alex waved him off. "I couldn't accept something like that from you. Besides, it's not too expensive, and I wasn't thinking of it for me...." He trailed off, not taking his eyes off the bracelet.

"Oh, I see," Owen said. "Why don't you get it for him?"

"You think? I get nervous about this stuff. Like what if he doesn't like it but wears it for me? I don't want him to feel he needs to wear it," Alex said.

"I don't think Jacob would do anything he didn't want to do. He's a grownass man. Get it," Owen replied.

Alex laughed lightly but asked the woman to wrap the bracelet up for him.

Owen said nothing to Leo about their anniversary. He knew that Leo was aware it was coming up, but he had said nothing either. It was better this way for Owen. He had committed to the idea of making dinner for Leo that night. Except....

"Owen, where are you? You've got your head up in the clouds!" Yuri said, poking his arm.

"Yeah, sorry, Yuri. Today is my anniversary," Owen said.

Yuri's face and energy level completely amped up.

"Oh really! What are you two doing? Going out, hitting the town, dining at a classy restaurant, going on a moonlit stroll, kissing under the stars." She got caught up in her own fantasy.

Owen snapped his fingers to get her attention again. "I don't know. I was going to cook something," he said.

"Ah, a close, personal, romantic evening at home," she said, then paused. "Wait, why are you working, then?" she asked.

"Well, Leo said we could go out later tonight, and he had no one to cover for me, so I'll be leaving a bit early," he said.

Yuri pouted. "Making your lover work for you on their anniversary is not very romantic. Say the word and I'll have words with Mr. Ellis."

Owen laughed, patting her shoulder. "If I ever need to have words with *anyone*, I will come to you first," he said.

Yuri laughed and waved Owen off as his drink orders were filled.

OWEN WALKED into the apartment at seven.

"Leo! What time are we...?"

He glanced up and froze. Leo was standing in the kitchen, wearing an apron—which was way sexier than he would have thought—and stirring something in a saucepan.

"Wow, you did this by yourself?" he asked, awed.

Leo mocked a look of offense. "Of course I did. I even looked up the recipe myself," he said.

"What is it?" Owen asked.

"Your favorite," Leo answered.

Without skipping a beat, Owen exclaimed, "Fettucine alfredo."

"Yup," Leo said. "It's almost done too."

"Where are we eating?" Owen still didn't like the dining room, but Leo probably wanted to...

"On the floor," he said.

"On the floor?" Owen repeated.

"Yeah, you can pick a movie, and we can watch it on the floor so we don't get sauce on the couch."

Owen loved this man. He had to say that there was nothing more romantic than eating a home-cooked meal he loved with the man he loved while watching *The Notebook*. Because that was definitely his choice.

"Ready?" Leo asked, mixing the pasta into the sauce and filling two heaping plates.

Owen took his plate and set it on the counter. He smelled it, then tasted one noodle.

"Are you sure you made this?" Owen asked, "Did someone make it and bring it up? No offense, but this is good, and you stink at cooking."

Leo laughed.

"I took lessons from Tyler. I remembered that he started out as a cook in the Spades restaurant," he said.

"Was this before or after he left?" Owen asked.

"After." Leo still sounded sore about that.

"So I'm going to guess—"

"Yes, that pain in the ass was there. Being his usual self," Leo said, sounding tired thinking about it.

Owen laughed, imagining Marcus's energetic comments and input.

"But it was worth it. I mean, if you like it?"

Owen frowned down at the plate like he was thinking. He could feel Leo's glance becoming worried.

"Leo, it's great! I'm going to give kudos to Tyler," he said.

Leo looked relieved.

Owen took both plates to the floor in front of the TV.

"What are we... wait. Let me guess. We're watching *The Notebook*. Again," Leo said. feigning annoyance.

"Well, if you insist," Owen said innocently.

Leo laughed and popped the movie—which was conveniently located right on top of the player—into the Blu-ray player.

Owen ate all of his pasta and sent Leo to get seconds since he didn't want to miss anything. Owen went on an emotional roller coaster through the movie, finally crying tears from deep within his soul when the movie ended.

Owen noticed that, as usual, Leo didn't shed a single tear.

"Leo, you're a brick wall," Owen said.

Leo pulled his sleeve over his hand and wiped away the tears falling down Owen's cheeks.

"Why do you watch something that upsets you so much?" Leo asked.

"It doesn't upset me. It *moves* me," Owen replied.

"I know. You have a good heart," Leo said, turning Owen's head and lightly licking the tears on his cheek, before kissing his closed eye.

Owen enjoyed the sensation until Leo pulled away. Owen was slightly disappointed. He could think of other places he would like Leo to kiss.

"So, did you think I wouldn't make dessert?" Leo asked.

Owen perked up. "Now, I know you didn't bake anything. You suck at baking," Owen said.

Leo winked at him.

"I did, in fact, bake for you. But Marcus helped me with that. Apparently, Tyler is a cook and Marcus is a baker," he said.

Leo went into the kitchen and opened one of the cabinets. Inside was a cake box.

"In honor of the first dessert you ever made for us, I have made you cupcakes," Leo said happily.

Owen was moved. He felt tears in his eyes… again. But this time he managed to blink them away.

"That's the best gift I've ever gotten!" Owen exclaimed, hopping up and giving his hug to Leo a running start.

Leo swayed back for a moment after impact, then embraced Owen in one of the tightest hugs he ever had. Owen felt so safe. And loved.

"That's not your gift, though," Leo said after a moment.

"Oh, I have something for you as well. One second." He dashed into the bedroom and retrieved the jewelry box he hadn't bothered wrapping.

"Here. I'm sorry if you want to be unique because I got the same one for myself," Owen said.

Leo opened the box and smiled. "I needed this, but I was too lazy to shop for it. And you have one too?" Leo's gaze turned lascivious. "We match now."

He put the chain around his neck. Owen pulled out his own chain, which was resting under his shirt.

"Owen, its perfect. Thank you," Leo said genuinely.

"Okay, what do I get?" Owen asked, a little bit leery. He was never one to like getting gifts.

Leo touched Owen's hand with his own. Owen was confused until he heard it. He heard *Leo*.

Marcus taught me to let down my guard for you, at least this much.

Owen was shocked. He drew his hand away quickly. He tried to read Leo's emotions, but they were still blocked. Yet he could hear him.

"It was Marcus's idea. He apparently knew that you couldn't read me, so he taught me how to lower my defenses, at least enough for you to read my thoughts," Leo said.

Owen gaped at Leo. It was like he couldn't process what was happening. He grabbed Leo's hand again.

What changed? he asked in his mind.

Lots and lots of meditation and focus practices.

Owen was thrilled. "Can you turn it on and off? That I can read you?"

"It's actually pretty hard to turn on," Leo responded, "but I can let you in on the important stuff."

"This is the best present I have ever gotten," Owen said, smiling widely.

OWEN LEANED back in his lawn chair and looked up at the stars. He'd never come up to the roof. He was never interested. But now that he was here, he wondered why he hadn't done it sooner. There were plants and trees cascading all around them. The sky was dark, with a new moon. The stars shone out even brighter for it.

It was the perfect night, in the perfect place, with the perfect person. Owen had never felt happier than he felt in this moment. Leo sat beside him, his total attention on the starry night above them.

Owen took Leo's hand and kissed it. In response, Leo pulled him in for a lazy kiss.

He felt complete.

Who knew that getting caught cheating would be the best thing that ever happened to him?

DEAR READERS.

Thank you for taking this journey with Owen and Leo—and me! Just for you, a bonus short story that follows our guys a few years into the future, after the events in *Spades*. I hope you enjoy it.

FOREVER

An Owen and Leo short story by Rose Masters

OWEN WOKE before the sun was even up. Alone. Still. He looked over to Leo's side of the bed and found him missing. Leaning over, he saw pajama pants carelessly thrown on the floor. So at least Leo had gotten some sleep.

Owen wasn't sure what was going on. Leo didn't talk about work, and Owen never asked. It was a good system. But now Owen wished he knew why Leo was in bed after him and out before him. Sometimes he didn't come back at all.

Whatever was going on, Owen was starting to get lonely. Sure, he had Alex, who was actually in the same boat as him. Whatever Leo was up to, Jacob was involved. It took more of a toll on Alex than it did on him, though. He walked around like he was ready to snap if someone looked at him wrong.

Whatever it was, Owen hoped it would be done with soon.

"I swear to God, Owen. This is nonsense," Alex lamented. They sat at the kitchen island eating omelets that Owen had made.

"Do you know what's happening?" Owen asked.

"Of course," Alex said, "but it's not really interesting."

AKA none of his business. Owen brushed the comment off.

"Wasn't Leo working on something with Marcus and Maribelle?" Owen asked.

Alex shrugged. "It got put on the back burner. I think Marcus has an illegal gambling business that he's trying to make legit. But other things have come up. It's all pretty boring," he said.

"Do you know how long this is likely to go on?" Owen asked.

"Maybe a month? Two months?" Alex frowned like a kicked puppy.

Owen stared at him. "Should we do something today?" he suggested.

"Like what?" Alex asked.

"I'm pretty bad at bowling if you want to do that," Owen said.

Alex laughed. "That's something I'm really good at, if you don't mind getting your ass kicked," Alex said, a smile filling his face.

"Good," Owen said. "And hey, you never know. I might beat you."

"Whatever you have to tell yourself," Alex replied.

OWEN GOT his ass kicked.

But the game had worked to lighten the mood. Alex at least was smiling again. And he stayed cheerful all through dinner. Obviously it was chicken parm. No matter what Owen tried to feed him, Alex loved his chicken parm.

Owen wasn't due at work for another hour, and Alex left on some errand or another. Leo had dropped security precautions for the most part. He basically paid Alex to hang out with Owen rather than guard him.

He sat on the couch, careful not to wrinkle his uniform. The TV was off, and he watched the overhead fan turning ever so slowly. He counted as the fan circulated. God, he was bored.

"I'm surprised you're still here."

Owen shot up on the couch. "Leo! Where the hell have you been?" Owen asked, more surprised than accusatory.

"Working. Do you want to play hooky from work?" Leo asked, hanging his coat neatly on a coat hanger.

"Fuck yes," Owen said right away. "So how are you going to make your absence up to me?"

"There's a new rooftop bar-and-grill type restaurant if you want to check it out. It's right up your alley," Leo suggested.

"Let me change. This is casual, right? Because sometimes your version of casual is not casual," Owen double-checked.

"As I said, bar and grill," Leo said.

"I'm wearing the new leather pants. And you…. I'm going to go ahead and lay out your outfit," Owen said.

"Don't trust me?" Leo asked.

"Not even a little. You overdress, and everyone stares at you like you just stepped off the runway. It's too much attention," Owen said.

"How do you know that it isn't you they are looking at?" Leo asked, smiling slightly.

"Okay, sure. You tell yourself whatever you want. I'm still picking out your clothes."

LEO HAD no casual clothes. No jeans, no T-shirts. The man liked his fashion, and he kept it classy. This didn't work for Owen's vision. He imagined Leo in dark jeans and a black band T-shirt. He knew Leo would never go for it, but Owen would die to see that outfit on him.

After creating a pile of clothes on the floor, earning Owen a frown from Leo, Owen finally came up with a pair of slacks and a cotton long-sleeved white shirt. It flowed nicely. Owen was proud of himself.

Leo took the outfit, but stared hard at Owen. Owen looked at the mess he'd made and sighed.

"You should clean it up as payment for my assistance with your fashion," Owen said, but he bent down and started picking up shirts and pants and putting them where they belonged.

He was distracted, so he missed Leo getting changed. He felt kind of ripped off. Like, he made the outfit; why couldn't he see Leo undress first?

OWEN AND Leo boarded the elevator for the rooftop. There was a huge line to get on, but the doorman whisked the two of them to the elevator and sent them up immediately.

"This is really new, right? I don't remember this," Owen said.

He was slightly nervous. Elevators seemed like deathtraps to him. The higher the floor, the more worried he became that he would fall to his death. His apartment wasn't bad; it was only six floors. But this was going up twenty-four floors, and as each floor passed, Owen considered how much more likely they were to die if the elevator were to fall.

Leo took Owen's hand and rubbed his thumb over his knuckle.

"You know there is a safety mechanism if the elevator were to start to fall," Leo said quietly. It really didn't matter, because they were the only ones in there.

"I know that, but I don't believe it," Owen said, but he found himself smiling anyway. Leo always knew how to calm him down.

The elevator finally dinged, and Leo ushered Owen out with a guiding hand.

"Mr. Ellis! What a pleasure to have you. Your table is all ready for you," a man said, leading them to the table with the best view of the city. He didn't look like an employee.

"Is he...?" Owen started.

"He's the owner," Leo said.

Owen looked at Leo thoughtfully. "Is this your restaurant?" he asked.

Leo laughed. "No. I loaned the owner a hefty sum of money, though. Hopefully he does well," Leo said.

Owen hoped he did too, for his sake.

Leo poked Owen's nose to get his attention.

"Aren't you going to admire the view?" he said.

For a moment, Owen thought Leo was talking about himself, but when Leo put his palm on Owen's cheek and turned his head to face the city, Owen was struck.

The sun had gone down, and the city was a sea of lights. They really did have the perfect seat. He could see their apartment building from where they sat.

"Wow," Owen said.

"Wow, indeed," Leo agreed.

Owen sat for a few minutes, completely enthralled with the view. A waitress interrupted him.

"What can I get for you?" the woman said, all of her attention on Leo. Owen sensed the greed coming off of her.

He wasn't one to get jealous, but he didn't like this girl's tone.

"Owen, pick," Leo said.

It wasn't Owen's imagination that the waitress actually pouted.

Owen hadn't even glanced at the menu, so he quickly scanned it.

"Oh, we'll get the buffalo chicken wrap. His with onion rings, and mine with fries," he said.

The waitress turned her attention back to Leo and beamed. "That'll be right out for you." She gave Owen one last blank stare before walking away.

Bitch.

"Onion rings?" Leo asked with a smile on his face.

"I told you I was going to make you try them. Now seemed as good a time as any," Owen said simply. "Ah shit. I forgot to order drinks."

Leo looked past him and waved the owner over. Owen could imagine that he was paying close attention to them.

"Hello, John. Can you please have someone get me a merlot and my partner whatever IPA has the most hops?" he asked sweetly.

The owner smiled despite his obvious nerves. Leo had that way about him. Like a snake with puppy-dog eyes.

"Right away, Mr. Ellis," he said, walking away just shy of a run.

It didn't take long for a petite woman to come over with their drinks.

"Thank you," Leo said, tipping her before she left.

"So, Leo," Owen said.

"Yes, Owen," Leo responded.

"What have you been up to?" Owen asked.

Leo immediately rubbed his fingers over his eyes.

"It's got to do with internal affairs. You know I have a ship to nowhere for gambling, right?" Leo asked.

"Yeah, that I knew," Owen said.

"Well, our system got hacked, and on top of that, we also realized that someone was cooking the books. Now it's a big headache, trying to see who did what and coordinating everyone involved. We're almost done, though. Should nothing go wrong, we'll have normal hours again come next week," Leo explained.

Owen nodded. It's not like he had any idea what was going on, but he kind of figured it was internal. Otherwise Leo would be all over Owen, keeping him safe from the bad guys.

Owen was happy that he could bring good news back to Alex.

"Here's your food, gentlemen," the waitress said, eyes focused directly on Leo as she laid the plates down.

Owen gave her kudos for somehow getting his meal directly in front of him without looking.

"Thank you," Leo said. Owen noticed Leo didn't tip her before she walked away.

"What happened? She didn't catch you in her snare?" Owen said, smiling.

"She has poor taste," Leo said, brushing his hair behind his back.

"Really," Owen said, confused.

"Anyone with any taste should be looking at you," Leo said.

Owen smiled but felt his face heat.

"Okay. So taste the onion rings," Owen encouraged.

Leo stared at his plate before picking up a greasy onion ring. He took a careful bite before looking up at Owen and smiling.

"Disgusting," he said, laughing.

"Well, at least you've tried it now," Owen replied.

"I no longer trust your taste credibility,". Leo said.

"Que será,"

Owen reached over the table to snatch an onion ring from Leo's plate.

"WHY AM I here, Marcus?" Owen asked.

Owen had gotten a text from Marcus that simply said, *Come over right now! It's an emergency!*

When Owen had texted back, he got no answer. Instead, he was informed by staff that a car had been sent for him. But when he got to the house, he walked in to find Marcus lying on the floor in the living room with his hands over his face.

"Owen," Marcus said as if he didn't already know that Owen was coming.

"Come, come," he whispered. It was hard to know if something was really wrong or not because Marcus was the biggest drama queen he had ever met.

Marcus got up, led them onto the patio, and closed the door. Owen was surprised to see they were alone. There was almost always a guard posted outside.

"Owen, I think Tyler hates me," Marcus lamented.

Owen stared at him.

"That, or he's cheating on me. Or both! God!"

"Okay, why the hell do you think that?" Owen asked.

"Because he keeps slipping out. And yesterday he smelled like perfume," Marcus said.

Owen raised an eyebrow.

"He doesn't wear cologne, Owen!"

Marcus sprawled out dramatically on the tile. Owen sat next to him. He brushed a stray curl off of Marcus's forehead.

"Marcus, you know Tyler is mad for you, right?" Owen said.

Marcus looked up at him, his eyes wet. "Yeah?" he said quietly.

"Yeah. I know you can't always feel it, but I do. There's an explanation—I guarantee it," Owen said.

Marcus wiped his eyes and shot up into a sitting position so quickly that he almost knocked Owen over.

"Obviously. I mean, who wouldn't love me? Right?"

Owen was a little surprised Marcus didn't sound as confident about that as he usually did.

"Come on, Marcus. Leo is working right now, so you can come over for lunch. I have leftover paella," Owen said.

"Paella! God, I wish you were my personal chef," Marcus said.

Owen didn't cook for Marcus as much as he did for Alex and Jacob, but he always got so excited about Owen's food. Owen thought he could make cereal and Marcus would be like a kid at Christmas.

"OWEN, HOW are you? Isn't your birthday coming?" Yuri started before Owen put a finger to her lips.

"Yes, my birthday is coming up. But I don't want anyone to know," he said quietly.

"But Owen," Yuri said softly, "you get the best tips on a birthday! From the regulars at least."

"No. Really no," Owen said.

"Ugh, fine. But I'm baking you cupcakes anyway," she said.

"Thanks, Yuri," Owen said.

THE NEXT day both Leo and Jacob were pulled away to work. Rather than sitting inside again, Alex and Owen decided to go shopping. Well, truthfully, Owen decided to go shopping. Alex was just along for the ride.

"So what are we looking for," Alex asked as Owen led him on a determined path through the outlet mall.

"Clothes," Owen said simply.

"What else is new?" Alex said with a sigh, but his aura spoke of happiness.

"I'm shopping for you too," Owen said.

Alex looked surprised. "I don't need clothes," he said.

"This is the same problem I have with Leo. You all think that you don't need new clothing, that you can wear the same suit down to the ground. If I can help it, you will all look as good as me and Jacob with our nice new outfits," Owen said.

Because Jacob was like him. He liked to be impeccably dressed, and when a suit or a shirt or jeans got old, they were donated. Not true for the other knuckleheads.

"You know I hate trying clothes on," Alex said.

"I know your measurements. You can hold things up to get an idea," Owen said.

Owen still felt kind of uncomfortable with the shopping arrangements that Leo had set up. Rather than having to leave a store with bags and bags of clothing, everything was shipped right to the apartment. In one sense, it was easier when Owen wanted to buy a lot. In another sense, it *encouraged* Owen to buy a lot.

Owen definitely had the money to spend. He basically spent his own money on nothing but clothing, because he didn't really buy anything else. Leo covered restaurants, living expenses, groceries, and basically anything else that cost money.

But somehow, Owen always felt guilty about how much he was spending. Well, it was his money to spend, but he had always lived on a tight budget, even growing up with the professor.

Still, his desire to dress himself and his compatriots outweighed the guilt.

Owen would tell no one how much money he spent that day.

"YOUR BIRTHDAY is coming up too?" Owen asked Marcus, who sat on the floor in Owen's living room.

Marcus didn't seem to like furniture.

"Yeah, our birthdays are the same week this year," Marcus said.

"I feel like your birthday is a different month every year," Owen said suspiciously.

"I do that to keep people on their toes. I honestly don't know when my real birthday is. We never celebrated stuff like that when I was growing up. I always declared myself a year older on New Year's Day," Marcus replied.

"Huh," Owen said.

"So what are you doing for your birthday? How old are you going to be anyway?" Marcus asked.

"I don't know yet. And thirty-four."

"Oh, you're younger than me. I'm going to be thirty-eight. I think." Marcus looked deep in thought. "Yeah, about that."

Owen said nothing, but he suddenly realized what Tyler must be up to.

"Has Leo said anything to you about my birthday?" Owen suddenly asked.

Marcus looked sly. "As if I would tell you that," he said.

Which meant he did know something.

"Is it a good surprise?" Owen asked.

"I don't know what you're talking about," Marcus countered.

Owen rolled his eyes and lay back into the couch cushions. He hoped it was nothing too over-the-top.

THE DAY of Owen's birthday was a workday. Owen wasn't working, but Yuri had begged him to stop by. He wasn't expecting Leo for a few hours anyway, so he showed up at the beginning of her shift.

"Owen! Happy birthday," she gushed. "Here, I got something for you."

Yuri went behind the bar and pulled out a Tupperware and a small wrapped present.

"As promised, cupcakes," she said.

"Yuri, you really didn't have to do anything for me," Owen said, taking the gift and pulling off the paper.

Inside the box was a gorgeous goldstone bracelet with lava rocks on both ends.

"Please, do you think that I would do any of this if I didn't want to?" Yuri scolded.

Owen laughed at her tone. "This is gorgeous. Thank you, Yuri," he said, giving her a hug.

"So I'm assuming you're going out to celebrate with your man?" Yuri asked.

"Unfortunately," Owen said.

Yuri smacked his arm. "That man loves you. You entertain him, and you do it with a smile," she said.

Owen laughed. He wasn't sure why he found that so funny, but he almost had tears in his eyes.

LEO HAD simply told Owen that they were going out. So Owen dressed up, thinking they were going to some fancy restaurant or another.

"That's not appropriate," Leo said when he got home.

Owen looked down at his outfit. It wasn't super formal, but it would work for the types of places that Leo liked to visit.

"Not fancy enough?" Owen asked, confused.

"No. Too fancy. We're going to the Crab Shack," Leo said with a smile.

Owen's whole body froze. That was his favorite restaurant, but, well, it was more of a dive than a restaurant. And Leo *hated* eating there.

"Really?" Owen said excitedly.

"Yeah. You can pick my outfit," Leo said.

Owen felt like a balloon that was about to pop. After fantasizing about Leo in jeans and a T-shirt, Owen had taken the liberty of buying some. And now, finally, he was making Leo wear them. When he laid it out, Leo actually pouted.

"Jeans? Really?" he complained.

"Yes. It's my birthday, so you wear what I tell you," Owen said.

Leo sighed and obediently pulled his clothes on.

It was kind of funny to arrive at the Crab Shack in an expensive sleek black car. They got a few looks as they stepped out and the car drove away.

While Owen was rarely able to convince Leo to come here, he had often come to eat with Marcus or Alex and Jacob. So he knew the waitress immediately when she came to seat them.

"Owen! Welcome back," she said.

"Hi, Dolores," he said.

"And you must be Leo. We have your table all ready for you," she said.

Owen eyed Leo curiously. This place didn't take reservations.

Dolores led them to a table right next to the window, offering a view of the water and the city beyond.

"Can I start you with some drinks?" she asked.

"Merlot for him, and Goose Island IPA for me," Owen said.

She smiled sweetly. "Coming right up."

Of course, they got raw clams. It wasn't a real seafood experience without them. There were so many delicious things on the menu, but whenever they came or ordered takeout, they got the lobster mac and cheese. They were enjoying their food when suddenly Leo poked Owen's lips.

"What?" Owen asked, giving him his attention.

"I have a question for you," Leo said, smiling slightly.

Owen took a good look at him. He looked happy but also kind of nervous. His body posture was rigid, and his smile was a little tense.

"Do you want to get married?" he asked.

Owen's brain shut down for a moment. But quickly, warmth suffused throughout his body, and he smiled widely.

Leo appeared relieved.

"You're going to propose here?" Owen teased. "And you're not going down on one knee, huh?"

Leo rolled his eyes. "You would hate that," he said.

"I would," Owen agreed.

Leo reached into his pocket and took out two silver bands with a pattern of ivy wrapped around them.

"So what do you say. Do you want to be stuck with me forever?" Leo asked, a quiver in his voice despite his smile.

Owen didn't even pretend to think about it. "Absolutely," he said, slipping a ring on his finger. "How did you know my ring size?"

"Do you remember when Marcus was getting rid of rings and he kept making you try them on?" Leo asked.

"Oh. Good plan. It's so the norm for him that I never would have guessed the real reason," Owen said.

"Exactly," Leo replied.

"So, marriage, huh? You don't think you'll get sick of me in a few years?" Owen asked, only half joking.

"I won't be sick of you even when we're old and wrinkly," Leo assured him.

Owen couldn't contain his excitement. He jumped out of his seat and hugged Leo from the back of his chair.

"Well, I guess you're stuck with me, then," Owen whispered.

People were starting to look at them, but Owen really, *really*, did not care.

"If you're done eating, I made you a birthday cake," Leo said.

"You made me a cake? I can't wait to see how that came out," Owen said, still on cloud nine.

Leo smiled and stood up. It was a little awkward because Owen refused to let go of him. Leo pulled Owen off of him and held his hand.

"Let's go," he said.

Leo paid the bill and left Dolores a generous tip. They waited a bit for the car to arrive in comfortable silence. Owen kept looking at the ring on his finger, trying to make sure that he wasn't imagining it.

They got in the car and made it to the apartment and up the elevator in total silence. When they entered the apartment, Leo shut the door behind them, then grabbed Owen and shoved him against the wall.

Their lips crashed together hard. Leo backed off a bit and licked Owen's lip as if in penance. Owen took a shaky breath, and Leo used this opportunity to slip his tongue into his mouth.

Leo kissed his way down to Owen's neck. He sucked and bit the skin there. Owen knew that he would have a mark. He knew that he would care later, but at that moment? He couldn't give a shit.

Leo finally pulled away, and Owen whined at the loss.

"Let's not do this against the wall," he said, taking Owen's hand and leading him to the bedroom.

Owen's eyes lit up, and he ran ahead of Leo, pulling him along and reveling in the sound of his laughter.

"OH GOOD! You said yes," Alex exclaimed.

"It wasn't exactly unexpected," Jacob added.

It was the first time that Owen could have both Alex and Jacob for dinner in months. He was surprised by how much he had missed Jacob.

"Was it super romantic?" Alex asked excitedly.

"Um, not really," Owen admitted. "But I like it that way."

"So there was no grand gesture? Did he get on one knee? Did he have flowers?" Alex asked.

"Nope. He just asked me," Owen said.

Alex looked disappointed.

"Just because that's what you want, doesn't mean that Owen wants it," Jacob scolded, but he was smiling.

"Jacob is actually very romantic," Alex told Owen quietly, even though Jacob could clearly hear him. "He buys me flowers all the time."

"I'm not the romantic one in this relationship," Jacob said.

Alex blushed. "Okay, well, that's true. But you put up with me, and that's what counts," Alex said.

"Oh, Jacob, since I haven't seen you in a while, I have a surprise," Owen said.

Jacob immediately perked up. Probably having guessed what the surprise was.

"I made you cupcakes," he exclaimed.

"Like the first time I met you," Jacob said cheerfully.

"Yup, true," Owen said. He hadn't been thinking of that.

"What are the two of you doing as far as a wedding?" Jacob asked, already going to the kitchen and helping himself to a cupcake.

Owen thought for a moment. "I'm not sure. I don't really want to do anything at all, but I don't know if that's what Leo wants," Owen said. "I think I'll leave it up to him. So long as it's nothing too big."

Jacob nodded. Probably because his mouth was stuffed with cupcake.

"I imagine that Leo feels the same way," Alex said.

"Huh." Owen didn't want Leo to miss out on the wedding he wanted in order to appease Owen.

Owen's phone buzzed, and he took it out of his pocket.

How was your birthday? Marcus sent.

Owen rolled his eyes. *I said yes.*

OMG am I going to walk you down the aisle????

Don't be an idiot.

Oh, come on! Oh! And I found out that all of Tyler's sneaking around was for my birthday! Do you want to know what we did?

No.

We went to a fancy restaurant and he gave me this epic necklace. Apparently the perfume was from one of those perfume-counter attacks.

Attacks?

You know, when they spray you when you don't expect it.

Ok, Marcus.

Let me know what's going on with the wedding. I'll prepare my best man's speech!

Owen rolled his eyes and put his phone away.

But that was interesting. Owen hadn't thought anything about a best man or ceremony or whatever. He was nervous now because he really didn't want all that. And who would even be his best man? Who would be *Leo's* best man? Owen had never met any friends of his, if he even had any.

Pushing those thoughts away, Owen joined Jacob in the kitchen and took a huge bite out of a cupcake. Frosting stuck to his face, and he tried to cover his mouth with his hand to hide the mess he was sure was there.

Alex sat back on the couch.

"Can we at least have flowers?" he asked suddenly.

Owen laughed.

"'We' is a very odd choice of words," Jacob said.

"Oh, come on. I love weddings!" Alex said.

Owen ignored them. He was too busy running this wedding business through his head.

"SO WHAT exactly are we doing?" Owen asked, sitting on the bed next to Leo.

Leo looked up from his laptop.

"Doing?" he asked.

"You know, for a wedding," Owen said.

Leo was quiet for a moment. "What do you want to do?" he asked.

"Nothing," Owen answered immediately.

Leo laughed. "Then we'll do nothing," he said.

Owen stared. "That's it?" he asked.

"That's it," Leo responded.

"Huh. Well, maybe we could take our friends out to dinner or something?" Owen said.

"Whatever you want. I honestly never thought I would even want to be married."

Owen felt the same way.

"So, when do you want to go to city hall and get paperwork done?" Owen asked.

"How about tomorrow?" Leo asked.

"You're not working?" Owen asked.

"I don't have to be," Leo responded. "Then do you want to get sandwiches after?"

"That's probably the perfect way to do it," Owen said with a smile.

OWEN LOOKED down at the paperwork for their marriage.

"What's the last-name situation?" Owen asked.

Leo shrugged. "Whatever you want it to be," he said.

Owen eyed him. "Yeah, but your name is known," Owen said.

"Hart could be known too," he said.

"You really don't care?"

Leo shook his head.

Owen thought for a moment. On the one hand, he had gotten his name from the professor. On the other hand, it would be kind of cool to take Leo's name.

"Okay. I'm going to be Owen Ellis," he finally said.

Leo smiled. "I love it," he said.

"All finished. You two are officially married," the clerk said, eyeing Leo like he knew who he was. Which he might.

Leo bent down and gave Owen a sweet, chaste kiss and then ushered him out of city hall. The car took them right to Lola's.

Leo ordered the Lion, as per usual, but Owen was feeling adventurous and opted for the Cajun chicken wrap.

"So that's it? We're married?" Owen said.

"Disappointed?" Leo asked.

Owen smiled. "Not even a little," he said.

"So can I kiss you whenever I want now?" Leo smirked.

Owen rolled his eyes. "I am amazed at your lack of shame. Married or not we are not going to be making out wherever you want," Owen countered.

Leo didn't seem to give two shits about what other people thought. It was both endearing and annoying.

"We going for dinner tonight?" Owen asked.

"Yeah. I already arranged it," Leo said.

"I'm guessing that it's fancy?" Owen asked.

"Of course," Leo said. "This time you have to appease *me*."

"Who's coming?" Owen asked.

"Well, you fell out of contact with your friends, right? Not that you had many to begin with," Leo said.

Owen wasn't insulted. It was the truth, and it never bothered him.

"So, of course I invited Yuri and her wife. Then Alex and Jacob and Tyler and Marcus," Leo said, making a face when he said Marcus's name. Owen didn't understand why Leo was still not fond of Marcus after all this time. Not that Marcus was helping in that respect. He loved upsetting Leo. He was one to stir shit up.

"You told them no presents, right?" Owen asked anxiously.

"Of course," Leo replied.

Owen smiled to himself. He was really married. To Leo Ellis. Not that his name meant a thing to him. He loved Leo's kindness and occasional immaturity despite the serious demands of his business. He loved the way Leo pretended not to be hungry so that Owen could eat his french fries. He loved Leo's eloquence, even when they argued. And he loved how every night Leo kissed him, even when they fought.

He was so happy to be married to Leo.

Leo was watching him as he was lost in thought. He poked Owen in the forehead to get his attention.

"You know I love *you* more than I ever have and more than I ever will, right?" he said quietly.

Owen smiled, willing the tears in his eyes to get sucked back up into his head.

"I know," Owen said. "Me too."

"OWEN! HAPPY marriage!" Marcus yelled.

Owen watched as the people around turned to look at them.

"Marcus, inside voice," Tyler scolded, coming up behind him and guiding him to the table like a child.

Owen often felt sorry for Tyler.

"Thanks for coming," Leo said quietly to them.

"Good to see you, sir," Tyler said, extending a respectful hand that Leo took.

"Good to see you, sir," Marcus mimicked. Owen felt the playfulness coming off of him and knew that he was just being an asshole. Leo seemed to realize this as well as he opted to pat his head instead of shaking his hand.

Marcus beamed, and Tyler shook his head.

"Owen," Yuri whisper-yelled as she and Rebecca walked up to the table. "I know you said no gifts, so I didn't really get you anything. Sort of." She pulled out a small photo album. Owen took it and scanned the pictures. They were all really cute photos of him and Leo.

"How did you even get these photos?" he asked.

"Well, I asked Jacob, because you guys seem close, and he got all this for me," she said.

Owen smiled. "It's wonderful. I love it. Thanks, Yuri."

Yuri beamed and sat next to Rebecca.

Owen sat between Marcus and Leo. He glanced up to see Alex and Jacob coming toward them. Jacob held a vase of red roses in his hands.

"Hey! Um, what's up with the flowers?" Owen asked.

Jacob looked amused.

"It's a wedding. You need flowers," Alex said firmly.

"I couldn't talk him out of it, so please, humor us," Jacob added.

Owen smiled. "Thank you, Alex. You may have your flowers," he said.

Alex beamed and deposited the flowers on the table such that they wouldn't be in the way.

The group chatted as they waited for their food. Owen was not surprised at all to see Yuri hitting it off with Marcus. Jacob and Tyler spoke. Owen was realizing that their personalities were quite similar. Owen was watching Leo talk to Tyler and Jacob when Marcus poked him in the side, hard.

"Hey," Owen said, shifting his attention.

"Stop ogling your husband and answer Yuri's question!" he exclaimed.

"I'm sorry, what did you say?" Owen asked Yuri.

She smiled like she hadn't been ignored. "So who took who's name?" she asked. The table grew quiet as, apparently, everyone heard the question.

Owen looked to Leo, who was no help at all. He smiled and waited for the answer like the rest of them.

"Uh, I took Leo's name," Owen said, waiting for the reaction.

Alex and Tyler each made a noise of defeat and took money out of their pockets. They handed it over to Jacob and Marcus respectively.

"I'm sorry, am I missing something?" Owen asked.

"We had a bet going. Me and Jacob had bet on the right name," Marcus said cheerfully.

Owen turned to Leo, who rolled his eyes but didn't break his smile. It actually seemed like Leo hadn't stopped smiling since they'd signed their marriage certificate.

"What are you doing for your honeymoon?" Jacob asked.

The attention of the table was drawn back to Owen and Leo. Leo gazed at Owen.

"I'm thinking we're going to go back to the private island. Owen likes the ocean," Leo said.

Owen nodded. "Yeah, we're doing that!" he said excitedly.

A few weeks on the beach and playing in the water? That was Owen's idea of a good honeymoon.

The conversation began to flow at the table. It was a good group; everyone seemed to get along well.

Finally the night was over, and everyone said their congratulations.

"Owen," Marcus hissed, gesturing for him to come closer. "I got you something."

Marcus reached into his pocket and pulled out a bottle of lube.

"It's fancy. It tastes and smells like green apple," he said. "Figured it might be good for your honeymoon."

Owen took the lube and slipped it in his pocket.

"I think I could know you for a million years and not know what goes on in that head of yours," he said. Owen thought for a moment, then turned back to Marcus. "Thanks. It's the thought that counts," he said.

Marcus smiled. "I'm telling you, it's gonna come in handy!"

Tyler passed Owen and took Marcus's hand to guide him away. He turned for a moment and smiled at Owen. "I wish happiness for the both of you," he said.

"Thanks," Owen said, kind of surprised by the sincerity he felt coming off Tyler.

As they turned away, Owen sensed Alex's joy right before he hugged Owen from behind.

"I knew this was destiny since day one," Alex said proudly.

"Sure you did," Jacob said skeptically.

"Owen, I'm so happy for you," Alex said, coming around to face him.

"Marriage means nothing. It's the two of you that count. And I think you do well with each other," Jacob said, summing up Owen's feelings about the whole thing.

"Congrats, Owen," Yuri said, giving Owen a kiss on the cheek.

"Congratulations, Owen. It was lovely to meet you," Rebecca said before guiding Yuri to the parking lot.

Finally alone, Owen looked behind him at Leo. He closed the distance between them and kissed him gently on the lips.

"What happened to no PDA?" Leo asked against his lips.

"This is an exception. So don't get any ideas," Owen said, pulling back and taking Leo's hand. They walked together to the car, neither one willing to break eye contact.

Owen leaned against Leo's chest the whole way home.

"LEO! GET into the goddamn water," Owen called, hip deep in the ocean. The waves were high enough that Owen had to jump to stay above the surface.

"No," Leo said simply from the safety of the sand.

"You're lucky I'm not willing to come out after you," Owen said.

Leo sighed and came out from under his beach umbrella. He walked toward Owen until his ankles were submerged.

"There, happy?" he asked.

Owen waded to Leo. Rather than leave the water, Owen sat down next to him with his legs splayed out and let the waves wash over his body.

"Fish," Leo commented.

"I don't know my father. For all I know he could have been a mermaid," Owen joked.

"Merman?" Leo corrected.

Owen gave him the finger.

"So, Mr. Ellis. How is your happily ever after going?" Leo asked, actually sitting down next to Owen.

"It could be better," Owen answered, earning a deep frown from Leo.

Owen leaned over and gently kissed Leo's lips. "There it is. Now it's perfect," he said. And he meant it.

Leo smiled and cupped Owen's cheeks in his hands.

"Here's to forever," Leo said against Owen's lips.

Owen couldn't agree more.

Keep Reading for an Excerpt from
In His Sights – Book #1 in the
Second Sight Series by K.C. Wells

CHAPTER 1

Boston, MA. Tuesday May 15, 2018

DETECTIVE GARY Mitchell took one look at the naked dead man lying facedown on the bed and his day officially went to shit.

Aw Christ, not another one.

The bedroom was an eerie carbon copy of the previous crime scenes. A small bottle sat on the nightstand, and Gary didn't need to see the label to know it contained GHB. On the bed beside the body were a tangle of red rope and a pair of handcuffs. He glanced at the rug, and sure enough, there was the soiled condom. Gary returned his attention to the deceased, noting the marks on the wrists and ankles, just like the previous victims.

This one struggled too. At least until the drugs kicked in. It was all supposition until the autopsy, but Gary saw no reason why the killer would change his MO. It hadn't gotten him caught so far, right? Why change a winning formula? The thought made Gary's blood run cold.

But what made his heart sink was the bloodstain on the corner of the white sheet that covered the guy's lower back.

"We've already taken photos of the scene." Detective Riley Watson picked up the condom with his nitrile-covered hand and dropped it into an evidence bag, then sealed it. He scowled. "God, I wanna catch this bastard." He scribbled on the label, noting the time.

Gary didn't respond. There was no need. They all wanted that.

Detective Lewis Stevens stood next to Del Maddox, the medical examiner. Lewis stared at the sheet, then raised his gaze to meet Gary's. "Wonder what it's gonna be this time?"

"Maybe he's obliged us by signing his handiwork," Del muttered. He pulled back the sheet with care and sighed. "Here we go again."

A letter *X* was carved into the victim's lower back.

"Done before death occurred, like the others?" Gary inquired. The amount of blood pointed to that conclusion.

Del nodded. "Looks like he used the same implement too."

Lewis grimaced. "Jesus. I hoped we'd seen the last of this guy."

"You and me both." Riley peered at him. "I bet it's days like this that make you sorry you ever left Vice. Chelmsford PD get a lot of these kinda cases?"

Lewis shook his head. "Never saw anything like this."

"Give it time," Del observed. "You've only been in Homicide for what, four years? Wait till you've been at it for as long as I have." He gazed at the deceased, and Gary noted the compassionate glance. "He could be my age."

"Can we save the chat for later and concentrate on doing our jobs?" Gary's stomach roiled, and a rock had taken up residence in his chest.

Lewis was silent, but his scowl said plenty. Riley gave a respectful nod and withdrew to talk to the uniform boys.

Del glanced at the nightstand. "Thoughtful of the killer to leave the drug. Now I know what to look for in the tox screen. Except if he's anything like the previous victims, there'll be a whole cocktail of drugs inside him." He addressed Gary. "How many of these guys do we have so far?"

"He's number five." Another one to add to the board. *Any more and we'll need another board.* Gary couldn't suppress his shiver.

Del pursed his lips. "So, five letters now. Anyone succeeded in making a word from the previous four?"

"None that make any sense."

"The killer's probably a Scrabble player with a list of obscure words." Both Gary and Lewis gaped at him. Del pushed out another sigh. "Sorry, guys. I'm as gutted as you are, but humor is my default when I don't want to think about a maniac being out there." He gestured to the body. "Help me roll him so I can take a look at the front."

The three men gently rolled the body with a care that was almost reverential. The man's wide staring eyes threatened to unravel Gary's self-control, and he had to force himself to shut off his emotions and look at the body objectively. The victim was maybe in his mid to late forties, with a salt-and-pepper beard and dark brown hair tinged with silver at the temples. A handsome man who'd clearly kept himself in good shape.

I hope you didn't suffer. Except Gary knew it was a false hope. The knowledge that he'd been cut before death and the bruising on the guy's wrists and ankles were grim indicators to the contrary.

Del gestured to his assistants who were standing to one side, maintaining a respectful silence. "Okay, boys." They lifted the corpse and placed it in an open body bag. Gary watched as they zipped it closed, obliterating his view of that staring face. They hoisted the bag onto a stretcher before carrying it out of the apartment. Riley bagged up the cuffs, rope, and bottle and handed them to one of the assistants, along with the bag containing the condom, to accompany the body to the morgue.

Del stripped off his gloves. "I'll get onto this one first thing tomorrow morning." He peered at Gary. "I'll see you there?"

Gary nodded. He knew Lewis wouldn't attend. He'd barfed at his first autopsy, and that was the last time he'd visited the morgue.

Del followed his assistants to the front door. The police officer let them through before reattaching the yellow tape that barred entrance to those neighbors who tried to get a glimpse. The officer was polite but firm, and the rubberneckers soon gave up.

Gary's hackles rose. *Yeah, someone is dead. You can read all about it in the media tomorrow.* Christ, number four had made the headlines before the ink was dry on Gary's report. He breathed deeply. His energies were best directed to the case.

Riley came over. "The victim's name was Marius Eisler, age forty-five." Gary's stomach clenched, but he pushed down hard on the momentary flash of nausea that always accompanied a surge of grief.

Keep focused.

Riley continued. "The body was discovered at twenty-three-hundred hours by the guy from the apartment next door, one Billy Raymond. He had a key. He said Marius had a habit of working late and not eating properly, so Billy regularly dropped by with food. He didn't see anyone. Uniforms have questioned everyone on this floor, but no one saw our man."

"Too much to hope there are cameras?" Gary asked.

Riley snorted. "Sure, they have cameras in the hallway downstairs, but they don't work. The neighbors said there were always guys coming and going."

Lewis rolled his eyes. "Another queer? Now *there's* a surprise." Riley fired him a disgusted glance.

Gary didn't bother reining in his glare. "I'm going to pretend I didn't hear you say that. Now why don't you go speak with Sergeant Michaels? See what else you can learn about the victim, the building...."

Lewis's brow furrowed, but he went without a word.

Gary breathed a little easier. He didn't need Lewis's shit right then. He scanned the bedroom. "No sign of a cell phone?"

Riley shook his head. "Just like the others. We've searched the whole apartment." He gazed at the rumpled sheets on the bed. "I'll bag these too." Riley glanced toward the door with a distant stare. "This was one talented guy. Did you see his paintings?"

Gary hadn't seen a thing. He'd been in too much of a rush to prove that nagging feeling in his gut wrong.

One look at the blood on the sheet had confirmed his fears.

"Our killer's not in any hurry, is he? Five bodies in two years." Riley's shoulders slumped. "I really thought he was done. Nothing since December."

Gary had hoped the same thing. "What worries me is those letters. How many bodies are there going to be before whatever it is he's spelling out begins to make sense and we get a lead?" Because so far they'd had precious few of those.

He walked into the living room, leaving Riley to remove the sheets from the bed, and paused to get a feel for the place. The heavily varnished wooden floor and oak furniture gave the apartment an elegant appearance. It wasn't cluttered, and judging by the size of the windows, Gary imagined it would be a light, airy room in the daylight. Every inch of available wall space was taken up with paintings of men. Some of the models were clothed, but most were nude or seminude, and all of them were good-looking. An easel stood by the window, a table next to it on which sat an open box filled with squeezed tubes of oil paint. A glass jar filled with dirty liquid held three long thin paintbrushes, and there was a palette covered with blobs of paint, a layer of clear wrap laid over it. A couple of rags smeared with colors sat beside the palette, and the odor of turpentine lingered in the air.

Gary went closer to look at the canvas sitting on the easel. It was a detailed study of a middle-aged man, clothed, sitting in a wide armchair, the same chair that stood beside the comfy-looking couch. The artist had yet to work on the clothing; the model's shirt was blocked in solid colors, shades of dark and light.

And now he'll never get to finish it.

Riley joined him. "According to the neighbor, this is how the victim earned his living. I googled him. Pretty well-known artist. I'll see what else I can find out tomorrow." He inclined his head toward the door. "The CSIs are here to dust and document the scene."

Beside him, Sergeant Rob Michaels cleared his throat. "I'll secure the scene once all the evidence has been removed."

"Thanks, Rob."

Lewis came over to them. "I don't think there's anything else we can do here."

Gary had to agree. The day had almost ended, and he was in dire need of sleep. "I'll see you both in the morning. You can write your reports then." He bade a good-night to Rob, and once the officer at the door had let him out, he hurried along the hallway to the stairs, stripping off his gloves and stuffing them into the pocket of his jacket. Some doors were open, and residents peered out as he passed.

Gary paid them no mind. He was too busy thinking about their victim.

Please, God, let us catch him. Don't let there be a number six.

GARY LET himself into his apartment and bolted the door behind him. The silence that greeted him held none of its usual comfort.

He knew why. All the way home, his head had been filled with thoughts of Brad. No, even before that. Memories of his late brother had suffocated him all day, to the point where he'd struggled to maintain his focus.

He'd have been forty-five today. The same age as Marius Eisler. It had taken every ounce of effort not to react when Riley had revealed the victim's age.

Gary trudged into the kitchen and peered into the fridge, not that he wanted anything. The neatly stacked microwave meals, bottles of iced tea and water, and foil-wrapped lump of cheese made the fridge's interior appear as minimalist as his apartment.

Despite his fatigue he wasn't ready for bed yet. Gary filled the kettle, then opened a cabinet to remove the box of chamomile tea. Its fragrance always soothed him, and right then he was in need of soothing.

When are we going to get a break? He loathed the hollowed-out feeling that pervaded each time he confronted their lack of success. The killer was either blessed with unholy luck or phenomenal planning skills. *How can he slip by unnoticed? Surely* someone *must have seen him.*

If they had, they had yet to come forward.

Sure, the police had the guy's DNA, thanks to the condoms, but he wasn't in the files. He left no prints, a fiber here and there, and appeared to have chosen victims who had a steady stream of male visitors. Lieutenant

Travers had already intimated that the chief was making noises about bringing in more men. The shit had hit the fan after the discovery of victim number three, Geoff Berg, when some bright journalist had worked out all the victims were gay men.

Worked out, my ass. Someone leaked it.

The headlines had screamed Killer Targets Gay Men! for a couple of weeks, but as the months passed and no more bodies turned up, things quieted down. Thank God the letters had remained confidential. They had one tool left for weeding out the crank confessors. But that didn't relieve the resulting pressure Gary and his team found themselves under once news had gotten out.

The kettle whistled and he turned off the gas. As he poured water onto the tea bag, his phone pinged, and he glanced at the screen.

Still coming Sunday?

What the hell was his mom doing awake at this hour? Except he knew that was a stupid question. She'd been a poor sleeper for the past twenty-three years. As usual, cold fingers traced a path around his heart at the prospect of the monthly ritual of Sunday lunch. He hated himself for even thinking like that. Seeing his parents shouldn't be a burden, shouldn't fill him with apprehension.

But it did. And he knew he'd go, because not to would be unthinkable. Unforgivable.

He typed with his thumbs. *Sure.* There was no reply, but that was typical of his mom. Her texts were always succinct and infrequent.

Gary took his tea and went into his bedroom. He placed the cup on the nightstand. The closet door stood ajar, and Gary moved toward it without thinking. He stepped into the closet and headed for the built-in drawers. He paused, his hand on the knob, his heart racing.

Will it help?

He ignored the quiet inner voice. He opened the drawer and removed the folded sweater, inhaling as he held it close. Whatever scent it had possessed had long since disappeared.

Gary returned to his bed and sat in the center, pillows stuffed behind him. He buried his face in the soft yarn.

I'll find him, Brad. I promise. I haven't forgotten about you.

The reminder was etched onto Gary's skin.

CHAPTER 2

I PICKED UP the red pen and walked over to the wall. "Goodbye, Marius," I intoned as I crossed out his face. Where the two thick strokes met, they obliterated his mouth. "Pity I couldn't have done that when you were alive." Anything not to have to listen to him drone on about his painting.

The four photos to Marius's left bore the same red cross. I gazed at the image on the right, enjoying the tingle that started in my chest, then spread outward. My stomach fluttered. Waiting was murder.

I grinned at my own joke. I had time to enjoy the intoxication a while longer, to bask in the radiant, fierce joy that had accompanied each death.

Marius's departure had been particularly delicious.

Once he'd gotten over his initial surprise—like the rest of them—he clearly relished the prospect of getting me in his bed. He wasn't on his guard. Why would he be? He knew me, after all. So easy to slip the Rohypnol into his glass and watch as he drifted into unconsciousness. And when he awoke, bewildered to discover he was naked, bound, and gagged, he'd pulled against his bonds. The sharp scratch as I administered the ketamine only added to his befuddled state.

I saw him resign himself to the act that was to follow. It was almost a pity to disillusion him.

Almost.

I waited until I'd filled him to the hilt before leaning forward to whisper in his ear.

Enjoy it. This is your last fuck. Because when I come?
You die.

And there it was, the ultimate thrill. Not penetrating that tight hole, not driving myself deep into him—that was an act to be *suffered*, not enjoyed. Even carving into his flesh brought merely a trickle of expectation. No, the anticipation of taking his life, of knowing he was unable to struggle against his bonds... *that* aroused me to the point of ejaculation.

I shivered. There would be time enough to dwell on Marius. The elation was still overwhelming. Another one gone.

I was in no hurry. My days had taken on a familiar pattern.

Erase one of those sluts from the planet.

Watch the news.

Add more names to the list.

Cross off the names of those who'd eliminated themselves.

Lay the groundwork for the next one.

Wash, rinse, repeat....

Only seventeen more to go. Seventeen men, out of a field rich with possibilities. The world would be all the better for the loss of those twenty-two souls. I'd have preferred a total of twenty-six, but it wouldn't fit.

Then again....

I might change my mind when I reach twenty-two. There are plenty of men to choose from, after all. And why stop if I'm getting away with it?

I gazed at the photo that took center stage, framed with bare wall, the images of my victims—actual and potential—kept at a distance so as not to taint it with their presence. Men like them had tainted him enough.

They're going to pay for what they did. And I've got nothing but time.

My gaze alighted on the image I'd already picked out. A definite possibility. My only difficulty?

I'd waited five months between victims, and it had been torture. It didn't matter that it had been the shortest time span thus far. I didn't think I could wait that long again. Not while the heightened emotions of the kill lingered still. Not with all those faces staring at me from the wall.

Not with *his* face gazing at me. His voice in my head.

"I'm doing this for you," I whispered. "To avenge you."

I had another motive too, one that suffocated me, haunted me, but I knew of one way to assuage that emotion.

I smiled at the image I'd selected. A handsome face with bright eyes and a firm jaw.

"You're next."

CHAPTER 3

Wednesday, May 16

DEL ARCHED his eyebrows as Gary walked into the morgue. "I thought I'd have seen you earlier than this. You're three hours late." He gestured to the sewn-up Y-incision. "Or did you stop by to complement me on my needlework?"

"I'm here for the edited highlights."

Marius Eisler lay on his back, the Y-incision the only visible evidence of the autopsy. Gary had watched Del at work on a couple of occasions and knew the reinforced thick twine that closed Del's cuts concealed the heavy-duty, leak-proof plastic bag containing the organs, hidden from sight in the empty chest cavity.

"Body fluids have already gone to Toxicology, but we know what I'm looking for."

"Your initial findings?" Gary knew better than to ask for more than that: It would be a while before the full autopsy report was finalized.

"As you correctly surmised, the letter was carved into the skin prior to death." Del's gaze bored into him. "And we know this how?"

"By the wound. Prior to death, the heart is working and blood is sent there. It has a different color, and the wound is significantly bloodier. After death, it's paler, more… withered, and there's less blood."

Del smiled. "Full marks, Detective. Good to know you've been listening. Although I'd expect nothing less from one of Boston's finest homicide detectives."

"I know there was a condom, but—"

"But you assume nothing, which is how it should be," Del interjected. "And yes, penetrative sex took place prior to death."

"Can you tell if it was nonconsensual?" The bruising on Marius's wrists and ankles appeared darker against the pale skin.

"Hard to tell." Del frowned. "Who's to say rough sex isn't consensual? There's some abrasion, some internal bruising, but nonrough sex can create some injury. What *you* want to know is if there was an overabundance of injury. There wasn't. As for the body fluids, I'll test for GHB, Rohypnol, ketamine, and barbiturates, although we found no GHB in the previous victims." His gaze flickered to the body on his table. "This one likes his routines." He frowned again. "So why does he leave the GHB at the scene? He doesn't leave any trace of the other drugs he uses. Is it some kind of message?"

Gary glanced at the table before meeting Del's gaze. "I'll be sure to ask him—once I catch the bastard."

"WHERE HAVE you been?" Lewis demanded as soon as Gary walked into their office space.

Gary came to a halt. "One of us had to go talk to Del. Did *you* want to do it?" As if he didn't know the answer to that one.

"Okay, so I had a weak stomach that one time," Lewis countered. His mouth went down at the corners. "Travers wants to see us all, ASAP. Riley's already in there."

Aw crap.

Gary had a feeling a ton of shit was about to roll downhill, aimed right at him.

Without a word, he followed Lewis to the lieutenant's corner office. Riley sat facing Travers's desk, its surface invisible to the eye, hidden beneath an explosion of paper, folders, and coffee cups. Gary gave it a cursory glance before meeting Travers's stern gaze.

"It may look like the aftermath of a robbery, but trust me, it's organized chaos. I know where everything is, and I can lay my hand on anything in seconds."

Gary held up his hands. "Hey, I didn't say a word." He knew better.

"Your expression said enough." Travers pointed to the empty chairs next to Riley. "Sit." No sooner had Gary's ass touched the worn leather seat than Travers launched into his controlled rant. "So now we've got five bodies, and we're no closer to discovering who's trying to wipe out Boston's entire gay population." As usual, Travers didn't raise his voice. He didn't need to. His clipped tone was sharper than a razor, honed by years of practice.

"Hey, we don't know—"

Travers cut Riley off. "He's killed five. Who knows when he'll stop?" He picked up the folded newspaper from the top of a pile of others and tossed it at Gary. "We made ink again. Only now it's worse. The press has gotten hold of the stuff about the bondage gear. Great. That's just great." He squeezed the words through his teeth.

"I know you're pissed," Gary said, "but—"

"Pissed?" Travers glared at Gary. "I'm not pissed. Trust me, when I reach pissed, you'll know about it. The only thing saving your asses right now is that it hasn't gotten out yet about his little calling card. We've already had three guys stroll in here to confess to the killings, and Lord knows, that's only the start."

He sounded as weary as Gary felt, and Gary was bone tired. He'd slept little the previous night. Every time he closed his eyes, two men's faces swam there: Marius, staring at him before they'd zipped him into the body bag, and Brad.

Except Brad was never far from Gary's mind. There were occasions when he'd realize with a hot flood of remorse that he hadn't thought about Brad for a couple of days.

That was when the sweater would come out of the closet.

"We're exploring every avenue," Gary ventured. "We've pulled all the records—"

"I know what you're doing. I've read the reports." Travers scraped his fingers through his graying hair. The lines around his eyes seemed deeper than usual. "You're in here because the chief feels we can be doing more."

"Hey, if the chief has any suggestions, let's hear 'em." Gary folded his arms, his jaw stiff, a dull pain pulsing through his temple.

Travers mimicked his stance. "Actually? He has one. There's a psychic who's worked with NYPD and Chicago PD."

What the fuck?

Gary gaped at him. "You're kidding."

"Nope, not even close. Chief says this guy's gotten results. So he thinks we should bring him on board. Guy by the name of Dan Porter."

Lewis snorted. "Hey, we could give my grandmother a call. She reads stuff in tea leaves. Or there's this woman who claims she can tell the future from dropping asparagus onto the floor and looking at the patterns it makes when it falls. Maybe *she* can find our killer. Want me to go to the store for a shit-ton of asparagus?"

Travers glared at him. "I'll try to remember not to repeat your suggestions the next time I get called into the chief's office." He sat in his chair, elbows on the desk, his fingers steepled, his gaze locked on Gary. "I know how it sounds." His low, earnest voice was clearly an attempt at mollification. "I was as incredulous as you, but I've done some checking. Dan Porter appears to be a genuine psychic."

"Is there such a thing?" Lewis retorted.

Travers ignored him. "His results aren't flukes, that's for damn sure. I don't claim to know how he does it, but he's helped cops solve crimes. And *that* came from the chief. He's been in contact with NYPD and Chicago to make sure the reports were accurate." Travers sagged in his chair. "All I'm saying is, maybe we should talk to the guy. It can't hurt, right?"

Gary struggled to breathe evenly, his stomach clenched. "No. We are *not* resorting to mumbo jumbo, voodoo, or any other new age happy crap."

Beside him, Lewis nodded. "The chief may go in for all that hogwash, but come *on*. We're the professionals here. We know how to catch this guy, and it's by good old-fashioned detecting."

Gary had to fight hard not to stare at Lewis. *Well fuck, we agree on something.*

Travers's face hardened. "Then get out there and detect. I don't want you coming in here and telling me victim number six has just shown up." He stood, reached for a coffee cup, and went over to the pot that sat in the corner.

Apparently they were done.

SCAN THE QR CODE
BELOW TO ORDER!

ROSE MASTERS is a full-time advocate and teacher for those living with mental health conditions. She does presentations in schools, businesses, and generally wherever people are open to learning more about mental health. She also teaches an eight-week course about mental health and how to cope.

Writing, for her, is a means of stress reduction and self-expression. Writing is simply fun. Rose wants every character in every story to be relatable and every relationship to be fun to watch. Rose started her writing journey with poetry and Teen Wolf fan fiction. She graduated on to creating her own characters

As someone who lives with a mental health condition, Rose has always found comfort in books and movies. Being a part of that is so important to her. She wants to encourage other people who struggle like she has to feel like they are capable of reaching personal goals, as she has by writing.

Through hard work and lots of support, Rose has graduated with a bachelor's degree in psychology and a master's degree in social work. Bringing joy and comfort to others is extremely important to Rose, and she hopes that she can spread some joy with the stories she has written.

CharmD Saga: Book One

Former chef Jasper Wight has been magically ensnared in his apartment for over three months. Cabin fever doesn't begin to cover it. All he can do to pass the time is indulge in his hobby—painting portraits of his neighbors. But once a handsome new man moves into a swanky nearby penthouse, Jasper is no longer content merely to watch. Following his gut, he reaches out through astral projection….

Finn Anderson is the CEO of a food app funded by his parents, but he struggles to believe in the dream. When a mysterious someone starts leaving messages on his mirror, he learns the world holds more possibilities than he ever imagined.

When a chance encounter brings Finn to Jasper's door, the pair are soon as enamored with each other as Finn is of the magic he's just discovering. But navigating a relationship that spans two worlds is only the tip of the iceberg. They still have to figure out how to free Jasper from his apartment, how to make Finn's business into a success, and whether an outsider can be trusted with the secrets of the magical world.

SCAN THE QR CODE
BELOW TO ORDER!

KISSING FROGS

Terry Wylis

All he needs is a kiss.
And to escape that damn vacuum.

Modern-day American "prince" Ellis Faraday has a problem: he's been a frog for a year, his time before hibernation is ending, and he's afraid there will be nothing left of him come spring. The castle-house up the hill seems like a promising place to start looking for a cure... if he can convince a human to take him seriously. A conversation—and maybe a kiss—with the pretty man who owns the koi pond might do the trick.

On a Friday night, Galen Townsend just wants to curl up and read in the backyard of the house he shares with his brothers, but the frog addressing him from the wall of the koi pond has him questioning his sanity. Moreso when he gives the frog a peck on the nose—just to be nice—and the frog becomes a handsome, precious man.

Unfortunately, Galen's "cure" proves temporary. After a few hours, Ellis is back to hopping and croaking, but at least he has an ally and a warm place to stay. Now they just have to keep Galen's brothers from discovering a frog in the house while they work out how to break the spell. How many kisses can it possibly take?

SCAN THE QR CODE
BELOW TO ORDER!

AMY LANE
Sometimes the best magic is just a little luck…
THE RISING TIDE
THE LUCK MECHANICS BOOK ONE

The tidal archipelago of Spinner's Drift is a refuge for misfits. Can the island's magic help a pie-in-the-sky dreamer and a wounded soul find a home in each other?

In a flash of light and a clap of thunder, Scout Quintero is banished from his home. Once he's sneaked his sister out too, he's happy, but their power-hungry father is after them, and they need a place to lie low. The thriving resort business on Spinner's Drift provides the perfect way to blend in.

They aren't the only ones who think so.

Six months ago Lucky left his life behind and went on the run from mobsters. Spinner's Drift brings solace to his battered soul, but one look at Scout and he's suddenly terrified of having one more thing to lose.

Lucky tries to keep his distance, but Scout is charming, and the island isn't that big. When they finally connect, all kinds of things come to light, including supernatural mysteries that have been buried for years. But while Scout and Lucky grow closer working on the secret, pissed-off mobsters, supernatural entities, and Scout's father are getting closer to them. Can they hold tight to each other and weather the rising tide together?

SCAN THE QR CODE BELOW TO ORDER!

AUGUST LI

TALES OF STARLING HALLOW

GRANNY BUCHANAN'S
OTHER HELPER

Tyler has the mountains in his bones, and he can't leave sleepy Starling Hollow even if everyone else has. He has no prospects other than helping out Granny Buchanan, the local conjure woman, and trying to keep the old Greenbrier Inn from falling down. He knows neither one's long for the world, and he dreads the idea of being alone.

Granny Buchanan's as stubborn as the mountain, with a memory almost as long. She has no plans to leave Tyler alone—there's somebody right in her backyard who'd be perfect for him, and she's learned some tricks in her life.

But things more mysterious than Granny haunt the old mountain, and they have tricks of their own.

SCAN THE QR CODE
BELOW TO ORDER!

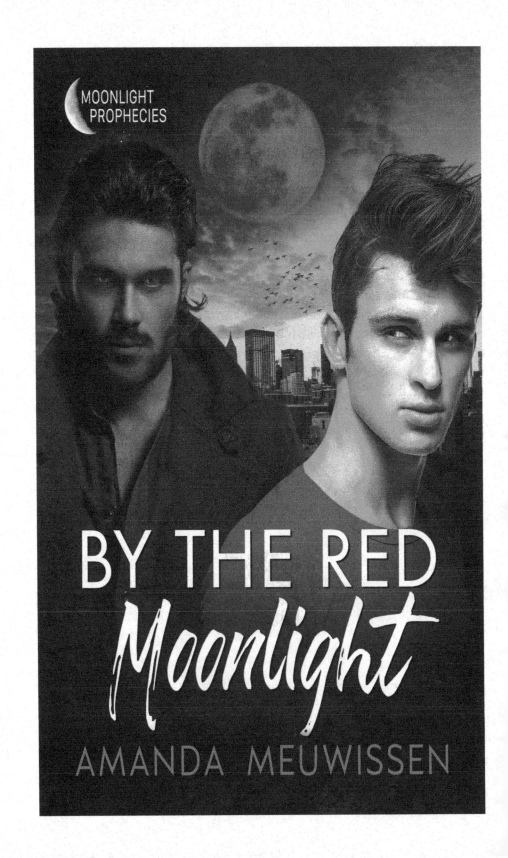

MOONLIGHT
PROPHECIES

BY THE RED
Moonlight

AMANDA MEUWISSEN

Moonlight Prophecies: Book One

Alpha werewolf, crime boss, and secret Seer Bashir Bain is neck-deep in negotiating a marriage of convenience with a neighboring alpha when a tense situation goes from bad to worse. A job applicant at one of Bash's businesses—a guy who was supposed to be a simple ex-cop, ex-con tattoo artist—suddenly turns up undead.

A rogue newborn vampire would have been a big wrench in Bash's plans even without his attraction to the man. After all, new vampires are under their sire's control, and Ethan Lambert doesn't even know who turned him. When Bash spares his life, he opens himself up for mutiny, a broken engagement, and an unexpected—and risky—relationship.

Ethan just wants a fresh start after being released from prison. Before he can get it, he'll need to turn private investigator to find out who sired him and what he wants. And he'd better do it quick, because the moon is full, and according to Bash's prophecy, life and death hang in the balance.

Scan the QR Code Below to Order!